Dear Reader,

I've been hearing from readers how much they are enjoying the Harlequin Duets stories and how they're finding our 2-in-1 format convenient. Keep your comments coming, so that we can keep publishing the kinds of stories you want.

BEST OF THE WEST features exactly that: three exciting, sexy cowboys tamed by the love of a good woman. Written by Cathie Linz, a nominee for a *Romantic Times* 1998 Reviewer's Choice Award, *The Rancher Gets Hitched* has a generous dose of humor and sex appeal. Look for the second title in January 2000.

Then we're pleased to welcome Marissa Hall to Harlequin. She pens a delightful tale of two driven workaholics with no time for love, but plans for a perfect affair. In *An Affair of Convenience* these plans, naturally, go awry.

Then we have two books about people on unusual journeys to love. A runaway bride pretending to have amnesia in Renee Roszel's *Bride on the Loose* finds herself trapped on an island overrun by eccentric characters, too many animals and one very sexy veterinarian. Then Colleen Collins returns with another quirky story about the most unlikely opposites who attract: a millionaire and a showgirl. Their dizzying courtship is captured in *Married After Breakfast*.

Keep those letters coming!

Malle Vallik

Malle Vallik
Senior Editor
    Harlequin Duets
    Harlequin Books
    225 Duncan Mill Road
    Don Mills, Ontario
    M3B 3K9 Canada

No matter how she might tempt him,

Zane wasn't going to give in. Not this time. Not with this city girl or any other.

He imagined Tracy thanking him for the massage with a come-hither look. Her full lips would smile in a way meant to make a man melt.

He'd resist.

She could stand stark naked in front of him and he wouldn't flinch.

She could...what was she doing now? He cautiously moved forward to get a better look at her face. Her long lashes were velvety dark against her creamy skin and her lips were parted as she...snored?

Oh, it was delicate and dainty-like, but it was definitely a snore.

So much for him thinking Tracy was lying there concocting some scheme to seduce him. She'd told him she was no more interested in having a relationship with him than he was with her.

Maybe it was time Zane believed her.

For more, turn to page 9

An Affair of Convenience

"Neither of us is any good at relationships, I guess."

"It's not us, Mallory. It's just that everyone else has unreasonable expectations. We work long, hard hours." Cliff frowned. "But I like going out with women. I like dating. I like—"

"Sex?" she asked sweetly. "Are you saying you can't go without it?"

"I happen to like women. So sue me," the lawyer in him responded.

Her smile faded. "Maybe you just need to have an affair."

Cliff sighed. "Every time I date, the woman pulls the same old your-work-means-more-to-you-than-I-do routine. I haven't even made it to first base with anyone in ages."

She nodded. "You know there's a solution to all this. We merely have to find someone to...to..."

"Have sex with occasionally?" he inserted silkily.

She tipped her chin upward. "Yes. Good clean sex." Mallory took a deep breath. "Why don't you and I have an affair?"

For more, turn to page 197

HARLEQUIN DUETS

ISBN 0-373-44075-8

THE RANCHER GETS HITCHED
Copyright © 1999 by Cathie L. Baumgardner

AN AFFAIR OF CONVENIENCE
Copyright © 1999 by Maureen Caudill

This edition published by arrangement with Harlequin Books S.A.

® and TM are trademarks of the publisher. Trademarks indicated with
® are registered in the United States Patent and Trademark Office, the
Canadian Trade Marks Office and in other countries.

Visit us at www.romance.net

Printed in U.S.A.

CATHIE LINZ

The Rancher Gets Hitched

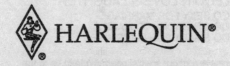

HARLEQUIN®

TORONTO • NEW YORK • LONDON
AMSTERDAM • PARIS • SYDNEY • HAMBURG
STOCKHOLM • ATHENS • TOKYO • MILAN • MADRID
PRAGUE • WARSAW • BUDAPEST • AUCKLAND

I confess that I have a "thing" for the West, just like my heroine Tracy. When I was a little girl, my big brother was a huge fan of TV Westerns like *Gunsmoke* and *Bonanza* (Little Joe was my favorite). Usually in our reenactments I played the role of the bad guy who gets shot. Now that I'm all grown up, I no longer have to "drop dead" at my brother's command. Now I get to write my own zany Western legends for this BEST OF THE WEST trilogy, all set in Colorado where I spent several summers and where my aunt still has a ranch. I hope you enjoy Tracy and Zane's story!

Cathie Linz

P.S. Several of the cooking disasters in this book are taken from my own family's chronicles of "Recipes Gone Wrong." Live And Learn is my motto in the kitchen.

Books by Cathie Linz
HARLEQUIN LOVE & LAUGHTER
39—TOO SEXY FOR MARRIAGE
45—TOO STUBBORN TO MARRY
51—TOO SMART FOR MARRIAGE

For Bill Phillips—my local cowboy poet
and punmeister

1

"SON OF A BUCK!" a grizzled old man declared in a gravelly voice. "Look what we got here."

Blinking at the bright pool of light spilling from the open door, Tracy Campbell swatted at the raindrops on her eyelashes. Her long hair was plastered to her head and cheeks like strands of sticky seaweed. She felt like a drowned rat and had no doubt that she looked the part. She'd been driving around in circles for hours in a raging downpour that would have sent Noah heading back to the ark. Tired to the bone, she managed to ask, "Where am I?"

"On our front porch," a younger man replied.

Great, she thought. Of all the ranch houses in Colorado, she had to end up on the doorstep of a comedian.

Tracy wasn't in the mood for laughing. What she was in the mood for was a full-blown crying jag. However, she refused to turn into a blubbering idiot in front of these two men. They were already staring at her as if she'd landed from outer space.

The older man had a shock of white hair and piercing light blue eyes. He reminded her of Lloyd Bridges. She hadn't gotten a good look at the younger man yet.

Gathering her composure along with the damp skirt of her denim dress—she figured everyone in Colorado wore denim—and without waiting for an invitation, she walked inside.

"I don't care where I am," she stated with a look that dared either man to cross her. "I'm *not* going out in that downpour again."

"Nobody asked you to," the younger man noted, his voice shimmying down her spine like a hot toddy.

"I got lost looking for the Best ranch," she said.

"You've found it," he replied.

Sending up a silent prayer of thanks, Tracy extended her hand before realizing the navy cotton sweater she was wearing over her dress had stretched until it limply drooped beyond her fingertips.

Yanking the saturated sleeve up to her elbow, she introduced herself. "I'm your new housekeeper."

"Well, if that don't beat all." The older man slapped his thigh and chortled.

She sensed the younger man's eyes gleaming with amusement as he surveyed her from dripping head to muddy feet.

"She probably cleans up pretty good," the older man added with another chortle.

"Forgive my father, he has a peculiar sense of humor. I'm Zane Best." His warm hand engulfed hers in a handshake that was startlingly powerful. Not that he squeezed her fingers too hard or anything like that. Still, her chilly fingers were humming with awareness.

This was Zane? Her rancher employer? He wasn't what she'd imagined. She'd pictured him looking like

J.R.'s father in the TV series *Dallas*—silver-haired, distinguished-looking, tall.

The only thing she'd gotten right was that last one. He had to be at least six-two and his ruggedly lean build was enough to make an advertising account executive like herself want to cast him in a jeans commercial.

But Tracy wasn't an account executive any longer. She wasn't an about-to-be-bride, either. That life was behind her, left back in Chicago along with the sterling-silver tea set and the Austrian crystal decanters. She was on her own now. On her own as a housekeeper, on a ranch in Colorado.

It had seemed like a good idea when her aunt Maeve had suggested it to her back in Chicago. Her aunt's new husband, Herbert, had a dear cousin out west who was looking for a housekeeper. Hadn't Tracy always wanted to live on a ranch?

At the time, Tracy's first priority had been getting away from the nightmarish mess her heretofore well-planned life had become, and to do that as quickly as possible. She'd jumped at the job, asking no questions. Maeve had offered to call ahead and tell them Tracy was coming.

Tracy had driven out west instead of flying and had spent more time behind the wheel of her beloved red Miata than she probably should have that day. But, after enduring a rough night in a no-name motel in the middle of Nebraska, she'd wanted to reach her destination by day's end.

The car was packed to the gills. She imagined her

ex-fiancé, Dennis, had noticed a few things missing by now, not the least of which was her.

Tracy's frantic telephone conversation with her aunt had led her here to the wilds of Colorado and to this rugged man who was eyeing her with equal parts of amusement and wariness.

"You still awake in there?" he inquired dryly.

Despite the fact that they were inside, he still wore a cowboy hat so she couldn't tell what color his eyes were. He had a classic profile. Above his right ear, she could see a few inches of his hair—dark hair. He had chiseled cheekbones and a jaw that could have been carved out of Mount Rushmore. Altogether it made for a sexy and craggy face, like the guys that posed for those cigarette ads in the sixties. Back to advertising again? She closed her eyes.

This man was supposed to be a middle-aged widower, with two angelic children of indeterminable age—Aunt Maeve hadn't been real clear on that detail. In her glowing description, her aunt had bestowed the mild and easygoing disposition of a saint upon Zane. Tracy was getting the feeling her aunt had exaggerated. Greatly.

THE WOMAN HAD "tenderfoot" written all over her—from the tips of her muddied beige suede boots to the top of her sopping wet blond hair. What kind of idiot wore suede boots to a ranch? Apparently the kind he'd hired, Zane noted with a sigh.

Beggars can't be choosers. It wasn't as if he'd received tons of applications for the position of housekeeper. Everyone in the county knew about his situation and they'd rather eat rattlers than work in his household—thanks to the wild stories put out by the two housekeepers he'd already gone through in the past month.

He hadn't expected Tracy Campbell to just show up on his doorstep tonight. She was suppose to arrive tomorrow. He didn't know exactly what relationship existed between himself and the woman dripping in his hallway. Her aunt had married his father's favorite cousin, which made her...there was probably some word for it but he didn't know what. Second cousin niece-in-law?

Who knew? Who cared? He needed a housekeeper and he needed her pronto.

His dad and his cousin Herbert, or Herb as he preferred to be called, talked on the phone all the time, and Buck had told Herb about the trouble they'd been having keeping household help. Still, Zane didn't know much about Herb's new wife. When he'd gotten the call saying that she had a niece who was coming to fill the job of housekeeper, he'd been too relieved to question his luck, not wanting to look a gift horse in the mouth.

This woman's mouth was worth looking at, even if it was a little blue around the edges from cold or exhaustion, he wasn't sure which. Her long hair was beginning to dry at the ends, and as it did so it turned a warm gold. Her denim dress clung to a body that was curved in all the right places. And she had eyes as green as grass.

"You should get out of those damp clothes before you catch a chill." The image of her without those clothes was enough to make him take a step back, as if she'd just zapped him with a cattle prod. "Uh, did you bring your luggage with you?"

"In the car," she said.

"You don't look so good," Buck stated bluntly. "Maybe you better sit down."

"You know what I could really use? A bathroom."

"It's over there," Zane said, nodding his head toward the door beneath the staircase leading upstairs. "It's not real big, but it should suit your needs."

After brushing her hair and drying her face with towels that could give sandpaper a run for its money, she felt only marginally more presentable.

"Appears to me, son, that a good wind would knock her over. She looked like a crazy wild woman, pounding on the door that way."

"She's not crazy. She's just tired from the trip."

Hearing Zane's words through the bathroom door, Tracy decided that exhaustion was as good an excuse as any. The truth was that she definitely was not at her best, but then who would be after what she'd been through the past few days? Being an unemployed runaway bride would make any woman look crazy and wild. "You're allowed," she assured her reflection in the tiny mirror.

From the other side of the door, she heard Buck's bellowing voice saying, "Son, she's in the john talking to herself! Maybe you should check on her."

"I'm fine," Tracy shouted back. "I'll be out in a second."

It took her several tries to undo the lock on the bathroom door, which probably dated back to the last century. She was just about ready to admit defeat when the lock finally gave way, and she nearly tumbled into the hallway, where Zane and his father stood waiting for her.

Gathering her battered dignity around her, she straightened her shoulders and said, "I think I'll go rest now, if you don't mind. It was a long drive out here."

"I'll take you up to your room," Zane said. He already had two of her bags in hand, the damp patch on his shirt indicating that he'd been out in the rain to get them from her car, which she'd left unlocked.

"Thanks." Tracy followed him up the stairs that creaked with every step they took. Zane was two steps above her, which put his denim-clad behind right about at her eye level. His jeans fit him like a second skin. He had a narrow waist and lean hips to go with his long legs—thirty-four waist and thirty-six inseam, if she wasn't mistaken. Not that she was paying attention to such things. Not anymore. Still, she couldn't help noticing that he moved with the cowboy swagger of the guys on *Bonanza*.

She should know, she'd seen every episode of the classic western TV show. She'd always had this secret desire to live on a ranch, and during the long drive west she'd told herself that maybe Dennis's cheating had been fate's way of guiding her here to live out her ranch dream. She just hoped this didn't turn into a nightmare the way her dreams of a life with Dennis had.

"The housekeeper's quarters are being...uh... being remodeled. So for the next few days you'll have to stay in the guest room," Zane said, kicking the door open with his booted foot.

The bed was big and looked comfortable, even if it was old. It had a quilt of some kind on it instead of a bedspread. There was a nightstand and a chest of drawers along with a straight-backed chair. Not exactly The Ritz, but it would do.

"I'll just put your bag here," Zane said, placing the smallest carry-on bag onto the bed, where it bounced several times on the creaky mattress.

Looking at it, Tracy longed for her own luxury mattress in storage back in Chicago. "Do you have a bathtub?" she asked Zane.

"Sure. But the hot-water heater is out of commission right now. Sorry," he said regretfully, with a tug on the brim of his hat. "It should be working again by morning."

"That's okay," she murmured, her hope of taking a hot bath gone.

"I'll turn up the heat for you. If you don't have any other questions, I'll let you get some sleep. We get up early in these parts. Breakfast is at five-thirty."

"Fine," she mumbled around a yawn, not really hearing him. "I'll see you then."

"The kitchen is at the back of the house downstairs," Zane added. "You can't miss it."

"Mmm, good night."

As she closed the door in Zane's face, the last thing she saw were his eyes. Finally she was close enough to see their color. They were blue.

TRACY WAS DREAMING that she was being rocked by gentle waves in the Caribbean. She and Dennis were on their honeymoon. They had the beach all to themselves. The ocean was getting rougher. A storm was coming. She could hear the thunder. It rumbled over her as she bounced like a cork in the rough seas.

"Wake up!" the thunder rumbled.

She tried to call out but couldn't.

"Wake up!" the thunder rumbled again.

Tracy opened her eyes to find a man looming over her in the semidarkness. Her scream was automatic.

Afterward, she didn't know which of them was more unnerved.

"Damn it, you scared ten years off my life!" the man grumbled as he retrieved his hat, which had gone flying when she'd let loose her startled yodel. "All I was trying to do was wake you up. You were supposed to have breakfast ready ten minutes ago. I've got hungry ranch hands downstairs waiting to be fed."

Completely disoriented, Tracy blinked at him, trying to place her surroundings. Where was she?

Then it came rushing back to her. She was at a ranch in Colorado. The one her aunt told her would be the perfect place for her to recover from the mayhem of her life. But no one could recover from anything at this ungodly hour! And the man staring with interest at the thin spaghetti straps of her nightgown was Zane.

"What are you doing in here?" she demanded, pulling the sheet up to her chin.

"I told you. I was just trying to wake you up."

"It's too early. Come back later," she moaned.

"Listen, lady," he growled as he hit the light switch on the wall, "I'm not running a health spa here. Last I heard, I'm the employer and you're the housekeeper and cook. Which means you're supposed to be downstairs making breakfast, not up here under the covers."

She groaned, then sat up in bed. "I guess this means breakfast in bed is out, huh?" Seeing his expression darken, she added, "I'm only kidding. I'm awake now. I'll be downstairs in a few minutes."

Tracy waited until Zane left before crawling out of bed, only to stub her toe on one of her still-unpacked suitcases. Tears sprang to her eyes as she grabbed her foot and did a one-footed hop.

This wasn't how she'd planned on starting her new life. She felt like a fish out of water, a very sleepy, tired fish, and she didn't like it. Anger washed over her, mixed with the pain of betrayal. Dennis had cheated on her, and Zane had stolen several hours of sleep from her. The two crimes might not be at all equal in seriousness, but for the moment they marked both men as guilty in her mind. Guilty of being men too used to having their own way.

"They should ban all males from this planet," she declared darkly. "Now where did I pack my jeans?"

In the end, Tracy had to wear beige linen slacks and a coral silk blouse. It was either that or risk having Zane come ranting back into her room. Her jeans must be in one of the bags still in the car.

She found the kitchen with no difficulty. Turning on the stove did not prove to be as easy, however.

Whenever she turned the knob, all she got was hissing gas.

The moment Zane walked in the kitchen, she told him, "Your stove is broken."

"It's not broken, you've got to light it with a match." When she gave him a blank look, he swore under his breath and lit it himself. "Just make a batch of scrambled eggs this morning and some bacon." He handed her a bowl of eggs and what looked like a pound of bacon.

"Do you know what this does to your cholesterol level?" Tracy said in disapproval.

"Just cook it," he growled.

She did, but not very well. The eggs were runny on top and burned on the bottom, while the bacon looked like cinders. Who could have guessed that making scrambled eggs and bacon would be so tricky? It was a good thing she'd brought a few cookbooks with her.

She didn't dare go out and ask the men how they liked the meal she'd made for them. So she stayed in the kitchen, trying to decide where she'd put the gourmet appliances she'd brought with her. She heard some muttered complaints from the other room, but didn't pay any attention to them.

There was no ignoring Zane when he strode into the kitchen. His face was as stormy as the sky had been last night.

"I was told you could cook," he said with remarkable calm, given his expression.

"I *can* cook," Tracy righteously maintained. One thing. Shrimp de Jonghe with angel-hair pasta. As for breakfast, Tracy rarely had anything more elaborate than coffee and a bagel with cream cheese. And she'd always bought that from a deli around the corner from her place.

There was nothing around the corner in this neck of the woods, though. Okay, so her first morning hadn't turned out as she'd thought it would. No big deal. She had an MBA. She could figure this out. How hard could being a housekeeper and cook be?

Turning her attention from Zane to the kitchen, she surveyed the mess she'd made. Bacon grease was spattered in a two-foot radius from the stove. Some of it had even hit her hand. She absently rubbed the spot while belatedly noticing that the eggs she'd broken into the bowl had left a slimy trail from the countertop to the kitchen sink four feet away.

She'd looked for, but hadn't yet found, the switch for the garbage disposal. Opening the window had gotten rid of most of the smoke caused by the burning bacon. For a minute there, she'd been afraid she'd set the place on fire.

Seeing her wandering attention, Zane was hard-pressed not to yell at her in frustration. The kitchen hadn't been in great shape when she'd started cooking, but now the place looked as if a bomb had hit it. He was on the verge of shipping her back to Chicago, when he reminded himself that he didn't have a bunch of applicants standing in line. It was her or no one.

Telling himself to be patient, Zane was about to speak when a new storm crashed in, banging the swinging door against the wall.

Ten seconds later, the damage was awesome. The

bowl from the countertop had flown across the room before smashing on the floor. The canisters Tracy hadn't even noticed before now lay beside the ruined bowl, their contents strewn all over the kitchen.

The air was filled with flour dust, making Tracy cough even as she asked, "What was that?"

"My two kids," Zane ruefully replied.

2

"YOUR *KIDS?*" Tracy repeated, her eyes glued to the
empty flour canister still drunkenly spinning on the
floor.

"You knew I had kids, right?" Zane said in a defensive voice.

She nodded slowly, still unable to comprehend how
so much damage could be done in such a short time
by a pair of little kids. "Aunt Maeve told me that you
had two adorable and incredibly well-behaved children. I'm getting the feeling that she may have been
exaggerating just a bit." *To put it mildly,* Tracy
thought as she gazed around the kitchen. The place
may have been messy before, but now it looked as if
it would qualify for disaster aid.

Zane's kids obviously weren't the demure quiet
kind and Aunt Maeve clearly hadn't told her the
whole story about this gig as a housekeeper. Her aunt
had omitted a few important items—like the fact that
Zane was sexy and his kids totally wild.

"Lucky!" Zane bellowed, making Tracy jump in
surprise. "Lucky is my daughter's name," Zane
added before the kitchen's swinging door whipped
open, almost smacking Tracy in the face as a flour-
coated child, dressed in jeans and a red T-shirt, gal-

loped into the room, skidding to a halt in front of Zane.

Not sure what to do, Tracy said, "How are you, Lucky?" and automatically held out her hand, more accustomed to meeting business associates than children.

"This is my *son*, Rusty," Zane said, his voice filled with paternal outrage.

"I'm sorry. I couldn't tell." Indeed, the little boy looked almost identical to the other child who'd just raced into the room. Both had short brown hair dusted white with flour, while each wore T-shirts and jeans spattered with egg.

"They're not identical twins," Zane told her. "It's not that hard to tell them apart."

Twins? He had twins. She'd seen the movie *The Parent Trap* so she knew how much trouble twins could be. The kitchen was proof that two kids could do the damage of five. "How old are they?"

"Seven," Zane answered.

"And a half," Lucky said. Or was it Rusty? No, it was Lucky. She could tell because Zane had his hands on his son's shoulders and the comment had come from the other one.

"We don't need anyone to take care of us," the boyish-looking little girl added with a belligerent thrust of her chin.

"I can see that," Tracy replied with a wry look at the mess they'd made in the kitchen. She'd felt bad at the havoc she'd created while cooking, but it was nothing compared to what they'd done, and in such a short time, too. "You appear capable of taking care of things pretty well all on your own." Returning her attention to the twins, she said, "My name is Tracy and I'm the new housekeeper. I'm here to take care of the house and the cooking."

"Grandpa said your cooking was awful," Lucky said.

"Be nice," Zane warned.

"I was being nice," Lucky protested with an innocent look in her blue eyes. "I didn't even kick her or anything."

Kicking? They kicked? Tracy took a cautious step backward just in case.

Seeing her retreat, Rusty laughed. "She's scared," he said in a voice that held a remarkable amount of disdain for a seven-year-old. Or even a seven-and-a-half-year-old.

"Behave," Zane said, his look reprimanding. "And apologize to Ms. Campbell for making a mess in here."

"It was already a mess in here," Rusty pointed out.

Zane's look was stern. "You two made it worse. Now, say you're sorry."

"We're sorry," the two children said in unison.

Tracy could tell from the devilish gleam in their matching blue eyes that they felt no remorse for their actions. Instead, she detected a clear hostility toward her.

Not the best way to start off her first day of work. But then that's how her luck had been going lately.

"And you're going to help Ms. Campbell clean up in here," Zane added.

"Oh, Pa," both children groaned in dismay.

"After you go on upstairs and get cleaned up first." Only after they'd galloped out the door and up the stairs, leaving a trail of flour-studded footsteps behind them, did Zane admit, "Sending them upstairs may not have been the brightest idea."

"That's okay. Kids are kids." Whatever that meant. She didn't know what else to say. She was beginning to feel at a complete loss here. "When does their babysitter get here to take care of them?" she asked hopefully.

"Babysitter?" He gave her a startled look. "There is no babysitter."

She frowned. "I'm no expert, but they seem a little young to be unsupervised. Or does your father look after them?"

"Sometimes he does. But watching them is part of the housekeeper's job. *Your* job."

This came as news to her. Another little detail her aunt had omitted. She'd told Tracy about the kids, but not that she'd be expected to take care of them. "Wait a second here. I thought housekeepers just took care of the house and the cooking."

"You thought wrong."

Tracy sank down onto a rickety kitchen chair, more than a little overwhelmed by this latest bit of information. "And your previous housekeeper did all this?"

"Yes. No problem."

"Then you won't have a problem getting someone else to do this job," she said with a sigh. "I'm not sure I'm the right person for it."

"I'm not sure either," he muttered. "But you're all I've got."

She recognized desperation when she heard it. Giving him a suspicious look, she said, "Why don't you tell me what's really going on around here?" On a hunch, she added, "How many housekeepers have you had?"

"Since when?" he hedged.

"How about in the past year?" she asked, her confidence returning.

"Several."

"How many is several? More than six, less than twelve?"

"That's right."

"And may I ask why they left?"

"For various reasons," he said.

"Named Rusty and Lucky?" she astutely guessed.

He shifted uncomfortably. "Look, maybe I should have told you more about my kids when you first came last night, but then you haven't exactly been completely honest with me, either." Lifting his head, he gave her a direct look, his blue eyes just a tad accusatory. "Telling me you can cook when it's obvious that you can't."

He had her there. "Okay," she admitted, "so I may not have tons of experience at this sort of thing but I'm willing to learn."

"That's what I'm counting on. Just for the summer. In September the kids are back in school and my dad can handle them after class. But I need you to promise that you'll at least stay the summer."

Tracy realized she was in no position to criticize

Zane for not elaborating about what he expected from a housekeeper. Even if he had given her a detailed job description last night, she'd been too tired to have paid much attention.

He was right. She hadn't been completely honest with him. She'd been so eager to get away from Chicago and experience life on a ranch that she'd glossed over her own shortcomings and hadn't bothered checking out the details of the position herself, leaving it to her aunt to phone and say she'd take the job.

But she was an intelligent woman. She could learn how to cook. It was simply a matter of following instructions, right? How different could it be from setting up a new program on her laptop computer? All she had to do was simply follow the instructions. And she'd brought enough cookbooks and cooking paraphernalia to choke a horse. She could manage this. She *would* manage this.

Because the bottom line was she wasn't about to fail here. Not after failing where her engagement was concerned.

And while she was no expert regarding kids, even *she* could tell that the twins could benefit from a woman's touch instead of being allowed to run wild. Especially Lucky. Growing up in an all-male environment had left the little girl looking and acting like a tomboy.

Tracy had worked on an ad campaign for a line of girls' clothing last year and worked with kids for that campaign. Lucky would look adorable in the B. Me clothing line—petite denim dresses and colorful hair bows. More importantly, Tracy was responsible for the ad campaign for Tyke Bikes, making them the hottest item on children's Christmas lists two years ago.

Everything she knew about kids she'd learned from those two campaigns, the only two she'd worked that had involved children. The rest of her accounts had covered the spectrum from wine to nuts—Spring Hill Winery to Pete's Pistachios, to be specific—from big-ticket items like motorcycles to small specialty items like a line of aromatherapy candles. She'd enjoyed the diversity and the new challenges.

Diversity and new challenges. Well, the job of housekeeper on Zane's ranch certainly was sure to provide both of those things in spades.

While working on the B. Me and Tyke Bike accounts, she'd spent several weekends with focus groups of kids. Granted, most of them had been a little older, and a whole lot more civilized, than the two hellions who'd blown through the kitchen. But that was just a minor glitch. She'd use her marketing experience to sell herself to his kids. And to sell them on behaving themselves.

With a nod, Tracy got to her feet. "Okay, you've got a deal. I'll stay for the summer."

The flash of relief on Zane's face would have been easy to miss if Tracy hadn't been watching him closely. But she had been watching him. It was all too easy to do so because he was the kind of man who demanded attention—not by anything he said or did but by his mere presence.

With his chiseled cheekbones and lean build he was just too darn easy on the eyes. It was a good thing she'd sworn off men for the time being. Her life was complicated enough right now without falling for a sexy rancher with an attitude.

She'd come out west to escape and do something completely different. She needed to rethink her life. She needed to clear her thoughts. She didn't need to develop a thing for her employer.

Studying her surroundings, instead of Zane, she decided she'd feel better once she'd restored some order to the place. The remains of scrambled egg were already congealing in the breakfast dishes. "Where's your dishwasher?"

"I'm looking at her," Zane replied, with a pointed look in her direction.

"So you've got a broken stove, no dishwasher, and—just a wild guess here—no garbage disposal, I suppose?"

"We've got a hog named Beauty. She's the garbage disposal."

A hog? They were big, weren't they? Not small and cute like the little pig in the movie *Babe*.

"Don't worry," Zane added. "Feeding Beauty isn't part of your job."

"Thank heavens for small favors," she muttered.

"And the stove isn't broken. It's just old. There's no pilot light, so you have to turn the gas on and light it with a match. Immediately. Otherwise the place fills with gas."

"And you don't have a stove with a pilot light, or own a dishwasher because…?"

This time he was the one who muttered. "Because

I don't have the time or the inclination to get new stuff.''

She translated that to mean he hated shopping, a common male affliction she was accustomed to. In the world of advertising, her job was to make people want to buy things. "What if I did the shopping for you?"

"I'm not made out of money," he warned her.

"I realize that. But if I could get you a good deal on some new appliances it would certainly make life easier. For all of us." She nodded toward the sign on the wall that read "If the Cook Ain't Happy, No One Ain't Happy." She wondered which of the string of departed housekeepers had left that little memento behind.

"This isn't Chicago," he reminded her. "We don't have lots of stores out here. In fact, there's only one place in Bliss that sells appliances, and even then it's out of a catalog."

"Bliss?"

"The closest town."

"Right. I wasn't exactly paying attention to the road signs last night. I was just relieved to get here in one piece."

"Whose cool car is outside?" Rusty demanded as he and Lucky burst into the kitchen. He skidded to a stop a few inches from his father while Lucky slid on a slippery spot on the black-and-white-checked linoleum. Cleaning the slick egg white from the floor was clearly high up on the agenda, Tracy decided. Zane had already picked up the broken shards of the bowl and thrown them away.

"If you're referring to the red car, then it's mine," Tracy replied, grabbing a bunch of paper towels and blotting up the worst of the egg mess on the floor before dumping the dripping paper towels in the trash.

"I don't like it," Rusty said, even though his voice had been eager with excitement a few seconds before. Now it was sullen, as was his expression. And he had his father's stubborn chin.

Well, Tracy could be just as stubborn. "I'm staying."

The twins didn't look at all pleased with her declaration. In fact, they looked so downright dismayed that she almost felt guilty. Trying to make it up to them, she spoke to Rusty. "After we clear things up around here, maybe we could drive into Bliss and you and your sister could show me around town."

"I'm not sure that's a good idea," Zane inserted.

"Why not?" Tracy asked. "I thought we agreed that ordering new appliances would be the thing to do."

"Only if you can find them for under five hundred dollars. For both the stove and dishwasher. Including delivery. And no weird colors. White or black only."

"Done," she promptly said, knowing she had connections in the business. "But first we need to clean up the kitchen."

"Good idea. The twins will help you. I'll leave you to it then." A moment later he was gone, leaving Tracy alone in the kitchen with two very militant munchkins.

"Well," Tracy began and then didn't know what to say next. How did one approach hostile children?

Cautiously, that was for sure. Yet, she couldn't afford to let them get the upper hand.

Think about how you deal with difficult clients, she told herself, recalling how she'd sometimes likened some of them to stubborn children. And she'd won over those clients in the end. She could do the same with these two.

She knew practical techniques to defuse confrontations. Granted, she hadn't used them on Dennis when she'd gone to his apartment to tell him she was having second thoughts about their engagement, only to find him in bed with another woman. But then she hadn't wanted to defuse that situation, she'd wanted to hightail out of it. And she had. By running off to Colorado, cappuccino machine in hand, to become a rancher's housekeeper.

Which brought her back to the twins. "I'm sorry you're not happy about having a housekeeper taking care of you. As you've guessed by now, I've never been a housekeeper before so I don't exactly know what I'm supposed to do and not do."

The twins' expressions immediately went from combative to crafty. As they advanced on her, she could easily imagine them rubbing their hands with glee.

"You're not supposed to make us do housework," Rusty stated.

"Yeah, and you're supposed to let us eat whatever we want, whenever we want," Lucky said.

"No green vegetables," Rusty declared. "A good housekeeper never serves green vegetables."

By now they had Tracy backed against the rattling

refrigerator. But still they kept coming, their words tumbling out.

"And always bakes chocolate cake every night," Lucky said.

Rusty nodded. "Yeah, and doesn't make us clean our rooms."

"Or make our beds," Lucky added.

"Or say we can't eat in our rooms," Rusty tacked on.

Tracy gazed at them with awe. Standing there in clean jeans and yellow T-shirts, they looked so angelic as they lied through their teeth. She was impressed.

"I'll keep that in mind," she said, sliding away from the fridge and making a clean getaway. At least the twins were no longer glaring at her with daggers in their eyes. "But first we better do as your father said and clean things up in here. Where do you keep the mop?"

"In there." Lucky pointed to a pantry door.

Feeling more confident that she was getting things under control, Tracy opened the pantry door only to have a small furry animal scurry out between her feet.

"It's Joe! Get him, get him!" Lucky shrieked as she and Rusty both nosedived toward the streak of fur.

"That's a mouse. Don't touch it!" Tracy shrieked just as loudly. "Come back here!" She grabbed a handful of Rusty's T-shirt only to have him wiggle out of it a second later.

Bare-chested now, he joined his sister who'd slid

the hallway area rug into a pile near the front door as she did a right-angle turn into the living room.

"I got him," Lucky yelled in relief a moment later, holding up her hands and cuddling the mouse to her nose.

Tracy shuddered. She hated mice. She'd had a thing about them ever since Lenny Bronkowski had dropped one down her shorts in the second grade.

Tracy knew she shouldn't just stand there and let the twins hold a rodent to their noses, or even worse, to her nose. If she were a brave woman she'd just saunter over and toss that mouse right out on its skinny little behind. Too bad she'd used up all her gutsy moves getting out here to Colorado in the first place.

Salvation came in the form of Buck, who spoke from his seat in a leather recliner in the corner. "So you found Joe. He's their pet mouse," he added for Tracy's benefit.

Lucky stopped cooing to her mouse long enough to say, "I was so afraid that Precious had gotten to Joe."

"Precious?" Tracy asked, trying to tell herself that a pet mouse was better than a wild one, surely.

"Rusty's pet snake," Buck said.

Of course. She should have guessed as much. "What's wrong with a dog or a cat as a pet?"

"Couldn't get one to stick around," Buck admitted. "They kept running off."

Tracy suspected the twins' hell-on-wheels ways had something to do with that.

Buck confirmed her hunch. "Mighta had something to do with the fact that the twins were practicing their ropin' skills on them to the point where the animals were rope-shy and sleeping with one eye open. So we're left with Joe and Precious," Buck said. "They usually don't stray very far. You better put Joe back in his cage, Lucky."

"Oh, Grandpa." It looked as if Lucky was going to say more when the older man fixed her with a no-nonsense look that stopped her protest.

Tracy took note and wondered if she'd ever be able to duplicate that look—part frown, pure disapproval. If she tried it, she'd probably end up getting wrinkles.

"Why are you running around with no shirt, boy?" Buck asked Rusty.

"She tore it off me." Rusty pointed an accusing finger in Tracy's direction.

When Buck turned his frowning disapproval toward her, Tracy couldn't help getting defensive. "I was trying to stop him from running after the mouse. I didn't know it was a pet."

"Could have been worse," Buck told her with a slow grin that added more lines to a weatherworn face. "My great-great-granddaddy, Jedidiah Best, brought a pet armadillo with him clear up from Texas. We still got it stuffed and on display in the den. You can take a gander at it if you'd like. Family legend has it that the armadillo brought him good luck."

Speechless, Tracy just shook her head, indicating she'd take a pass on viewing the stuffed armadillo. She was still recovering from the mouse.

"That stuffed armadillo didn't bring Cockeyed Curly Mahoney much luck, though," Buck continued.

"Not that he was family, exactly. More like a friend of the family. You ever heard the stories about Cockeyed Curly the bank robber?"

"Can't say that I have," Tracy replied.

"Legend has it that Cockeyed Curly hid the gold coins from his last heist in these parts. Unfortunately, shortly thereafter he choked on a piece of steak and died, taking the secret of his treasure's hiding place with him. So you see what I mean about him not having very good luck in the end."

"Grandpa knows lots of stories about Cockeyed Curly," Rusty said.

"Of course the most famous story is the one about the treasure map," Buck said. "My great-great granddaddy saved Curly's hide in a barroom fight over in Leadville. To repay Jedidiah, Curly drew him a map supposedly showing where he'd buried his treasure. Then Curly went to eat that fateful steak dinner where he choked and died. But that map, if it ever existed, has long since disappeared."

"Maybe it was written on invisible paper," Rusty suggested.

Buck chortled at the idea before his expression turned serious. "I can tell you that some of that money would come in handy right about now. Family ranching isn't exactly a booming operation these days. The little guy is fast becoming a thing of the past, just like the other legends of the west," Buck noted with a brooding expression. "Doggone corporations are taking over the world."

"Grandpa don't like corporations. Don't like city

folks, neither,'' Lucky added with a pointed look in Tracy's direction.

"Doesn't like city folks,'' Tracy automatically corrected.

"That's what I just said. You want to pet Joe before I put him in his cage?'' The little girl held up the mouse and practically waved it underneath Tracy's nose.

Tracy could feel the blood draining from her face even as she hid a shudder, imagining little mousy feet scuttling and scratching against her skin. "No, thank you.'' Did her voice sound faint? She certainly hoped not. If the twins sniffed out her fear of mice they'd pounce on it in an instant. Or have the mouse pounce on her.

Everyone was allowed one weakness. It was just her luck that mice was hers.

"I thought I told you to get on upstairs and put Joe back in his cage,'' Buck reminded Lucky. "Unless you want Precious to make a meal of him.''

"What kind of snake is Precious? And where is he or she?'' Tracy quickly added, looking around the living room and only now realizing how messy the place was.

Last night she'd been so glad to have a roof over her head after the long drive and torrential rain that she hadn't really been paying attention to the decor. Not that she could see much of the decor, what with the newspapers and toys strewn around the place.

There was no missing the huge fieldstone fireplace that filled most of one wall. A pair of matching green leather chairs faced each other like gunfighters at high noon, while a couch stood off to one side as if it were an uninterested bystander. Buck's brown leather recliner had seen better days and appeared to be held together with duct tape. The carpeting may have once been green as well, but it was hard to tell as most of it was covered with papers, socks and an assortment of stuff. If there was a snake in the room, it would be hard-pressed to find an inch of wiggle room.

"The kids wanted a boa constrictor," Buck said. "But I put my foot down and said no. So Precious is just a garden variety snake. And she's kept in the kids' room nowadays."

Tracy picked up on that qualifier right away. "Nowadays?"

"Precious has gotten into the housekeeper's bed a few times," Lucky announced with a grin that wasn't intended to do Tracy's peace of mind any good.

"Yeah, but your pa made you promise that Precious wouldn't do that ever again, remember?"

Lucky's cockiness evaporated at the sound of Buck's reprimanding voice. "Right, Grandpa. I remember."

"Good." Buck nodded. "Because it's too plumb upsettin' for the snake to be plunked down in strange places all the time."

Too upsetting for the snake? What about the *housekeeper?* Tracy wondered. Apparently she was on her own in this Wild West Best household.

3

IT TOOK A GOOD TWO HOURS to get the kitchen back in shape, even with the twins' so-called assistance. Most of the time the kids were more of a hindrance than a help, but Tracy figured that the work was good for their character. At the end of the exercise she had a newfound appreciation for the maid service that she'd had come in twice a week back in Chicago.

The silver lining was that she'd burned enough calories that she wouldn't have to do her aerobic workout. Who knew housework could be so tiring? And there was still the living room to be done.

But first she had to make lunch. She found a bottle of spaghetti sauce in the walk-in pantry along with several boxes of pasta. She warmed the sauce in the countertop microwave but forgot to put a lid on it, so tomato paste spattered all over. By the time she got that cleaned up, the pot of boiling water that held the spaghetti was frothing over.

Since the twins were doing nothing but laughing at her, she sent them into the dining room to set the table. She didn't have time to instruct them on how to lay a proper place setting, so she just gathered the silverware and stuck it in a nice looking ceramic pot big enough to hold it.

Tracy had worked as a waitress one summer in college, so she knew how to efficiently transport as many plates in one trip as possible. The table was set, the big bowls of spaghetti and sauce set in the center, when the men came in at noon. In the blink of an eye, the food had been consumed and they were outside again, heading back to do whatever it was cowhands did on a ranch. Things had no doubt changed some since the Cartwrights ran their Ponderosa ranch on *Bonanza,* where they'd had an excellent Chinese cook, as she recalled.

Which got her to thinking what she wouldn't give for an order of pot stickers and Szechuan chicken.

Zane made no comment about her spaghetti lunch, but he did eat it. He even brought his own dish, now empty, into the kitchen. He set it on the counter just as she was turning from the sink. Their bodies collided midstep.

Her startled gaze met his as awareness shot through her system. Did he feel it, too?

Zane looked into her green eyes and recognized trouble when he saw it, or felt it. And feel it he did, clear to the soles of his feet. It had been a long time since he'd had a woman's soft body pressed against his, or smelled the citrusy freshness of a woman's hair. Her hands were city-girl soft, her perfume expensive.

She didn't belong here. It was as obvious as the spaghetti stain on her ritzy silk shirt. So what if her eyes were the green of a mountain meadow or her lips just made for kissing. She wasn't for him. He'd already learned his lesson by getting hitched up with a city girl. His ex-wife, Pam. She lacked staying power and had run off when the twins were little.

Look but Don't Touch. That was his motto where city girls were concerned. Taking a step away from Tracy, he beat a retreat out of the kitchen, remembering that line about those not being able to take the heat, staying out of the kitchen. That was one piece of advice he aimed on taking.

"Is the hot water heater fixed?" she asked him before he could reach the door.

Hot water? That's what he'd be in if he hung around her much longer. "Not yet. But it should be fixed by tonight."

That was the extent of his conversation before he left the room.

Tracy watched Zane through the kitchen window as he strode toward the horse corral near the barn. Actually he was doing that cowboy amble she'd found so sexy the night before. Men are pond scum, she reminded herself and set to work on the sinkful of dishes. She broke two nails with her scrubbing. The continued lack of hot water made the washing more difficult and had her hands looking like prunes by the time she let the dirty water out of the sink.

Definitely the first thing she had to do was to go check out Bliss and get some 20th-century appliances.

No, she corrected herself, looking down at her clothing. First she had to change clothes. Her linen pants and coral silk shirt were goners. No wonder Zane had stared at her so strangely. It was because she was a mess, not because he was attracted to her.

Leaving the twins in Buck's care, she went upstairs

and managed to find her jeans and a denim shirt as well as a pair of designer athletic shoes in her luggage. Her suede boots had not recovered from the mud and rain the night before. She wasn't sure they ever would. She'd only been in Colorado twenty-four hours and already she'd ruined three hundred dollars' worth of clothing. At this rate she'd be broke and naked in no time—not really a lifetime goal of hers.

She would have liked to redo her hair into something fancier but she was running out of time, so she left it loose around her face. Some sunscreen and lipstick and she was ready to go.

It wasn't until she was downstairs that it occurred to her that both kids wouldn't fit in her two-seater Miata, something she hadn't considered at the time she'd made the offer earlier to give them a ride, so Buck told her to use the pickup truck out front.

Tracy had never driven a truck before, but at least it had an automatic transmission and not a stick shift. The thing was huge. It felt like she was driving a tank the size of a small country.

After making sure the twins had fastened their seatbelts in the passenger seats directly behind her, she drove out the long gravel driveway that led to the main highway. Looking out her rearview mirror she got her first real look at the exterior of the ranch house. It was painted white and had a wraparound porch that showed signs of sagging. Or maybe it was the mirror that was crooked. The two-story building was reminiscent of the farmhouses that she'd occasionally glimpsed while speeding along the interstate in Iowa and Nebraska—big rambling structures from a time when no one worried about fuel conservation or heating bills.

Which reminded her, she sure hoped someone had fixed the hot water heater by the time she returned from Bliss. She was about ready to kill for a hot shower.

At the end of the drive, right before it joined the highway, she slowed as the truck rumbled over something embedded in the road—a set of rails laid side by side and several inches apart.

"Somebody should fix that," she muttered.

"It's a Texas gate to keep the cattle from crossing over from the ranch to the road," Lucky loftily informed her. "Everybody knows that."

Stung, Tracy retorted, "We don't have cattle in Chicago, aside from the Bulls, and they play basketball."

"Grandpa said it was a load of bull that you'd ever done any cooking before." This charming comment came from Rusty.

"Your grandfather is a real character." Tracy just wished he was more like Ben Cartwright and less like Rodney Dangerfield.

IT WAS A HALF-HOUR DRIVE to the town of Bliss. *Town* may have been an overambitious description of the place 159 people called home, as was proudly displayed on the wooden sign with the town's name neatly printed on it. Bliss—the Little Town That Could. But Didn't, someone had scrawled beneath it.

Bliss had one main street, appropriately named Main Street. There were no traffic lights at the two intersections, but there was a stop sign at both First Avenue and Second Avenue. The town apparently didn't have a third avenue but just sort of petered out with a bunch of trailers set back from the road. Tracy was relieved to see that she wouldn't have to parallel park, something she'd finally mastered in her compact Miata but had no desire to even attempt in this tank. Instead the pickup trucks were parked head-in and at an angle. She had no trouble finding an empty space right in front of the Roxy Movie Theater, a throwback to the days when a box of popcorn was a dime and names like Clark Gable and Cary Grant headlined the fancy marquee.

Walking down the sidewalk with the twins at her side she passed an insurance office, the post office, an American Legion, and two bars—one of which had a sign on the door proclaiming No Knives Allowed on Premises.

It had obviously been a while since Zane had gone appliance shopping, as the catalog outlet store had a sign up in its window saying that it had gone out of business. It was dated six months ago, and there was a For Rent sign beside it.

Tugging her pocket-size computerized memo minder out of her purse, she punched in the name of a nationwide appliance store that she'd done work for a few months back. Sure enough, their headquarters were in Colorado Springs. A moment later she had her cellular phone in hand and was speaking to her contact.

As luck would have it, there was a warehouse in Denver and two discounted appliances could be trucked in for the five-hundred-dollar budget she'd agreed to. It paid to have connections.

Feeling confident now that she'd taken care of that bit of business, she decided to explore the rest of Bliss—as in the other side of the street. So she crossed back to check out the few stores. The twins were utterly disgusted that she insisted that they hold her hand while crossing the street.

"We're not babies," Lucky declared.

"Humor me," Tracy retorted, aware of curious looks from passersby—all three of them. In the end she barely hung onto the twins as they rushed her across the street.

The first establishment she stopped at, a dry-goods store with everything from cigarettes to china in the window, was closing as she arrived, the clerk hurriedly turning over the Welcome sign to its Sorry We're Closed side just as she reached the door.

Glancing at her watch, Tracy noted that it was only a little after three. Rather early to be closing up. Moving on to the next store, she was surprised to find their door already locked. The third place, a combination grocery-and-hardware store, was open but claimed they were about to close once Tracy and the twins were inside. The clerk gave them the bum's rush and Tracy found herself standing on the sidewalk facing yet another Closed sign.

She'd heard of places that didn't welcome outsiders, but this was ridiculous. It was as if they saw her coming and locked their doors and pulled down their blinds. Why? Why would they be so unfriendly?

Tracy didn't even realize she'd said the words aloud until Rusty answered them.

"Because we're accident prone. We broke something the last time we went in there," Rusty said with more pride than remorse.

"What did you break?" she asked.

"The front window."

She gulped. These Best twins didn't seem to do anything on a small scale. When they went after glass, they skipped the bottles and headed right for the big-ticket items. "How did you manage to do that?"

Rusty shrugged. "I hit it just right with my slingshot. I used a walnut in it."

"The window didn't really break," Lucky added. "It just got a big ol' crack in it."

"Pa wasn't happy when we did that," Rusty said in a hushed voice. "We're not allowed to play with our slingshots in town anymore."

"Or in the house," Tracy added for good measure.

"Or in the house," Lucky agreed before fixing her with a haughty stare. "But not because you said so. Because Pa did."

"Your father is a wise man."

"Well, actually I'm the wise one in the family," a man wearing a badge stated as he strolled up to join them.

"Uncle Reno!"

The twins launched themselves at him. Apparently he was used to it because he scooped one child up in each arm and twirled around, giving Tracy a good view of yet another good-looking denim-clad cowboy. He was taller than Zane and younger. Where

Zane projected a raw power, this man was more easygoing.

"And who's this lovely lady with you?" he asked the twins.

"Our new housekeeper," Lucky replied. "She's not staying long."

Taking matters into her own hands, Tracy introduced herself before tacking on, "And I am staying, for the summer at least."

Reno's eyes actually twinkled as he drawled, "You're a courageous soul."

Oh, yeah, this one was the charmer in the family.

"She can't cook," Lucky told Reno.

"Darlin', she doesn't have to cook," Reno murmured with a meaningful glance.

Unlike Zane's dark looks, Reno's charm did nothing for her, which meant he was less of a threat to her peace of mind than his older brother was. When Reno shook her hand, there had been no humming in her fingers and her heart hadn't even skipped a beat.

"Uncle Reno is the sheriff," Rusty informed Tracy. "He can arrest you if you do something wrong. Like feed us broccoli."

"Rusty here hates broccoli, but feeding him some isn't a hanging offense."

"It oughta be," Rusty muttered.

Tracy couldn't help it. She grinned. "We just came into town to get some groceries and take a look around, but it seems that the twins' reputation precedes them."

"Maybe you'll be able to civilize them," Reno suggested.

"That could happen. Let's just say that I can be as stubborn as they are and leave it at that."

"The stubbornness they got from Zane."

"I had gathered that much. He told me that he'd had a hard time keeping a housekeeper." A little late, she noted to herself, but he had finally told her.

"Yeah, the twins have a way of putting the fear of the devil into you while looking at you with the eyes of an angel. Look, they're doing it right now even as Lucky just tied your shoelaces together."

Tracy looked down to see that he was right. It appeared that she still had a thing or two to learn about dealing with the terrible twosome.

BY THE TIME Tracy found her way to the supermarket over in Kendall, where the twins weren't as well-known and therefore banned from the store, it was already five. Kendall actually had two traffic lights, both of which stayed red for five minutes while Tracy fumed behind the wheel. She'd never get back to the ranch in time to make dinner now.

"You're speeding," Lucky announced ten minutes later, jabbing an accusatory finger into Tracy's right shoulder. "I'm gonna tell Pa."

"You do and I'm making broccoli for dinner for the rest of the week."

Okay, so she was lowering herself to their level, not a good negotiating technique, but she was tired and hungry. She hadn't eaten her own cooking, which meant she hadn't eaten anything, aside from a granola bar in her suitcase, all day.

The broccoli threat seemed to work, for the twins

stayed quiet. But the momentary peace was soon broken by the sound of a police-car siren.

"I told you you were speeding." Lucky gloated.

Suffice it to say that the policewoman from Kendall was not as charming as Reno had been, citing Tracy not only for speeding nine miles above the speed limit but also for driving with a defective taillight. The fact that it wasn't her truck carried no weight with the policewoman at all.

"That was Sally," Lucky said after the policewoman had departed. "She used to date Pa."

"She gives him tickets, too."

Tracy aimed on giving him more than a ticket. She aimed on giving him a piece of her mind for sending her out on a wild-goose chase without taillights. It didn't matter that Buck was the one who told her to use the truck or that Zane hadn't been keen to have her go into Bliss in the first place. All that mattered was that Zane was a man who made her hand, not to mention the rest of her body, hum at a time when she wanted nothing to do with the male species.

TRACY'S BAD MOOD was tempered by the delicious smell of barbecued ribs wafting from the ranch house. Her mouth watered. Her nose led her through the house and beyond the kitchen to the backyard, if a ranch had such a thing. There she found Buck, master of all he surveyed, a big white apron covering him from shoulders to knees as he leaned over a smoking hot grill. He handled the pair of large tongs the way Wyatt Earp handled a gun, twirling it in his right hand before stashing it back in place.

"Will that taste as good as it smells?" Tracy asked.

"Son of a buck, it tastes even *better* than it smells." Buck added a chortle for good measure.

He was right. It did taste even better than it smelled. It was quite simply the best barbecued ribs she'd ever tasted. And she told him so.

"The secret is in the sauce," he confided. "It's an old family recipe."

Tracy helped herself to another delicious rib. "I don't see why you need a cook when you can make something this good yourself."

"My father's barbecue is great," Zane acknowledged, "but it's the only thing he cooks."

Tracy knew all about being a one-trick pony. The only thing she cooked was Shrimp de Jonghe.

"You should bottle this and sell it," she told Buck even as she licked the sauce from her fingertips.

"Pa, you're staring at Tracy." The accusation came from Lucky.

Turning her head, Tracy noted that Zane's sexy craggy face was now a shade of red not unlike that of the barbecue sauce.

"Is it because she got a ticket?" Lucky had an eager look in her eyes. "I told you she got a ticket, right?"

"Only about a hundred times," Zane muttered.

"So is that why you were staring at her?"

"I wasn't staring at her. I was just surprised that she talked about Grandpa selling his barbecue sauce."

"Why should that surprise you?" Tracy asked. "I was in advertising before I came out here and I worked with focus groups on a variety of products, including foods. Gourmet food items are very hot right now."

"Grandpa's sauce isn't hot," Rusty said. "You should taste Pa's salsa. It'll burn your mouth out."

"By *hot* I meant that they are very popular," Tracy explained.

"Our Pa is poplar," Lucky said, for the first time sounding like a kid.

"Popular," Zane automatically corrected her.

"A poplar is a tree, dummy." Rusty elbowed his sister.

"I'm not a dummy!" She elbowed him right back.

"I think these ribs would taste wonderful with broccoli." Another cheap shot at least but it ended the shoving match between the twins.

Returning her attention to Buck, she said, "I really think you should seriously consider bottling your barbecue sauce and selling it."

"Selling it where?" Buck countered. "Here? We don't get many visitors to these parts."

"Selling it in gourmet food catalogs. There are a number of them that specialize in products from the West and Southwest. Many of them have Web sites on the Internet as well."

"I'll give it some thought," Buck said, but looked doubtful.

"Maybe you could be more famous than Cockeyed Curly, Grandpa." Rusty looked pleased by the idea.

"As long as you don't choke on any steak." This bit of advice came from Lucky. "Or ribs."

"Or broccoli," Rusty added with a dire look in Tracy's direction.

She ignored it. "Where are the rest of the cow-hands?" Although she hadn't been formally introduced to any of them yet, she knew there had been half a dozen of them at lunch.

"They have Monday night off so they head into town," Zane replied.

"Into Bliss?"

Zane laughed. It was the first time she'd heard his laugh and she liked it. His voice might shimmy down her spine like a hot toddy but his laugh had more of a ripple effect.

"No, not into Bliss. They head over to Red Deer or Kendall."

"Tracy got a ticket outside of Kendall," Lucky piped in yet again.

"We know!" The words were spoken in unison by Zane, Buck and even Rusty.

Lucky's glare told them that she was not amused.

Join the club, kid, Tracy thought, still brooding over her reaction to Zane's laugh.

Her mood was only slightly improved after doing another sinkful of dishes—the hot water heater had finally been repaired, thank heaven—while Zane put the twins to bed. Buck asked about her ideas for his barbecue sauce while she worked. When Zane came back downstairs he passed by the kitchen to grab a cup of coffee from the coffeemaker she'd been told to keep brewing at all times.

"Would it be okay if I took a shower now that the hot water heater is fixed?" she said, not wanting to do anything that would make it break down again.

He looked at her as if she'd just asked him if she could dance nude on the kitchen table.

She frowned. "Is there a problem?"

"No, no problem." His voice was rough and a tad curt. "You can take a shower, just don't spend all day in it or the hot water will run out."

"I'll be sure to save some hot water for you." The thought of him in the shower—minus the jeans, shirt and boots, with droplets of water rolling down his bare body—was enough to make her eyes widen. And to make her wonder if that's why he'd looked at her so strangely a moment ago. Because he'd been imagining the same thing about her?

Or maybe he was just aggravated by her lack of ability in the housekeeping department. It was getting pretty bad when she couldn't tell whether a man's look was aggravated or aroused. She'd gotten out of practice while she'd been engaged to Dennis. He'd chased her from the first moment he'd met her at a professional function. He'd swept her off her feet. It had been intoxicating. She'd found him compatible and their lifestyles and interests meshed, so she thought he must be the man for her.

She'd only been interested in him. Sappy though it sounded, she hadn't even noticed other men.

Which was one of the reasons why her response to Zane worried her a bit. Well, maybe it wasn't so much a response as an *awareness*. Yes, she liked that term. It didn't sound as serious. Awareness was okay. After all, she was a free woman now. It was perfectly normal for her to appreciate a good-looking man.

After her quick shower she retired to her room to use her cell phone to call her aunt.

"I'm so glad to hear from you!" Aunt Maeve had a booming voice. Wincing, Tracy moved the phone a little further from her ear. "Did you get to the ranch safely? Were Herbert's directions helpful?"

Herbert was Aunt Maeve's third husband. Growing up, Tracy had been convinced that the movie *Mame* was based on her Aunt Maeve. When her own parents had died right after she'd graduated from high school, Aunt Maeve had stepped in—or swept in and taken over, to be more accurate. Aunt Maeve was like a bird of paradise, all bright colors and showy moves. She had a heart of gold and the memory of a sieve. "You didn't give me Herbert's directions."

"Surely I did."

"No, you gave me your directions."

"How could you tell the difference?" Maeve demanded.

"Because Herbert's directions would have been more specific than 'you take the little road after the big road.'"

"Did you get lost?"

"I found it in the end," Tracy replied, stretching out on the bed after pulling back the covers to make sure there was no mouse hidden underneath the sheets.

"Well, then, my directions weren't so bad after all. And how are you settling in?"

"Okay, I guess." She gingerly explored the shadowy foot of the bed with her toes, still not one hundred percent confident she was alone. "It wasn't exactly what I expected."

"Why is that?"

Tracy curled up and bent over to take a peek under the bed before replying to her aunt's question. "Because you told me that Zane was a middle-aged widower with two angelic children."

"And?"

"And I come here to find out that the twins are hellions and Zane is..."

"Yes?" Maeve's voice perked up.

"No more middle-aged than I am. Oh sure he may be a few years older, but not by many."

"Funny, one would expect that having twin hellions would age a person," Maeve noted dryly.

"It hasn't aged him. He's got this cowboy swagger... Anyway, I was expecting J.R.'s dad from *Dallas* and instead he's..."

"Mel Gibson in *Maverick?*" Maeve suggested.

"Only harder."

Maeve's earthy laughter was positively wicked.

"I mean darker," Tracy stammered, feeling like a teenager. "Jeez, you're making me blush, Aunt Maeve."

"I told you that heading for the ranch would be good for you after your broken engagement."

"I know you did." Feeling restless, Tracy got up and started pacing the room. "The ironic thing is that I went to see Dennis that afternoon to tell him that I had doubts about us getting married. After finding him in bed with another woman, I could understand where my doubts were coming from,'' she ended tartly.

"You suspected that Dennis might be cheating on you?"

"No," Tracy admitted. "It wasn't that I had doubts because I thought he was cheating on me. I had doubts about whether or not I loved him. Or whether or not he really he loved me."

"And now?"

"Now I know he never loved me, at least not the way I want to be loved. As for my feelings, I think I wanted to love him rather than really loving him. I felt anger at his betrayal but a bit of relief as well now that I had a bona fide reason for calling off the engagement. He was very convincing in the beginning of our relationship in the way he chased after me." She paused in front of the window, the mountain range out beyond the large cottonwood tree reminding her once more that she'd come a long way from Chicago. "I'm certainly relieved that I found out what kind of man he was before I married him, glad that I trusted my instincts and went to see him when I did. Did I tell you that when I informed Dennis that our engagement was off, he didn't believe me?" She resumed her pacing. "He kept saying he could explain. He even tried to justify his behavior by telling me that she was a client and he was just trying to keep the client happy. When that didn't work he threatened to fire me if I didn't marry him. That's when I told him that not only was I breaking off our engagement but I was quitting my job as well."

"Good for you."

"And that's when I checked into a hotel and called you telling you that I needed to get away."

Maeve immediately picked up the story from here. "And I told you about Zane needing a housekeeper. You see how things all work out in the end? You had a need, he had a need, together you fulfill each other's needs."

The image Maeve's words created had more to do with sexual needs than practical ones. Tracy shifted, feeling incredibly warm all of a sudden. "I wouldn't put it exactly like that."

"Why not?"

"Because you make it sound like we're..." Tracy's voice trailed away as an erotic image took hold.

"Yes?" Maeve prompted.

Shaking her head, she booted the forbidden picture from her mind. "Nothing. I have to tell you that I still can't quite believe that I just packed up and came out here."

"Believe it, dear. And enjoy it."

THAT NIGHT Tracy didn't dream about Dennis at all. Instead she dreamt that just like Gulliver who had been tied down by the Lilliputians, she too had been tied down with incredibly tough ropes except hers were made of burned bacon, and her little tormentors were named Lucky and Rusty. Somehow she was wearing Dorothy's red shoes from *The Wizard of Oz* and wasn't able to click them to get back home again.

You'd better wake up or you're going to get a crick

in your neck. The thought permeated her foggy dream. *Unless you want to stay here all tied up.*

It's just a dream, she sleepily thought. *I want to see what happens next.*

The sound of pounding woke her up. She blinked owlishly. Dawn was just beginning to lighten the darkness of her room. Was it time to get up? She tried, only to be stopped in her tracks.

"Damn it, Tracy," Zane growled from the other side of her bedroom door. "You're late again."

"I'm all tied up at the moment," she shouted back.

"Just get yourself downstairs, pronto."

"Can't do that," she said.

"Why not?" he demanded.

"I think you should come in and see for yourself," she said.

Zane walked into her bedroom to find Tracy's bed completely covered with twine crisscrossing just a few inches above her body, effectively pinning her in place.

"It would appear that your little darlings were busy last night," she noted tartly. "Unless you find it necessary to tie all your housekeepers to their beds to keep them from running off?"

4

ZANE COULDN'T TAKE his eyes off Tracy. She was all creamy skin and lush curves. Her green eyes sparkled with irritation. She wore an ivory nightgown that displayed a generous amount of cleavage. More cleavage than he'd seen in some time, he realized as his body reacted to the sight.

"Stop looking at me like that," she muttered.

"Like what?" he said, unable to tear his gaze away from her for a moment.

"Like I'm on the menu for breakfast."

She did look good enough to eat, he decided, the thought of him lapping his way across her bare skin only adding to the already tight fit of his jeans. Did she taste as soft as she looked?

"Would you just untie me?" she said in exasperation.

"Oh, right." Feeling a tad bit guilty about his erotic feelings, Zane moved forward to try and tackle the closest knot. It happened to be near her waist. There wasn't enough wiggle room for her to shift out of his way as the back of his knuckles brushed against her satin-covered body.

He heard her inhaled breath. It matched his own. Muttering under his breath, he moved on to her ankles where he managed to get a few inches undone before running into another knot, this one along the side of her leg. He got that one undone and was starting to make headway when he suddenly found himself following the twine trail that lead him directly to…her breasts.

His fingers froze in the process of working on another knot, but that only meant that his fingers were now grazing the bare skin on the curve of her left breast. And yes, her skin was as soft as it looked. Sweat formed along his upper lip as he was consumed with the sudden urge to taste her, to take her.

A quick glance into her startled eyes told him that she felt it too, this chemistry pulsing between them.

TRACY HELD HER BREATH as Zane's fingers moved across her skin, exploring her instead of the narrow cord holding her captive.

Now it was no longer just the twine pinning her to the bed, it was also the heated intensity of his gaze, the raw temptation of his touch. His fingertips were work roughened and they didn't so much glide over her skin as they explored with a velvety touch—from her collarbone down to the lacy edge of her nightie and back up again.

The outline of her nipples was now clearly visible beneath the thin material of her nightgown as her body signaled its arousal. It was if her body had a mind of its own, for it certainly wasn't obeying her logical commands to behave.

This nightgown had been part of her trousseau. She'd planned on wearing it for Dennis. Instead here she was with a ruggedly lean and sexy cowboy seducing her with his fingertips, which were getting ever closer to the aching apex of her nipples. Would he…would she…yes! He grazed the peak of her breast with his thumb and her back arched as far as it would go given her twine prison. Her movement trapped his hand between her breast and the narrow cord, further embedding his touch into her body and her psyche.

Heat, exquisite and elemental, swept through her entire body. Her heart was soaring like a shooting star as excitement burned deep within her. The sound of his breathing coincided with hers—fast, shallow pants of anticipation. Or impending disaster.

The sensations buffeting her were as uncontrollable as a lightning bolt. Not a good thing.

"No," she gasped, trying to retain some semblance of sanity.

Zane immediately yanked his hand away, his stark expression making his chiseled cheekbones stand out even more than usual. They weren't the only things standing out, she noticed with a guilty look at his jeans.

Getting to his feet, he reached into his pocket and pulled something out. Light from the overhead fixture flashed on the silvery metal of…a knife! He'd just flicked open a pocketknife the size of Colorado! She'd heard of guys who got upset when a woman said no, but hauling out a sharp weapon was extreme.

Eyeing him warily, she said, "Now let's stay calm here and talk about this."

"What's to talk about? The knife is for me to cut the twine, not your neck," he retorted sharply.

She recovered quickly. "Of course. I knew that."

"Yeah, right. That's why you were looking at me like I was a serial killer or something."

"You forget, I'm from the big city. I don't trust people with knives."

"I won't forget you're from the big city," he said, the tone of voice making it clear that her origins were less than stellar in his book.

"You've got something against people from the big city?"

"You could say that."

"I just did," she said, annoyed by his comment. "What exactly do you have against city dwellers?"

He looked up from his work to pin her with his gaze, as intensely blue as a Rocky Mountain sky. "Why do you care?"

"Because I work for you, and it might help me understand you."

"Don't bother," he told her as he threw aside the last of the twine. "Understanding me isn't part of your job. Cooking and taking care of my kids is."

Having said those words, Zane closed his knife, jammed it back into his pocket and headed out of her room as if the hounds of hell were at his heels.

"And good morning to you, too," Tracy muttered as she finally sat up in bed, freed of the physical binds put on her by his children, but not freed of the memory of Zane's touch.

THE GOOD NEWS was that she didn't actually burn anything at breakfast, the bad news was that the eggs were overdone and the bacon rubbery. Which meant perfection was somewhere between yesterday and today. And she had no doubt that perfection would be easier to attain, or to at least approach, once the new stove was delivered in two days.

She now knew that she was cooking breakfast for six—Zane, his father, his two hellions, and two full-time ranch hands. There were two more temporary hands—teenagers working for the summer, Buck told her—but they ate before they got there. They needed to be fed lunch, however.

"Spring and fall are our busiest times on the ranch," Buck told her as she cleared the breakfast dishes from the huge oak table in the dining room. "Right now we've just finished up all the inoculations and branding. I reckon you already met Murph'n'Earl here." Buck rolled the two names together into one. "These two sons of a buck have been working here since Zane was knee-high to a grasshopper."

Tracy blinked at the image of Zane being anything but the ruggedly sexy man he was now. Meanwhile the two ranch hands, who stood shifting from one leg to the other, were nervously rolling up the brims of their hats in their hands with awkward shyness.

"Go ahead and talk to her, boys. She won't bite."

When the men just shuffled their feet, Buck grew impatient and elaborated on the introductions himself. "The tall hombre with no meat on his bones is Murph. The other fella with the silly grin on his face is Earl."

"I'm Murph," the taller of the two men confirmed,

his voice like tumbling gravel. "And this here's Earl." He nodded toward his friend.

By contrast, Earl was shorter and stockier although far from heavy. Both men possessed the kind of time-worn faces that told of years spent outdoors. She made a mental note not to go outside without plenty of sunscreen. While the lines on their faces gave them character, she doubted that the same would be said about her. Meanwhile their bashfulness endeared them both to her.

Tracy smiled at them. "It's nice meeting you both. I'm sorry the breakfast wasn't all that good this morning. But I'm still having trouble with that ancient monstrosity."

"You mean Buck here is giving you trouble?" Murph asked.

Tracy tried not to laugh. "I was referring to the stove, not to Buck."

"I may be ancient but I sure ain't no monstrosity," Buck grumbled. "You two layabouts best stop shooting the breeze and get to work. I ain't running no dude ranch here."

"Everyone thinks they're a comic," Buck added for Tracy's benefit as the two men shuffled their way out. "Truth is that no one had the sense of humor that Cockeyed Curly did. Now there was a man with a dose of brains. Wrote his own poetry, he did. Nowadays cowboys are famous for writin' poetry, but in them days Cockeyed Curly was something of a celebrity. Course that could have been because of all those trains and banks he robbed. At each one, he left a poem meant to drive the local constabulary plumb crazy. One of my favorites goes like this.

Curly was here to help you out,
That money is heavy there's no doubt.
So I lift it from you to lighten your load.
Make it easier for you to get down the road.''

When Tracy laughed, Buck was obviously thrilled with a ready audience and immediately launched into a long-winded poem of his own that lacked Curley's wit and seemed to go on and on.

When he finally paused long enough to draw breath, she quickly inserted, ''I'd better go see what the twins are up to.''

Pushing open the kitchen swing door, her mind was already focused on how she was going to deal with the children after their nightly prank on her.

They were waiting for her in the kitchen, where Zane had set them to work doing dishes as punishment. While appearing to be suitably chastened as they'd made their joint apologies to her beneath their father's steely gaze before breakfast, one look in the twins' eyes and she could tell that the battle wasn't over yet. In fact, it may have only just begun.

A small part of her was tempted to give them a taste of their own medicine, no matter how childish that might seem. But she suspected they'd be happy if she'd attack. It would put her on their home turf— which of course she already was by living in their house. But it would mean playing the game the way they liked to play it and the way they'd no doubt played it with all the other housekeepers they'd already run off.

When you react you are hooked, she reminded herself. The same could be said about her reaction to Zane that morning in her bedroom. She wasn't about to get hooked.

This wasn't about Zane, this was about managing his kids. She smiled as inspiration struck.

"I appreciate being included in your western welcome ritual," she told them, her voice deliberately friendly.

"What's a ritual?" Rusty asked suspiciously, lifting a soapy hand to shove a lock of brown hair out of his eyes.

"A ceremony," Tracy explained. "Like tying me to the bed so your father could untie me."

"That's not why we did it," Rusty said.

"No?" Tracy pretended confusion. "Then why did you do it?"

"To make you leave." Rusty plunked another dish in the murky water.

"Why would you want to do that? So you can cook and clean for everyone by yourselves?"

Both twins looked outraged by the idea. They both turned their backs to the sink to glare at her. "We're just kids!"

Tracy met their gazes head on. "You seem smarter than just kids to me."

"We do?" Lucky was clearly pleased by this news, while Rusty appeared more doubtful.

"Sure you do." Tracy smiled before leaning closer to confidentially confess, "You may even be smarter than I am. Because for the life of me I don't understand how getting rid of me helps you.''

Lucky looked at Tracy as if she were denser than a rock. ''Because then Pa will have to stay home all day with us.''

Bingo! So that was what was behind their shenanigans. She nodded slowly. ''Yes, I can understand how you'd want to spend more time with your father.'' *I wouldn't mind spending more time with him myself.* The wayward thought ran through Tracy's mind before she shoved it aside. ''How about if I help you spend more time with him?''

''How can you help us?'' Rusty scoffed.

''I've got my ways,'' Tracy assured them. ''Let's talk.''

ZANE WAS STANDING ankle deep in manure, which he considered to be a fitting reminder of the kind of deep cow patties he'd be in if he allowed himself to be reeled in by a city girl like Tracy. Been there, done that. He'd learned his lesson well after his ex-wife, Pam, had put him through the wringer.

He'd met her in a bar down in Denver. She'd wiggled up to him, all sultry like, in a pair of jeans that look as if they'd been spray-painted on. She'd claimed that she had a thing for cowboys and asked if she could buy him a drink. Instead he'd insisted on buying her one and she'd insisted that they dance afterward. They'd done more than just dance.

He'd been plumb loco over her. He'd gone down to Denver every chance he got, putting thousands of extra miles on his new truck. She'd gazed at him with her baby-blue eyes as if he was the best thing since sliced bread, and he'd believed her when she'd said she loved him and would love to live on a ranch.

But the reality was that after two years Pam had had her fill. She'd up and told him that it was time for her to move on, to follow her dream of becoming a Vegas showgirl, a dream he'd known nothing about until that moment. Maybe he should have gotten suspicious when she'd insisted on naming the twins Rusty and Lucky after the lead characters in her favorite movie—*Viva Las Vegas*.

She'd said that the twins would be in her way in Vegas, packed up her rhinestone duds, and taken off in her sporty car with a hefty check in her pocket because, after all, she'd need money to set up her new life. And if she didn't get it, maybe she'd take one of the twins after all. Zane had given her the money. Gladly.

There were times when he still found it hard to believe that she'd chosen to leave her kids behind. He'd walk though fire for the twins and fight to the death to protect them, but Pam had never shown any maternal feelings for them. Instead she'd bitterly complained that they'd nearly ruined her figure and took too much of her time.

When Pam walked out, the twins had been a little over a year old. Just starting to walk and talk. And they'd been walking and talking nonstop ever since.

He'd never forget the pain in his kids' eyes when they first realized that other kids had a mom, while theirs had run off on them. They had no memory of Pam at all. Yet when she had died in a car accident last year, he'd seen in their eyes the loss of a dream he hadn't even been sure they'd had. The dream of having a mom.

The only good thing Pam had done was give him the twins—and teach him the lesson that this ranch was no place for a city girl, even one born and raised in Colorado. It was certainly no place for a silky blond from Chicago, a city that made Denver look puny.

Zane was in no rush to get married again, but he did aim on getting hitched one day. And when he did, it would be with someone like him, someone who had been raised with this kind of life. Not an outsider.

Muttering a curse, Zane tossed another shovelful of manure and straw into the wheelbarrow. Usually he had one of the ranch hands do this chore, but today he needed reminding of his roots and the deep pile of manure he'd be in if he got mixed up with a satin-covered city girl like Tracy.

ZANE HAD BEEN IGNORING her all day, but Tracy finally tracked him down in the barn. He'd left the dinner table before dessert, as if her chocolate cake was something to be afraid of. Actually the box cake had turned out fairly well, with simple mixing instructions that even she didn't mess up.

She'd brought him a piece of cake and planned on talking to him about the twins.

It was actually her first time in a barn. She'd seen them on TV of course. But you couldn't smell your TV screen, so you missed the sweetness of fresh hay and the warm smell of horses.

The evening was getting cool and twilight brought with it that magical light that, while pretty, made it hard to see.

She paused to get her bearings when, the next thing she knew, someone made a grab for her derriere!

Startled, she turned around only to discover that the culprit was a horse.

"I've got enough problems without a horse trying to get fresh," she muttered, taking several hurried steps away.

She'd never seen a horse laugh before, but she was convinced this one was doing just that as it shook its head and mane while making funny snorting noises.

"Very funny, buster. Just keep your nose or whatever to yourself."

Horses were in stalls on both sides. She tried not to jump as a horse on her right stomped its foot, or was it hoof? The chocolate cake on the plate she held slid dangerously to the side, but she managed to save it in time.

Continuing down the center aisle, she squinted into the gloom. Wasn't that Zane's shirt hanging from a nail near the back of the barn?

He was in the last stall, using a pitchfork to distribute a thick bed of fresh straw on the ground. He looked like the epitome of a cowboy, his bare chest and back displaying lean rippling muscle, while his lower torso was looking good in snug denim jeans.

"I...uhm," she cleared her throat. "I brought you something."

She no sooner got the words out than she felt something wet and cold and big smack her elbow, jostling the arm and hand holding the cake. Yelping in surprise, she leaned forward to catch the dessert before it slid off the plate. All that did was make her lose her balance and plow smack into Zane, who'd turned to face her and see what all the commotion was about.

Zane barely had time to toss the pitchfork out of the way before Tracy toppled him onto the bed of hay he'd just spread.

Tracy didn't know where the plate or the cake ended up. All she knew was that she was plastered against Zane, her breasts pressed against his bare chest, her left leg resting between his legs.

It was as if they were back in her bedroom again, heat flaring between them with instant fire. His heart was pounding beneath her, matching the throbbing within her.

Lifting her nose from the hollow above his collarbone, she tried to apologize for plastering herself against him like plastic wrap. But before she could get the words out, he kissed her.

5

TRACY'S LIPS were still parted when his mouth captured hers. There was no teasing introduction, no awkward pause or bumping of noses, just unadulterated hunger. He took her breath away.

Sliding his fingers through her hair, Zane linked them at the back of her head, his large work-roughened hands cradling her as he angled her mouth just so, ensuring even more sultry tongue fluttering. He tasted like the coffee he'd had with his meal.

Where had he learned to kiss like this? She was stunned, awed. She was inspired to kiss him back just as impressively.

It must have worked, because a moment later he rolled over so that he blanketed her. The change in position changed the kiss, for the better. Now he could nibble his way around her lower lip before devouring her mouth.

He flicked the tip of his tongue across the roof of her mouth in a move that should have been ticklish but was instead wildly seductive. Keeping one hand cupped behind her head, he slid the other one down the side of her neck, his fingertips brushing the line of her jaw on his way...where? She couldn't tell where he'd touch her next, and there were so many places on her body that ached for his touch.

His kisses kept her distracted as he moved his hand ever so slowly from the base of her throat, over the slick material of her blouse to her breast. He didn't grab her or boldly fondle her. All he did was graze her nipple with the ball of his thumb.

It was enough to make her insides melt and flow like hot honey. He did it again, this time adding a flick of his tongue to their kiss as she moaned into his mouth and eagerly responded with a few clever feminine thrusts of her own.

That first kiss had turned into many as their embrace became even more intimate, the roll of his hips making his arousal plain. He shifted again, reversing their positions so that she was once again draped against him. His hands were beneath her blouse now, having tugged it from the waistband of her jeans. Hers were all over his bare chest. He'd tugged her blouse up and had just undone her bra when Tracy felt heavy breathing on the bare small of her back followed by another wet nudge that most definitely didn't come from the man beneath her.

Lifting her lips from Zane's, she yelped. Startled, Zane dumped her off his chest and into the hay.

When she rolled onto her back, she stared up at a huge horse's head. It was just about nose to nose with her and looked as if it wanted to get closer to do more than just nibble on her.

"Stop that, Bashful," Zane growled, his dark hair ruffled and his hat nowhere to be found. It took her a second to realize she'd been the one who'd ruffled his hair when she'd run her fingers through it.

What had she been thinking of? This man was her employer. Scooting into the far corner of the stall, she stared at Zane with a mixture of dismay and lingering passion. He was looking at her in exactly the same way.

"That never happened," Zane said, his voice curt as he got to his feet, creating more distance between them.

"The horse startled me," she began when he interrupted her.

"That kiss never happened. It was a big mistake."

Tracy had never been a big mistake before and she didn't like it.

Zane welcomed the flash of anger he saw in her green eyes. It was better than the sexy warmth he'd seen in them a moment or two before. "Look, I already got burned by a city girl, my ex-wife. This time around I'm looking for a plain-Jane woman with no career aspirations, one who'll make my kids her top priority, one who is rock solid. You don't fulfill any of those qualifications," he ended bluntly.

Tracy was glad the pitchfork was at the other end of the stall, otherwise she might have been tempted to use it on him. "It was just a kiss." Okay, so that was a lie, but this next bit was the truth. "I can assure you that I'm no more eager to enter into a relationship with you than you are with me. After all, I've just broken off my engagement because, among other things, I caught my fiancé cheating on me. That's why I wanted to get away from Chicago for a while. Not to have a roll in the hay with an arrogant son of a...buck!'' Scrambling to her feet, she brushed the hair and straw out of her eyes before fixing him with a chilling look. ''This incident is already forgotten.'' She stomped out of the stall, marching through the missing chocolate cake as she did so, but not stopping for one instant. She considered herself lucky that all she'd lost in the episode was another pair of shoes. It could have been much worse.

Despite her words, it wasn't easy for Tracy to forget their kiss. Anger carried her back to the ranch house, where she kicked off her ruined chocolate-covered shoes in the mudroom at the back of the house. How dare Zane kiss her like that and then act as if it was all her fault.

''Did you talk to Pa?'' Rusty asked the minute Tracy entered the kitchen.

''Your father has the brains of a mule. No, that's probably not fair to a mule. He has the brains of a tick on a mule!''

Rusty's eyes bulged at the sight of her in a high temper. Lucky was equally not impressed. ''Don't you insult our pa!'' The little girl put both hands on her hips and glared at Tracy. ''He's the smartest man in the universe. He knows lots more than you do.''

''What's going on in here?'' Buck demanded. ''I could hear yelling clear in the front parlor. How's a man supposed to enjoy a John Wayne movie with all this caterwauling in here?''

''We don't have a cat,'' Rusty said, frowning in confusion.

''He means noise,'' Tracy translated.

"She was yelling," Lucky said, pointing an accusing finger at Tracy. "She said Pa has the brains of a tick."

"Oh-ho, she did, did she?" Buck's look was speculative. "I wonder what my oldest son of a buck has gone and done now. You care to elaborate, missy?"

Tracy primly shook her head. She'd said enough as it was. "Anybody want some homemade lemonade?" Without waiting for an answer, Tracy grabbed a glass pitcher and headed for the fridge, where she grabbed a handful of lemons and slammed them into the juice extractor she'd brought with her. It had been a wedding gift. Since it had come from a friend of hers, she'd taken it with her when she'd left.

"Try and keep things to a low roar out here," Buck suggested before returning to his movie.

Left alone with the twins, she poured sugar into the glass pitcher filled with lemon juice and water. No need for bottled water out here. Zane had told her that their water was spring fed. He'd also just told her that she wasn't rock solid, thereby implying she was a flighty idiot.

She'd mixed the drink so much that it had a foamy head on it as she poured some into glasses for the kids. After taking one sip, Rusty made a face and proclaimed, "You make lemonade like a city girl."

"City girls don't make lemonade, they buy it," Tracy retorted.

"You..." Rusty paused as a giant bubble formed on his parted lips. A *soap* bubble.

Uh-oh. Tracy belatedly realized that she must not have rinsed all the dishwashing soap from the pitcher when she'd washed it. Grabbing the lemonade away from Rusty and Lucky, she quickly emptied the glasses down the drain.

One sip of slightly soapy lemonade wouldn't hurt Rusty, right? In the old days, parents used to wash their kid's mouth out with soap when they were bad. But they didn't have them swallow it.

Should she call a poison-control center? No, she was overreacting here. It's not as if they drank the dishwashing soap, only a small residue of it greatly distilled by the water and lemonade.

"You were supposed to go out to the barn and talk to Pa about his spending more time with us, not poison us." Lucky's outraged words were accompanied by an affronted expression.

"I didn't poison you," Tracy denied, trying not to give in to the guilt just waiting to swamp her. She should have known that bubbles weren't supposed to form on top of lemonade. "And your father was busy, but I will talk to him." *If I don't sock him first.*

"Are you leaving?" Rusty belligerently asked Tracy.

"No." She frowned at him even as she made fresh lemonade, being very careful to rinse the pitcher thoroughly before using it again. "I already told you I was staying."

"Our mother left. She's dead," Rusty said out of the blue. "She didn't want us. She left us behind when we were just babies." His words were spoken with such a bald matter-of-factness that Tracy's instinctive response of denying them died in her throat.

"But that's okay because our pa wants us twice as much," Lucky quickly added.

"I can tell your father loves you both very much," Tracy said huskily.

"And we love him lots and lots. We don't need no one else. We don't need you here."

Lucky's defiant stance vividly reminded Tracy of how she'd reacted when her own parents had died in a car crash. She'd been determined to prove she was strong enough to go on alone. Like the twins, she hadn't thought she'd needed any help. And just like the twins, she'd been bluffing, hiding her fears behind a blustery bravado.

Aunt Maeve had sensed that and had swept into Tracy's life, ignoring Tracy's reserve and offering her love, warmth and friendship.

Oh, yeah, she knew exactly how the twins felt. They might not want her there, but they most certainly did need her.

TRACY WAS BEAT by the time she headed upstairs but she felt a sense of satisfaction that the kitchen was in order. She'd found a place for all the kitchen gadgets she'd brought—the juice extractor, the bread maker, the cappuccino machine. At least her wedding gifts would come in handy for something. She'd given the room a thorough cleaning, from the wooden cabinets right down to the black-and-white checked linoleum floor.

Zane had remained out in the barn the entire time. The twins had gone to join Buck in watching the John Wayne movie. Rusty had returned to the kitchen to grab a bag of potato chips, but that had been it. Tracy had worked alone, but she'd worked quickly and gotten a lot done.

Now her body was paying for it, her muscles aching from the workout. Not to mention the additional activity of rolling in the hay with Zane out in the barn.

Since the twins had told her about their mother's desertion and subsequent death, Tracy could better understand Zane's outburst. It couldn't have been easy on him, raising the twins on his own with only his father's help.

Enough soul-searching. What she really needed was a long hot soak in a bath. She had the water running and had already taken off her clothes when she realized she'd forgotten her nightgown in her room. Tugging on her robe, she opened the bathroom door, checking to make sure no one was around. She could still hear the noises of the twins and Buck and their movie coming from downstairs.

Her room was right across the hallway. Moving quickly, she grabbed her nightie from beneath her pillow—checking for Joe, the mouse, just in case. Then she returned to the bathroom, unaware that she was no longer the only resident.

ZANE WAS ALREADY on his way upstairs when he heard Tracy scream and came running, his boots pounding up the stairway. He found her in the bathroom, leaning against the door frame, holding her sides and laughing hysterically.

Not sure what in hades was going on, Zane said, "Are you okay? Why did you scream like that?"

She pointed a shaking finger. "There's an iguana on the toilet seat."

He should have guessed that a tenderfoot like her would be afraid of a little lizard. "It's just King."

"I didn't know the kids had a pet iguana. Or that it was toilet trained."

"They don't. King belongs to my dad."

"And your father toilet-trained his iguana?"

"Yeah," he said defensively, accustomed as he was to the previous housekeepers' dislike of King. "What about it?"

"My father would be so jealous," she said almost wistfully.

He figured she was babbling, because she sure wasn't making much sense to him. What did her father have to do with an iguana?

"My father worked at the reptile house at Brookfield Zoo in Chicago. He passed away when I was seventeen, both my parents did. A car accident. But he loved snakes and lizards. We always had them around the house. But he never had a toilet-trained iguana. I'm impressed."

"Then why did you scream?"

"I wasn't expecting to see him there. I was running my bath and realized I'd left my nightgown in my room."

Which meant she was wearing nothing under the robe she had on. The robe was the same satiny material her nightgown had been and it clung to her body the same way.

Tracy had curves in all the right places. He already knew that her breasts fit his hands as if made for them. And that she smelled like some kind of fruit, something exotic like those Hollywood types ate for breakfast. Mango or papaya or coconut.

He was nuts to be staring at her like a starving hound. But he couldn't seem to look away. His gaze was fixed like adhesive to the shadowy curve of her cleavage, impressively displayed by the neckline of her robe. He wasn't sure that she knew how much skin was showing, and he should probably tell her. In a minute.

Whoa, cowboy. The warning sounded in his brain. This was too cozy a setup, with her bed just down the hall from his.

"The housekeeper's quarters off the kitchen will be ready for you to move into by tomorrow night," he abruptly told her.

"You never did say what renovations you were doing on it."

"The twins sprayed the walls with ketchup, then lay on the floor as if they'd been shot by desperadoes. Scared the last housekeeper so much that she didn't even bother packing, just tossed her stuff in her car, saying she wasn't going to stay in any room decorated like some scene from *The Texas Chainsaw Massacre*."

"I know why the kids did that."

"So do I." Zane kept his eyes on King not Tracy. "To get rid of the housekeeper."

"So you'd spend more time with them."

Her words made him frown. "So now you're a child psychologist, huh?"

"I promised the twins I'd talk to you."

"They can talk to me themselves anytime they want," he said.

"They want to talk to you all the time."

"True enough," he acknowledged.

"The twins want you to spend time with them, so I thought it might be nice to have 'twin time' after dinner."

"To have what?" He looked at her. Big mistake. Her lips were parted and her green eyes glowed. He hurriedly shifted his eyes back to King, who was nowhere near as nice a shade of green as Tracy's eyes.

"Twin time. An hour or an hour and a half with just you and the twins. I could spend time with Buck then so he wouldn't feel left out. He could tell me more tall tales about the west and the adventures of Cockeyed Curly."

"I already spend time with the kids."

"You sit in the same room watching TV, but it's not the same thing."

He glared at her. Who was she to be telling him how to raise his kids? She hadn't been there when they'd both come down with chicken pox at the same time and he'd stayed awake for three days to take care of them. "And you figured this all out after only a day or two in my house?"

"I didn't have to figure it out," she replied. "The twins told me that if there was no housekeeper you'd have to stay home with them."

At a loss for words, Zane shoved his fingers through his dark hair. Why had his kids told this satin-covered city girl who'd only been on the ranch a few days something they hadn't told him? There were times he wished he could stay home with his kids and forget about everything else, but he had a ranch to run. If he didn't work, they wouldn't be able to keep a roof over their heads.

As if able to read his thoughts, Tracy said, "I'm not in any way trying to say that you're doing anything wrong with the twins, heaven knows I'm no expert, even if I did mastermind the Tyke Bike campaign."

"The what?"

"The Tyke Bike. It was the hottest item on every kid's Christmas list a few years ago. Remember, I told you that back in Chicago I was in advertising. Well, part of my job was making people stop and go wow about a product."

She'd certainly made him stop and go wow, as she put it.

Tracy finally became aware of the heated look Zane was giving her. She also belatedly noticed that the opening of her robe was gaping more than it should. She rectified that as the kids came clomping up the stairs.

"We heard her scream," Rusty said, his hair falling into his eyes. "Grandpa wouldn't let us come up till now. What happened?"

"She was just surprised by King," Zane replied, running a fond hand through his son's unruly hair. "King wasn't supposed to be loose until Tracy moves downstairs. I wonder how that happened."

"Only wimps are scared of iguanas," Rusty scoffed before his mouth dropped open in shock at the sight of Tracy picking up the iguana like a pro.

"Hi, fella," she cooed.

"Her dad worked in the reptile house of a zoo," Zane told the twins.

For the first time the twins gazed at her with approval in their blue eyes. They were clearly impressed.

And so was Zane.

Impressed by the cleavage she'd been showing earlier or her way with iguanas, she wasn't sure. She only knew that she liked impressing him, liked it far too much.

6

AH, EAU DE PAINT FUMES. She'd recognize that smell anywhere. The last ad campaign she'd done before leaving Chicago had been on Chic Celebrity Room Paint. She'd had to test the colors before being able to write the ad copy about them.

Here in Colorado, the paint wasn't Paul Newman Baby Blue or Marilyn Monroe Blond or Smashing Pumpkins Orange. Here Zane was tackling the job of repainting the housekeeper's room like a man possessed...and he was painting it white. Plain white.

The housekeeper's quarters were located down a short hallway off the kitchen, isolated from the rest of the house.

The twins had wanted to help their father, but Buck had taken pity on Zane and had taken the kids off on a trip to their Uncle Cord's cabin in the mountains. Only Buck's promise that they'd look for Cockeyed Curly's treasure map while they were there had drawn the kids away.

Before leaving, Buck had told her that Cord was the loner in the family, while Reno was the charmer. Which left Zane as what? she wondered. The responsible one, the stubborn devil of a cowboy whose kisses made her knees melt and her insides hum? An apt description in her view, but one she doubted the rest of his family shared.

Tracy had opened the kitchen windows to let in some fresh air. For once it wasn't because she'd darkened some pot or ruined some meal. It was because she was getting giddy from the paint fumes.

She certainly wasn't getting giddy about being alone in the house with Zane. Compared to the male models she'd worked with on advertising layouts, he wasn't even that exceptionally good-looking. Or even as good-looking as Dennis was in his smooth yuppie kind of way. Dennis lived for Italian suits and vintage California wines, for his own cappuccino and latte machines, his own coffee grinder and special blend of beans. Zane was nothing like Dennis.

She was still trying to figure out why she'd responded to his kiss the way she had in the barn last night. Here she was, thirty years old, and she'd never felt such passion, never desired a man more—not even Dennis. Despite those hormone-driven feelings, she'd spoken the truth when she'd told Zane she was no more eager to get involved with him than he was with her. She'd just been politer about it.

She hadn't told him he didn't fulfill any of the qualifications she had for a future mate. Partly because she no longer had a list of qualifications. Not after Dennis. He'd shot that theory out of the water. She'd thought he was everything she'd wanted in a man—but he was minus a few things, like integrity for one.

Zane seemed to have plenty of that. And a love and loyalty for his family that was admirable. Just like the Cartwright family on *Bonanza*. But come to think of it, none of those Cartwright boys ever did find the right woman for them.

Wiping down an already clean countertop, Tracy wondered who the right woman would be for Zane. Apparently it wasn't her. Which was just fine by her. She was just here for the summer, enough time to get a new perspective on her life and what she wanted to do with it—whether she wanted to return to Chicago or start fresh somewhere else.

For the time being, all she wanted was a cool drink of lemonade. The pitcher she'd made last night had plenty left. Maybe Zane would like a glass, too? It was only polite to ask him. What any housekeeper would do. Then she'd get to work on the living room while Buck and the twins were out of the way.

Last night Tracy's response to King, the iguana, had instigated a breakthrough of sorts with the twins. Rusty had actually shown her his snake, Precious, and had done so with pride rather than mischief in mind.

As for their father, well there was no telling what was on his mind. He wasn't saying, and she sure wasn't asking. When she brought him a glass of lemonade, he just took it from her and drank it all down, said thanks and then went back to working. He had a pair of painter's overalls on over his jeans and denim shirt.

"The painting would go faster if we both worked on the room," she noted.

"Painting isn't part of your job. Besides I'm almost done in here."

She tried to ignore the slight sting his dismissal caused. She'd never thought of herself as having a thin skin before. She'd always been able to blend her creative and her business sides together with a professionalism that precluded her having hurt feelings if a client didn't like one of her ad ideas.

The problem here was that she wasn't pitching an ad campaign, so the rejection wasn't of her work, it was of her. Personally. Not professionally. Not that he was all that impressed by her professionalism as a housekeeper. So what would impress him?

She needed to forget about all this relationship stuff and concentrate on cleaning the living room. Practical stuff like stacking old newspapers and gathering up dirty clothes. She had yet to tackle the wash, come to think of it. One peek in the laundry room and the mountain of clothes waiting there had sent her scuttling back to the kitchen.

Before leaving, she took a quick glance around the housekeeper's room, which was large and airy with a window facing the range of mountains. Since Zane had finished painting one side of the room already, he'd removed the tarp from the few pieces of furniture on that side of the room. The rustic pine bed, nightstand and chest of drawers were more intricately designed and crafted than the set upstairs.

Noticing her gaze on the furniture, Zane said, "My brother Cord made those."

"He's very talented. There's a huge demand for handmade western-style furniture," she added, running a hand over the smooth headboard.

"So he tells me."

"It must be nice having all your family live so close by."

"Family is important out here."

"Family is important wherever you are," she gently corrected him.

Looking away, he said, "I...uh...I told the twins we'd spend twin time together tonight."

Tracy smiled. "I'm so glad! What did they say?"

"They didn't have to say anything," he noted gruffly. "The look on their faces said it all."

"They were pleased."

"Yeah. They were pleased." Zane's blue eyes met hers, and for an instant she felt like she'd stuck a wet finger in the toaster, something she'd done the other morning and gotten a zing of an electric shock.

Don't get sappy, she warned herself. She was just suffering from withdrawal symptoms because she didn't have an ad campaign to work on, although she had already done a few sketches for a possible label for Buck's Barbecue Sauce. Just doodles really, but it kept her occupied when she'd had a hard time falling asleep last night. And it was better than thinking about Zane.

"Well, I should get back to work," she said, already taking a few steps toward the door. "Do you want me to start packing up my stuff to move it down here?"

"No sense packing it all up only to unpack it again. Just bring down the drawers and dump 'em in the drawers here. The room should stop smelling of paint in about another hour or two."

During that time, Tracy focused her energies on cleaning the living room. And she discovered that the carpeting was green, a yucky avocado green from the sixties, but a cleaner green than it had been thanks to some heavy-duty vacuuming from a machine that had probably been built when Kennedy was president.

When Buck mentioned that the house had hardwood floors beneath the grungy carpet she'd been tempted to suggest taking up the worn-out carpet and letting the flooring beneath take its place. She could already see it in her mind's eye—the mellow glow of oak flooring with the scattering of Native American rugs—Navajo maybe. In earth tones. It was enough to get her creative juices flowing.

It was probably too soon to go redecorating Zane's house. After all she'd only been there a few days. But she had already ordered new appliances for the kitchen, they were coming tomorrow. Maybe in a week or so she'd bring up the matter of removing the carpet and resanding the floors. How hard could that be?

Once the living room had been restored to some semblance of order, Tracy moved upstairs to get her things. She only had an hour or so before she had to start the evening meal. Was it too soon to have spaghetti again? She'd managed that fairly well, since all that was involved was boiling pasta and opening a jar of sauce and warming it up.

Wanting to be more efficient, she put all her things in two drawers, filled to overflowing, and then put one on top of the other to carry downstairs. She had just enough room to see over the top, if she was careful.

She was careful, but the combination of both drawers was heavier than she thought it would be. The top drawer was about to slide sideways when Zane came to her rescue halfway down the stairs.

"Here, give me that." He took both drawers from her and briskly made his way to her new quarters.

"Just set the drawers on the bed," she requested, trailing right behind him.

When he did as she asked, a mound of her silky lingerie slid out of the drawer. He instinctively grabbed for it, and a moment later her apricot-colored bra-and-panty set was dangling from his fingertips. He looked at the clothing as if it were a poisonous snake about to bite him.

The man had been married. Surely he'd seen women's underwear before? Just not her underwear. She snatched the clothing from his hands. The tips of her fingers brushed his, and she shivered at the contact.

Everything simple became rich with meaning when she was with him. Her startled eyes met his. She was close enough to see them darken. He could speak volumes with those blue eyes of his, and she was beginning to learn his visual language. He wasn't a man of many words, but with eyes like those he didn't have to be. They spoke for him, said what he couldn't or wouldn't. That she wasn't the only one who felt this intense attraction, that he was tempted by her, that she had power over him just as he had power over her. Sensual power.

Then he blinked and the moment was over. "What's for supper?" he asked as if nothing had happened.

"Spaghetti?" she said. "Or I could make my specialty, Shrimp de Jonghe, if you have any shrimp in the freezer.''

"Shrimp isn't exactly cowboy food."

"It's very healthy and good for you."

"You don't aim on changing our eating habits, do you?" he asked suspiciously.

"Other than having Lucky use a napkin rather than wiping her mouth on her shirtsleeve, no, I had no plans to change anyone's eating habits."

"I meant serving up those fancy yuppie meals with a spoonful of mystery food in the middle of an empty plate decorated with fancy swirls of sauce."

"You're not a fan of French cuisine, I gather."

"I prefer real food."

"Only because you've never eaten crème brûlée." She licked her lips just at the thought of the dessert.

Zane was not equally impressed. "It's just pudding with a sugary crust on top," he scoffed. "You think I've never eaten in a French restaurant? I went to college in Seattle. They've got plenty of French restaurants there. You don't have to look so shocked. You think I've never been off the ranch?"

"I don't know what to think." That much was true. Just when she thought she had Zane pegged, he went and startled her. She couldn't decide whether she liked that or not.

THE NEXT DAY Zane was in a bad mood for some reason, but the good news was that the new appliances were delivered without incident. That's how she'd like her life to be for a week or two—without incident.

But it wasn't meant to be. At least, not yet. While her spaghetti last night had been good, she'd ruined the eggs this morning—her last time cooking on the old stove. The new one hadn't been connected in time for lunch so she'd had to make tuna fish sandwiches. Cowboys weren't real fond of tuna fish, she quickly learned. At least not the cowboys on the Best ranch.

Once the appliances were installed and the workman had departed, she couldn't wait to show Zane how great the kitchen looked. She grabbed him the minute he walked in the mudroom, not even waiting for him to actually walk into the kitchen.

"Come look!"

"Look at what?" he asked as she dragged him over to the sink.

"Everything." She held her arms wide to embrace the entire kitchen, sparkling clean, with the new white stove and dishwasher. Standing before them like a game-show model, she waved her arms toward the shining appliances. "Self-cleaning oven, electronic-ignition burners. And the dishwasher does pots and pans, too. And I found room for the things I brought with me from Chicago. See, I came prepared. I've got a salad shooter, and a cookie shooter."

"The only thing we shoot around here are housekeepers who can't cook," Zane growled.

Fed up with his crabbiness—he'd been like this all day—she responded by sticking her thumbs in her ears and wiggling her fingers at him.

He stared at her in astonishment.

"A little something your kids taught me," she noted demurely. "Consider yourself lucky I didn't pour honey over you the way the kids almost did to me this morning. They had an open plastic bottle of it rigged to the top of the door frame into the pantry.''

Zane couldn't answer. He was all caught up in the image of her covering him with honey.

''They assured me it was a little something left over from when I first arrived and they wanted me to leave. I think it was a test of sorts and I passed it. Since you told them you'd be spending more time with them, things have been much better. In fact, aside from this honey incident they've been remarkably good, considering.''

''Considering?'' Zane's voice was raspy. He knew what he'd been considering. Tracy. Wearing honey and a wicked smile. Nothing else.

''Considering they are the Best twins, able to strike fear into the hearts of shopkeepers and housekeepers alike.''

He laughed.

She smiled at him, her delight evident. ''You should do that more often.''

He had a feeling he would be with her in the house. It was hard not to when she was so bright and chipper. Not to mention sexy. And he wasn't going to mention it or even think about it. Yeah, right. And pigs could fly.

FEELING CONFIDENT NOW that she was cooking on a new stove, Tracy decided to try out the new pressure cooker she'd brought with her and use it to make Potage Saint Germain, or split pea soup.

As she'd told Zane, her specialty was getting people to stop and say wow. And okay, so they were saying wow about her cooking because it was so *bad* right now, but that would change. She'd picked up a magazine called *Quick Cooking* at the supermarket the other day and had gotten plenty of ideas from that.

This recipe was from one of the cookbooks she'd brought from Chicago and it didn't call for cooking the soup in the pressure cooker, but she decided it would save time to do so.

Meanwhile, she had to get back to the wash, or more specifically, the dryer, which was buzzing at her as if mocking the fact that she hadn't been able to figure out how to turn that feature off when a load was finished. "I heard you the first time," she shouted as she headed for the vocal dryer.

"Who are you talking to?" Lucky demanded.

"The dryer."

"Do all city girls talk to dryers?"

"I didn't talk to dryers when I lived in the city." She used to drop her dirty clothes off at a laundry in the lobby of her condo building. They'd magically come back all clean and pressed.

"Then why do you talk to them here?"

"Because they talk to me first. Buzzing at me. Oops." She looked in dismay at the T-shirt she'd put in a half hour earlier, which was now twice as wide and half as long as it had been. She'd grown tired of reading all the labels on every item of clothing—all of them had said Tumble Dry, so after a while she'd stopped looking.

Meanwhile the washing machine had suddenly taken to shaking as if it was drunk and about to heave.

Something was definitely wrong with the spin cycle. This was only her second load of wash. She punched what looked as if it should be the off button. It didn't work.

"You open the lid and it turns off," Lucky told her as if she were the adult and Tracy the child.

"Right. I knew that." Lifting the lid made the machine grind to a shuddering halt. Peering inside, Tracy frowned at something that looked remarkably like...a pair of suede boots? Her boots. "What are my boots doing in the wash?"

"Getting clean," the little girl replied.

Tracy didn't have time to discuss why suede and washing machines did not go well together, because she'd suddenly become aware of a hissing noise coming from the kitchen. The rattling heaves of the washing machine had drowned it out before. Now she heard it with dread. Her soup!

Racing back into the kitchen, Tracy arrived just in time to see the vent on top of the pressure cooker bubbling ominously. Oh, no! She'd forgotten to put the weight thingamajig on top of the vent. Too late. A geyser of split peas spewed clear to the ceiling, where the steaming gooey green masses clung like something nasty and noxious.

"Why are you cooking snot?" Lucky asked from behind her.

"I'm not...it's split pea soup."

Gazing up at the glop on the ceiling, Lucky said, "Is that how you're supposed to split the peas?"

"I doubt it," Tracy muttered. "You stay back while I turn this thing off." Once the burner had been turned off, the pressure cooker eventually stopped its spewing.

So much for impressing Zane with her culinary skills. Not that he cared much for French cooking anyway. Especially when it was hanging from the ceiling.

Tracy plastered a bright smile on her face. "So...how about spaghetti for dinner tonight?"

In the end, she went with several family-size pizzas she found in the freezer instead of spaghetti. Add a large salad and presto—dinner, with not a minute to spare. Cleaning up the split pea mess had taken more time than she thought. Any hope of keeping the incident quiet went out the window when Lucky regaled everyone with the story.

The silver lining was that, once again, Beauty the hog would benefit from Tracy's mishap in the kitchen.

And the lesson was to always read directions all the way through to the end—where it said never to cook applesauce or dried peas in the pressure cooker. Now she knew why.

As Tracy loaded the dishwasher after dinner, the twins helped her by putting the silverware in the washing basket while keeping her up-to-date on her duties as housekeeper. It seemed, as far as they were concerned, pizza every night was de rigueur.

"A housekeeper can cook pizza for dinner all the time," Rusty said.

"Yeah, but she can't make us eat everything on our plates," Lucky added.

Rusty nodded his agreement. "Or get mad if we

feed our pizza or cake to our snake. A housekeeper would never get mad about that.''

"Son of a buck, you kids are full of hooey," Buck scoffed as he entered the kitchen, adding a cackle of laughter for good measure. "I'll tell you what a good housekeeper does. Follows orders. My orders. And is a good listener. Appreciates my poetry. Is a great cook. And it would be nice if she could play the fiddle or sing.''

"And she should be able to pitch a baseball," Rusty added.

"And know all the words to the songs on *The Lion King* video," Lucky inserted.

"And be able to bake an apple pie that'll melt in your mouth," Buck said wistfully.

"What's going on in here?" Zane asked as he joined them. "A family conference?"

"We were just telling her how to be a good housekeeper," Lucky said.

"*She* has a name," Zane pointed out. "It's Tracy. Or Ms. Campbell.''

"Tracy is fine," she said. *Especially the way Zane said it.* There they were again. Those forbidden thoughts. What was wrong with her? Not a week ago, she'd been engaged to be married and now here she was getting all gooey about the way some sexy rancher said her name.

It was one thing to notice that he'd look good in a jeans commercial, it was quite another to like the way he said her name or the way his fingers felt on her breast or the way his tongue tickled the roof of her mouth when he kissed her.

"Can anyone tell me why there's a pair of wet boots in the washing machine?" Buck inquired from the laundry room.

"They were dirty," Tracy replied, exchanging a grin with Lucky. The little girl grinned back as if they were co-conspirators.

Buck chortled. "That explains it then."

For the first time since she'd arrived at the ranch lost and soaking wet, she felt like part of the family. And it was a good feeling.

AS THE DAYS PROGRESSED, Tracy settled into a routine. And that old saying about practice making perfect did apply to cooking. Not that she was anywhere near perfect yet, but things were slowly improving.

By her third week on the ranch she'd actually mastered the art of having everything prepared at the same time, ready for the table. No more waiting around for the potatoes to be done while the meat got cold. She'd even managed to set a lovely table, including a centerpiece of wildflowers she'd gathered from around the house—stiff-stemmed black-eyed Susans and magenta spikes of fireweed. She'd found an easy recipe for fast-baked fish and dilled rice, which she served with honey-glazed baby carrots.

She'd no sooner placed the meal on the table and sat down when everyone started reaching and gobbling. Five minutes later the food was gone. She'd worked all afternoon on it, and they'd inhaled it as if it were fast food from a burger joint instead of the first perfect meal she'd ever made. There had been no savoring, no compliments.

Sure Lucky hadn't wiped her mouth on her sleeve and had used her napkin, and Murph'n'Earl had given her shy smiles, but that was it. She'd barely had time to eat a few bites, and they were ready for dessert.

"You ate it all!" she yelled at them all.

Buck blinked at her accusatory tone. "Something wrong with that?"

She blinked back tears. "No one even paused to enjoy it."

"We ate it, didn't we?" Buck looked and sounded aggrieved, as only a male of the species could. "That means we enjoyed it. You fixed us supper. It's supposed to be eaten."

"Eaten, not devoured," she retorted, deciding that men really were from Mars. "It was a masterpiece."

Buck frowned in confusion. "It was just fish and carrots."

"Yes, but made just right. My first perfect dinner!" she practically wailed. Sleep deprivation was starting to take its toll on her. She didn't finish her work until late at night, and then she had to get up before the birds the next morning.

A more experienced housekeeper could probably get things done in half the time, but not her. She'd had to resort to using twenty-five-watt bulbs in the living room because she had yet to dust in there, and the dimmer light hid that fact. A little tip she'd picked up from a housekeeping site on the Internet.

"I liked the fish," Rusty said, reaching over to squeeze her hand as if sensing she wanted to cry. "It didn't taste like a city girl made it. It was real good, and I had seconds. It was so good I wouldn't even give some to Precious or Joe because I wanted it all for me."

"You're right, it was wonderful," Zane confirmed in that shimmy-provoking voice of his. "Tracy, I apologize for our lack of manners. We've been without a woman's civilizing influence for so long that we've resorted to acting like a bunch of rowdy cowboys gathered 'round the chuck wagon."

"No offense intended, ma'am," Murph said.

"Best meal I've had in weeks," Earl added.

Since Tracy had been cooking their meals for weeks, she decided this was a backhanded compliment but an accurate one. Her dinner tonight had far exceeded everything else she'd done up to that point. That's why she'd been so upset that they hadn't noticed, although she supposed the fact that they'd eaten every scrap was their way of saying it was good. But there were times when she needed to hear the words, darn it.

To make up for it, Zane insisted on serving dessert—scoops of Rocky Road ice cream. He even stuck around afterward to help her tidy up in the kitchen, a first.

"I've been meaning to tell you," he paused to carefully replace the dish towel through the handle of the refrigerator the way she liked before continuing, "that you're welcome to ride any of the horses anytime you'd like."

"I don't exactly have a lot of free time."

A guilty expression flashed over his face. "I haven't given you a day off since you've been here, have I? Sorry about that. Time tends to get away from me. From now on you can have Sundays off. How does that sound?"

"Nice."

"And as I said, you're welcome to take one of the horses."

"I don't know how to ride," she interrupted him, still feeling out of sorts.

"I'll teach you. Think of it as my way of repaying you for the wonderful meal."

Tracy tried not to notice how good his denim-clad behind looked as he bent over to put a bowl in the dishwasher, before just giving up and letting herself surreptitiously enjoy the view. "You already pay me to make wonderful meals."

"Yeah, but this was your first perfect one. It deserves something special to mark the occasion." He straightened and smiled at her. "Besides, riding is one of those skills a good housekeeper should have, like knowing all the words to the songs on *The Lion King* video."

She eyed him suspiciously, wondering if she was being set up here. "You're telling me that your previous housekeepers could ride horses?"

Zane nodded. "All twelve of them could ride. Even old Mrs. Battle, who was eighty if she was a day."

"Well, if Mrs. Battle can do it, then so can I."

That philosophy sounded fine until Tracy found herself face to face with a giant of a horse a few days later. "Is this the one that gets fresh? Because I'm telling you that one of these horses copped a feel the last time I was out here."

"That would have been Randy," Zane said.

"An apt name."

Zane laughed. She liked his laugh.

"People treat horses the way they treat people," he was saying.

If that was true then Zane must be really great with people, because he was certainly magical with the horses, even with the feisty Bashful, who was anything but. Randy was the horse who'd laughed at her, but Bashful was the one who looked at her as if he wanted to bite a chunk out of her.

"Just a guess here, but riding means I have to get close to the horse, right?" Her nervousness was cloaked in humor, but he heard it.

"Are you afraid of horses?"

"Let's just say I have a healthy respect for something that is so much heavier and bigger than I am."

"I'm bigger and heavier than you are," Zane pointed out, "yet I don't see you showing me a lot of healthy respect."

The man was actually teasing her! Standing there, in his denim shirt with the snap closures and long sleeves rolled up to show his tanned forearms. She'd already memorized the fit of his jeans, the image indelibly imprinted on her brain. His cowboy boots were scuffed and worn, a working rancher's boots, not an urban cowboy's. His hat was white, like one of the good guys.

She wiped the damp palms of her hands on her jeans, suddenly at a loss for words.

Zane just smiled and said, "We'll start out easy with Mabel. She's very reliable."

Mabel might be reliable but she was still the size

of a house. Or that's how she appeared from Tracy's five-foot-five perspective. But Mabel did seem to have friendly eyes, complete with a set of gorgeous eyelashes.

"First off, I'll show you how to walk around a horse. Here, give me your hand." He took it, then frowned at the scrape at the back of her knuckles. "How did you do that?"

She mumbled her reply.

He leaned closer. "What did you say?"

"I said I scraped it on the brownies I made this morning." The look she gave him dared him to say anything. "I lost track of time and they overcooked. They were harder than rocks by the time they cooled down, and I had to scrape the pan to hack them out of there."

While she talked, he absently brushed his thumb over her knuckles as if to soothe the hurt. Once he realized what he was doing he quickly placed her hand near the back of the horse's rib cage.

"Okay, you stand here, with your rib cage against the horse's. No, get closer." As he positioned her, his fingers brushed her breast. "Sorry about that," he muttered. "Okay, now move around to the other side. This way." He walked around the back of the horse to the other side.

"You sure this isn't some kind of plot for revenge for that quiche I made the other night?" she asked suspiciously. "I mean, this isn't a setup where the horse is going to smack me in the face with her tail or something, is it?"

"Oh ye of little faith."

"I'm not the one who doesn't trust city girls." The words were out before she could stop them.

"No, you're the one who doesn't trust me."

"That's not true."

"Then prove it," he said. "Walk around the horse. I'll be right here. She won't hurt you."

And what about you? she wondered. *Will you hurt me?*

Only if you let him, her inner voice replied.

7

THREE HOURS LATER Tracy felt like a pro, standing next to Mabel and cleaning her hooves while chatting with the horse as if she were an old friend. "You're much nicer than Bashful or Randy. Do they give you any trouble?"

"They're geldings," Zane answered on Mabel's behalf.

She'd read enough Western romances to know what that meant. "Ah, so they've been fixed. You'd think that would have taught them a lesson, hmm, Mabel? But males do tend to be stubborn in their bad behavior, isn't that right?"

"Since you and Mabel here are getting along so well, how about taking a ride? I'll saddle her up for you, and we'll go out for a while."

"If it's okay with Mabel, it's okay with me," Tracy said. "Is what I'm wearing all right for riding?"

"Do your boots have a heel on them?"

"Not a platform heel, no. I bought these in Bliss." She held out her foot and wiggled it at him. "My beige suede ones had to be thrown out."

"Good thing." The tone of his voice let her know that he was no fan of her suede fashion boots. "Flat soles are no good for keeping your feet in the stirrup. Those Bliss boots will do fine, they've got a practical heel on them. As for the rest of your gear, jeans and a shirt are fine. We don't go in for fancy English riding here.''

"Good," she said, apparently the only one who knew her jeans and shirt bore the label of a trendy western outfitter. "I'd look stupid in jodhpurs and one of those funny little cap things they wear on their heads."

"Headgear is required around here, too." Zane plunked, there was no other word for it, a straw cowboy hat on her head. Then he stood back to survey her, as if she were livestock he was considering buying. "That'll do."

It certainly would do. He could just stop staring at her like that. You didn't see *her* looking at him, even though she might want to. No, she'd shown admirable restraint. Just a peek or two without him noticing, like now as he put the saddle on Mabel. Her heart only skipped a beat or two as she appreciated, for about the ten millionth time, how good he looked in jeans.

She likened her behavior to appreciating the view of the mountains out the back of the ranch house. The mountains were there, so she paused from time to time to admire them. No harm in that.

Not that Zane's gaze on her had been filled with masculine admiration. Come to think of it, he'd looked at Mabel with equal consideration.

"Okay, we're ready to go. I'll give you a hand up," Zane told her.

"That's okay, I can do it myself." She didn't want

him accusing her of trying to entrap him or some such nonsense. He could just keep his seductive hands to himself.

She'd seen enough westerns on TV to know that you grabbed the…thingamajig at the front of the saddle…the horn. Yeah, that's right. You grabbed the saddle horn with your hand and stuck your foot in the stirrup and then, presto, you were on the horse.

She was halfway up before realizing something was wrong. It wasn't until she was fully in the saddle, after an awkward scramble that left her feet dangling out of the stirrups, that she knew exactly what is was that was wrong. She was facing Mabel's rear end instead of her beautiful mane.

"This horse is going in the wrong direction," she said.

To give him credit, Zane didn't laugh at her, although she could tell by the quirk at the corner of his mouth that he was tempted.

"It's not the horse, it's you that has the problem. Here, come on down from there." Putting his hands up to her waist, he helped Tracy dismount more smoothly than she'd gotten up. "Rookie mistake," he told her. "When mounting a horse you put your outside foot in the stirrup, the one farthest away from the horse."

"You could have given me that useful bit of information a bit earlier," she retorted.

"I did. I guess you weren't paying attention."

"I always pay attention." At the time she may have been paying attention to his body instead of his words, however.

"Yeah, well, you ready to try again? I'll help you this time."

"I don't need your help." But she did. Once she got her foot in the stirrup it took more effort than she'd expected to get her inside leg up and over the back of the horse. His hands guided her, leaving a trail of warmth wherever they touched her.

Mabel, bless her heart, stood rock solid though the entire episode.

Tracy listened carefully as Zane reviewed how to use the reins to turn and to stop. Then they were moving. She and Mabel and Zane and Bashful...or was it Randy? She wasn't sure. She only knew that it was gloriously exhilarating to actually be riding a horse.

They were out of the barn, moving away from the ranch. Thin wisps of clouds were gathered at the edge of the sky as they set out across the meadow. They were headed toward the mountains, their peaks silhouetted sharply against the Wedgwood-blue sky. No, Wedgwood was paler and more delicate than this blue. It was more vibrant and intense than any sky she'd ever seen. Why hadn't she noticed it before?

Probably because she'd been too busy cooking and cleaning and washing. But she noticed now and was filled with delight as all her senses soaked in the freedom of being outdoors—the warmth of the sun hitting her back, the increasing scent of pine in the air, the plop-plop of Mabel's hooves against the ground.

The mountains looked close enough to touch but were actually farther away than they seemed, a common optical illusion in the mountains, where the clear thin air made distant objects stand out with clarity.

Zane also appeared close enough to touch as he rode beside her.

"You look at home on that horse," she said.

"I've been riding since I was—"

"Knee-high to a grasshopper, I bet," she inserted with a grin.

His smile matched hers as he said, "Seems my dad has been talking to you."

"Of course he has. Buck loves talking and he's good at it. He can tell some great yarns about the Old West and Cockeyed Curly."

"This part of the state has had its fair share of wild and wooly history," Zane agreed. "It's where outlaws like Butch Cassidy and his Wild Bunch used to come and hide out from civilization."

Tracy knew all about hiding out. That's what she'd been doing when she'd first come to the ranch. Hiding out from the mess her life had become.

Back in Chicago she'd been on the fast track to success in advertising, and her future had been all mapped out. First off, there would have been marriage to Dennis, then pursuit of the plum job of the Beeler Sparkling Water account and, after landing it, she would have gotten a full partnership in the firm. Then would have come buying a house, having a child in three years, continuing to work, getting a weekend cabin in Wisconsin and living happily ever after.

Dennis had used to tease her about the way she'd fanatically make lists. She hadn't thought there had been anything fanatical about it. She was just being organized.

But there had been no way to anticipate the curveballs, like finding Dennis in bed with another woman. Or to anticipate her own questioning of what she wanted out of life, of what made her happy. Was it life in the fast lane or life in the mountains?

"Are you falling asleep on me?" Zane said mockingly.

The idea had its appeal. Falling asleep with her head on his shoulder. "Absolutely not." Her voice rang out, firm in its denial.

"Glad to hear it," he said before reluctantly adding, "You've got a good seat for a city girl."

"Thank you, I think."

"We can go a bit faster, if you want."

Oh, she wanted to, all right. That was the problem. "That would be good."

"Hang on."

She did. The trotting stage in between riding and galloping was the only thing she didn't like. That's when her bottom bounced on the saddle like a basketball in an NBA game. Still galloping, even for the short amount of time they did it, was like rhythmic flying. She loved it.

When it was over, she said, "Let's do that again!"

Zane shook his head. "You've had enough for one day. Your legs are going to be sore as it is."

She didn't know what he was talking about until she got off the horse and could hardly stand up. She soon recovered her balance and the trembling in her legs subsided, allowing her to feel the ache on her tailbone.

"Want to ride again?" he asked Tracy as he removed Mabel's saddle.

"Absolutely. Just not today." Grimacing, she rubbed her palm over her denim-clad bottom.

"Let me know if you stiffen up later on," he said. "I've got some salve that might help."

By eight that evening Tracy was walking as if she were eighty. She would have taken a hot bath after dinner, but she wasn't sure she'd be able to lower herself into the claw-foot bathtub in the housekeeper's quarters, let alone get out of it.

One thing she didn't have to worry about was wandering iguanas. It seems King hated stairs, so he limited his sojourns to the upstairs of the house. Which meant she'd have her bathroom to herself. Precious, the snake, managed to slither her way down the steps just fine but seemed disinclined to do so, while Joe had been confined to his quarters so far. Even so, she always made a point of checking under her covers and her bed each night just to make sure the mouse wasn't there.

But tonight she'd have to forgo the under-the-bed check. Bending down was definitely not a good idea in her current physical condition. Standing under a hot shower was a much better idea. And it did make her feel better, for a while. Then the stiffness and body aches quickly returned.

Who knew there were so many muscles in her inner thighs? Actually it felt as if there was just one giant concrete muscle right now.

She slowly moved...okay, she slowly hobbled from the bathroom to her bed, where she carefully sat down and then rolled onto her back.

She was never moving from this bed. They'd find

her body in the morning and on her tombstone they wouldn't put anything clever like the tombstones Buck had told her about. Nothing like Here Lies Lester Moore. Four Slugs from a .44—No Les, No More.

No, on her tombstone they'd inscribe "City Girl Couldn't Hack It." Or maybe "City Girl Fails Big-Time." Or how about "Here Lies Tracy Campbell. From a Bed, She Couldn't Scramble."

Hey, that last one wasn't half bad.

A knock on her door interrupted her self-authored epitaphs. "I'm off duty now," she yelled out. "Come back during regular business hours."

"I've got that salve I told you about," Zane said through the door.

She could either be both modest and gutsy by braving the physical pain and telling him that she was fine, or she could be a wimp and ask for his help. Pain or no pain? No contest. "Come on in."

He did. She heard him but couldn't see him because she was staring up at the ceiling. Moving required too much energy, not to mention discomfort.

"This is all my fault," Zane said, his voice reflecting his regret. "I should never have let a tenderfoot like you ride more than a few minutes."

"Watch who you're calling a tenderfoot, cowboy," she growled.

"I'm watching," he murmured in reply.

Something in his voice made her risk moving her head to the side so she could get a good look at him. The empathy in his blue eyes almost made her cry. "I'm not a failure," she told him fiercely.

"No, you're not a failure," he readily agreed. "I, on the other hand, should have my head examined."

"For hiring me, you mean?"

"No, that didn't turn out as bad as I thought."

"Despite rock-hard brownies and runny eggs?"

"Just the way I like them."

"Since when?" she scoffed.

"You mean I never told you that old cowboy rule?"

"You mean the one about shooting housekeepers who couldn't cook?"

"No, the one that says anybody who complains about the food has to do the cooking."

"I'd definitely remember if you or Buck had told me that one before."

"Well, consider yourself told." She wondered if this was his way of telling her she was doing a good job. "Now do you want me to help put some of this salve on you?"

There was a time for modesty and a time for pain relievers. This was definitely the time for the latter. "Yes, thank you."

"Can you roll over onto your back?"

"Sure thing." She did and ended up with her nose buried in a pillow, which Zane kindly removed for her. She felt the mattress dip as he sat down beside her.

Zane looked at her satin-draped body and felt lower than the belly of a snake. She was hurting and it was his fault. For once his first thought wasn't that this was proof that she didn't belong out here. Instead his first thought was to make her feel better.

He rubbed the salve onto his hands and began rubbing it onto her legs, working his way up from her calves to her thighs. She didn't say a word, which wasn't like her at all. Normally she could talk the ear off a mule. She had an opinion on everything. Sometimes he was even surprised that they shared the same opinion.

He'd also been surprised by the way she'd taken to riding today, by the way she'd bonded with Mabel and seemed to take pleasure in being in the great outdoors.

Her skin was softer than a summertime breeze or a butterfly's wings. Fragile. And like the breeze or a butterfly she was fleeting—passing by, but not lasting.

And when the summer was over she, like the warm breeze and the colorful butterflies, would be gone.

But for now she was warm and inviting beneath his hands. The last time he'd really touched her had been in the barn, when they'd kissed. The intensity of her response had surprised him. What was she feeling now that he was touching her again?

"Is this helping?" he asked.

"Mmm," she murmured, her voice like a purr from one of the barn cats that the twins had yet to discover.

He had his hands beneath her robe, his splayed fingers within touching distance of her silky underwear and the curve of her bottom. He could feel her relaxing beneath his ministrations.

It might be helping her, but it was definitely hurting him. Well, not hurting exactly. More like causing an itch that couldn't be scratched. Because no matter how she might tempt him, he wasn't going to give in. Not this time. Not with this city girl or any other.

He refused to give in to her siren call.

He imagined her thanking him for the massage with a come-hither look over her satin-covered shoulder. Her full lips would smile in a way meant to make a man melt.

He'd resist.

She could stand stark naked in front of him and he wouldn't flinch.

She could…what was she doing now? He cautiously moved forward to get a better look at her face, turned sideways with her cheek pressed against the back of her hand. Her long lashes were velvety dark against her creamy skin, and her lips were parted as she…snored?

Oh, it was delicate and daintylike, but it was definitely a snore. She'd fallen asleep on him, just as he'd teasingly accused her of doing when they'd gone riding.

So much for him thinking she was lying there concocting some scheme to seduce him. She'd told him she was no more interested in having a relationship with him than he was with her. Maybe it was time he believed her.

TRACY WOKE the next morning feeling more rested than she had in weeks. She didn't remember what happened after Zane had started rubbing his miracle salve on her. She only recalled a sense of peace and relaxation.

Perhaps once she'd successfully marketed Buck's

Barbecue Sauce she'd add the miracle salve to the roster of products she was trying to pitch.

After making a breakfast of bacon and scrambled eggs that actually tasted good, she did something she'd done every day since coming to the ranch. She checked her e-mail on her laptop computer while sipping a cup of cowboy coffee—strong and hot.

She got a reply from Keisha Washington in Chicago, a fellow advertising executive and friend. Keisha had acted as a sounding board for some of Tracy's ideas for Buck's Barbecue Sauce. They'd agreed on the label featuring a western sunset with a bucking horse silhouetted against it. Even Buck himself had been pleased with the outcome.

Now came the hard part, convincing western catalogs to carry Buck's sauce. Tracy had sent out a dozen sampler boxes but had yet to hear back from any of the mail-order retailers. She'd even put a brand on the box—Best of the West—to get their attention.

Which reminded her of the time she'd told Zane that in her line of work her job was romancing the brand.

He'd told her that out here brands had a different meaning, and Buck had gone on to talk about the over thirty thousand brands Colorado ranchers had registered.

But what she remembered most were Zane's words. So many things out here had a different meaning for him.

She didn't know why it was so important that he think well of her. She just knew that when he'd said she wasn't a failure last night, it was as if her heart had been bathed in sunshine.

Just a few words from him had more of an effect on her than all of Dennis's flowery speeches. Maybe because she knew that Zane's words were truly what he thought, while Dennis only said what he thought she wanted to hear.

Gathering her thoughts, she refocused her attention on her e-mail. Keisha had gotten her sample box of Buck's Barbecue Sauce and she'd loved it. She also liked the way Tracy had wrapped the bottles with bandanna bibs and raffia rope. The mild sauce was labeled Tenderfoot Mild—Buck's idea—while the spicy sauce was marked Rip-Snortin' Hot.

The next e-mail was from an address she didn't immediately recognize. Only when she clicked on it and started reading did she realize it was from *Southwestern Living* catalog, the biggest mail-order retailer in the area. The news had her shrieking in delight.

"Don't tell me that mouse got loose again," Buck grumbled as he ambled into the kitchen to see what all the commotion was about.

"It's not the mouse." Grabbing him by the shoulders, she gave him a huge kiss on the cheek. "We did it!"

"What the Sam Hill are you talking about, missy? You haven't taken to adding a little something to your coffee have you?" He shot her a suspicious look.

"I'm not drunk, I'm happy. *Southwestern Living* loved your barbecue sauce."

"Well, course they did," Buck retorted as if that was a foregone conclusion. "What idiot wouldn't?"

"You don't understand. They want to carry your barbecue sauce in their catalog. They've placed an order for three hundred bottles of both the mild and the hot sauce."

Buck stared at her as if she'd gone loco. "Three hundred bottles?"

"That's right."

"Son of a buck! How am I supposed to whip up three hundred bottles of the stuff?"

"We'll help you, Grandpa," the twins said from the back door.

"Son of a buck," he repeated, this time with awe in his voice as he shoved a hand through his thick white hair before grabbing hold of his suspenders and snapping them with pride. "Well, what are we all standing around here for? We've got to get working."

8

EVERYONE ENDED UP pitching in to get the sauce done. Buck was the only one who could actually concoct it, because he kept the recipe secret. But everyone else pitched in, even the twins, who put the adhesive labels on the hundreds of glass jars that Tracy had ordered via express delivery.

There had been plenty of errors the first day, with barbecue sauce spilling over everything, from the bubbling pots on the stove to the actual bottle labels themselves. No doubt the Food and Drug Administration would not approve. But once Tracy had gotten a streamlined, sanitary assembly-line process set up, things had smoothed out and the process went much faster.

By the Fourth of July, the first order of Buck's Barbecue Sauce was ready to send out and Tracy was ready to celebrate.

Buck seemed to share her sentiments because he said, "We finished just in time to clean up and go join the festivities in Bliss."

"Festivities?" she asked, wondering what a small town like Bliss did for the holiday.

"That's right. Go on now." Buck gently aimed her

toward the hallway leading to her room. "Get cleaned up, and we'll be heading off."

"Okay. Lucky, I could use some help if you'd come with me to my room."

The little girl, while appearing curious at the request, made no comment as she followed Tracy.

Once they reached Tracy's room, she told Lucky, "I have a surprise for you."

She handed her the package that had come yesterday. Lucky tore into it with the enthusiasm of a seven-and-a-half-year-old. Paper wrapping was tossed in the air as the little girl eagerly got to the bottom of the box to find...clothes.

"These are part of the B. Me clothing line. They're very popular. See, the dresses are denim with these cute little red-and-white polka-dot bows." Tracy held it up for Lucky's perusal. "I thought you could wear this today for the Fourth of July."

Thrusting out her chin, Lucky jammed her fingers in the back pockets of her jeans, as if even touching the dresses had somehow contaminated her with girly cooties.

"I ain't wearin' no dress," she said belligerently. "And you can't make me." The look in her eyes went on to say *You'd have to hog-tie me and pin me to an anthill before I'd be caught dead in those.*

"You don't like them?" Tracy stared at the clothing as if seeing it for the first time. Come to think of it, they did look a tad overdone. Had they always had so many frills? "Hmm, maybe you're right. They are a bit too..,"

"Girly." Lucky said the word as if it were the ultimate of insults.

"What's wrong with being girly? If there are no bows or frills involved?"

"My mom was a girl."

Tracy nodded, not making the connection. "That's right."

"And she left and hurt my Pa. He doesn't like girls as much as he likes boys."

A strangled sound from the open doorway was the only indication of Zane's arrival. "Hey, peanut." He scooped Lucky up in his arms. "It's not true that I like boys better than girls."

"I can attest to that," Tracy muttered, recalling that heated kiss in the barn.

"I love you just as much as I love Rusty," Zane told his daughter, his voice husky with emotion. "And I think you'd look mighty beautiful dressed up for the Fourth of July."

Lucky stared at him uncertainly, tweaking a strand of her short hair.

Ah, Tracy thought. Now I know why she has that cowlick of hair that stands straight up on top. It was the first time she'd ever seen the little girl actually tweaking her hair, but then it was also the first time she'd ever seen Lucky appear unsure about anything.

Two more nervous tweaks of her hair before Lucky said, "Does that mean I havta wear a dress?"

"Not if you really don't want to," Zane replied.

Tracy could tell that the little girl was at a momentary loss, torn between wanting to please her fa-

ther by wearing a dress and her own aversion to the
frilly bows.

Tracy offered her another option. "You can get
dressed up without wearing a dress. What about this
vest?" The denim vest was more toned down—no
bows, just a touch of colorful floral embroidery on
the front. "You could wear this."

The little girl reached out from her father's arms to
touch the article of clothing with a reverent yearning
at odds with her tough exterior. "The flowers are
pretty."

"Yes, they are," Tracy agreed.

"If I wore it, that doesn't mean I'm a girly girl."
Lucky's comment was meant to be a warning.

Tracy nodded solemnly. "Understood."

"You sure you love girls, too?" Lucky asked Zane.

"I'm positive, peanut." Zane gave her a fierce bear
hug before lowering her back to the ground and ruf-
fling her hair. "Now I'll let you and Tracy here get
all prettied up. Don't take too long, though. We need
to be leaving in fifteen minutes."

Back home in Chicago it would have taken Tracy
fifteen minutes just to blend her eye shadow. But
since coming to the ranch she'd learned to speed up
her beauty routine.

Those first few days, she'd arranged her long hair
in an intricate French chignon as she'd done back
home. Not only had it come undone before half her
workday was done, but it had also required that she
get up half an hour earlier to fix it that way.

Forget that.

Next she'd settled for putting her hair in a French

braid, but even that required too much time and effort. In the end Tracy settled for a simple ponytail, which seemed to suit her new lifestyle best.

Lucky was already wearing clean jeans and red T-shirt, so all Tracy needed to do was add the vest and then turn the little girl so she could see her reflection in the bathroom mirror. While in the inner sanctum, Lucky gazed in both awe and disdain at the bottles of perfume, bubble bath and body lotion that were on the counter next to the sink. Tracy didn't say anything as she redid her own ponytail, adding a colorful red hair barrette to fasten it.

"My hair is too short for a ponytail," Lucky said.

Tracy searched the little girl's face for a clue as to whether or not that pleased her. She thought she caught another flash of that same yearning she'd seen before, when Lucky had touched the floral vest.

"It is too short for a ponytail," Tracy agreed. "But I have some—" she almost said cute but decided that description would be the curse of death as far as Lucky was concerned "—some cool hair barrettes you could wear." She showed the little girl the small star-shaped designs.

"Can you help me put them on?" Lucky asked with something almost resembling shyness.

"You bet."

She picked Lucky up and set her on the counter so she could get a better handle on what she was doing. Once she'd put the barrettes on either side of Lucky's part, she used a brush to smooth out the girl's hair, swirling it around her cheek. "There. What do you think?"

Turning to look over her shoulder, Lucky stared at her own reflection, her pleasure clear to see in her blue eyes. But aloud all she said was, "Looks okay." Then she reached out to give Tracy a kamikaze hug as short as it was unexpected.

It was the first time the little girl had made any physical overtures to her.

Just as Tracy felt tears coming to her eyes, Lucky released her and hopped down from the counter. "Thanks," she added before scooting out of the room.

Five minutes later, Tracy joined them outside. She didn't have time to do more than change into clean jeans and a red T-shirt and add some sterling silver jewelry—dangle earrings and a bracelet with bezel-set turquoise. But she felt happier than if she'd spent the day at a beauty spa. Because Lucky had hugged her and made her feel that the work she was doing here made a difference.

Lucky also insisted on riding with Tracy in her car instead of with her father and Buck and Rusty in the truck. Murph'n'Earl were driving a battered-and-faded blue pickup attached to a double horse trailer. Tracy's little red Miata stood out amid the monster trucks and trailers in Bliss, but she didn't care.

She met Zane at the predesignated gathering place of the corner of First and Main.

"I see you made it in one piece," he noted with a slow smile. He was wearing his standard attire—denim jeans and a long-sleeved shirt with the sleeves rolled up. Today the shirt was white, the pearlized snaps gleaming in the Colorado sunshine.

"I only got lost that first day," she replied. "Since then I've managed to find my way around pretty well."

"You've managed to do several things pretty well." His voice was unusually gruff. "I haven't thanked you for what you did for my dad. Finding that catalog company to carry his sauce. I never thought that would happen."

"I told you I'm good at what I do."

"I'm starting to believe you."

"I should hope so." Her eyes meshed with his for a moment before she forced herself to look away. "So tell me about this parade. I'll bet it dates back to Cockeyed Curly's time, right?"

"As I recall, Curly did use the parade as a distraction for robbing the bank one year. We don't have that kind of trouble anymore."

"Because your brother is such a great lawman."

Zane appeared surprised by her words. "You've met Reno?"

"Sure. That first time I came into town with the twins."

"Oh, right. I forgot about that. You need to watch out for my youngest brother. He's a ladies' man."

"He's a charmer," she agreed and then wondered if she imagined the flash of jealousy she saw in Zane's blue eyes. He was wearing that darn hat again so it was hard to always get a clear look into his eyes, unless he tilted back his head and gave you the full impact. Then it was *sin city—full hormone alert*. For a man who was serious and responsible, he sure did have sinful eyes.

"Uhm..." She grappled for a topic of conversation. "What about your other brother? Is he coming to the parade?"

"No. Cord is working on a special furniture order for a bank down in Glenwood Springs. Besides he doesn't like crowds."

"This is a crowd?" she inquired with a teasing grin at the three dozen or so people lining the parade route.

"This is a bigger crowd than we used to get. One year everyone in town was in the parade, which meant there was no one standing along Main Street to watch it. So now we designate whether you're assigned to march in the parade or be a spectator, and then we alternate that assignment each year. Last year our family all marched or rode, so this year we get to watch."

"Watching is fine by me," she murmured, surreptitiously keeping her gaze on him as he collared Rusty before the little boy stepped into the street. After a month out west, she had plenty of experience not only watching his kids but also watching Zane. Watching the way he moved with a cowboy swagger that was less about arrogance and more about poetry in motion. Other guys walked, Zane *moved*. And as a result, he moved her heart. Or was threatening to.

As the parade began with the Bliss Volunteer Fire Department truck at the forefront, Tracy couldn't help thinking that she could use a cooling off as the firemen got things rolling by spraying everyone with a mist of water, to the great delight of the warm crowd. The intense sunshine was making the day a hot one.

Or at least she liked to think it was the sun, and not Zane.

The parade was short and sweet, going to one end of the route and then turning around and coming back again, to make it seem longer than it actually was. There were high-stepping horses with fancy saddles and riders, the veterans from the American Legion in their uniforms and the high school marching band from Kendall, complete with baton-twirling and pom-pom-waving girls. And everywhere there were American flags, festooned from the light posts and waving in the crowd.

After the parade, everyone headed over to Bliss Park, the area behind the trailer that housed both the sheriff's office and city hall. There, numerous picnic tables had been set up and the smells of summer—hot dogs and mustard, fries, cotton candy and fresh-cut watermelon—filled the mountain air.

The twins headed right for the watermelon area, where they competed in what was apparently a Bliss tradition, The Watermelon Contest. Lucky won the watermelon-seed-spitting contest for her age group while Rusty took top honors in the watermelon-eating segment—done in one minute, face first, with no hands. Lucky decided not to enter.

Tracy suspected it was because she didn't want to mess up her hair, but Lucky wasn't saying. However, Tracy did catch her holding up a metal plate and looking at her own reflection, and then smiling.

After a lunch of hot dogs and fries topped off with strawberry ice cream for dessert, the games began. Tracy and Lucky came in second place in the three-legged race, while Zane and Rusty took first place. When Buck invited Tracy to participate in a game of horseshoes, she was willing to give it a try. She ended up winning.

There was no time to celebrate, because she was snared by the Women's Auxiliary to be a jam judge in the food tent. It seemed that Mrs. Battle, the same former housekeeper of Zane's who could ride a horse even though she was now in her eighties, had to cancel at the last minute because of indigestion.

After tasting all the various jams—peach, choke-cherry, wild strawberry and strawberry-rhubarb—Tracy proclaimed the wild strawberry by Contestant Three to be the finest of the lot. This created quite an uproar, as apparently every other year Mrs. Battle's sister-in-law had won this event, as Mrs. Battle had been the only judge. This year's winner was Annie Benton, a teacher in town.

Annie appeared stunned by the news that her jam was the best. The rest of the group applauded Tracy's choice as she awarded the purple ribbon to the young teacher. Only Mrs. Battle's sister-in-law looked as if she'd just sucked on a lemon as she huffed off.

"We've never had the nerve to stand up to Mrs. Battle's decisions before," one woman who'd introduced herself as Susan Grey said. "But you've given us the courage to do that."

"Me?" Tracy stared at her in surprise. "All I did was pick the best jam."

"That's right. You picked the best jam, without prejudice. Which is what we should have been doing instead of letting Mrs. Battle boss us around."

"I've never met her, but I get the impression she's a formidable woman," Tracy said.

"That's right, but even she couldn't handle the Best twins. And you've worked wonders with them." Susan nodded her approval before confiding, "Last year they knocked down the bunting over Main Street, and it fell on the marching band, where it got caught up in the tuba before wrapping around all the other brass instruments as the kids kept to their marching formation, even with the bunting swaddled all around them. It took them a long time to get everything sorted out."

Just then Rusty raced toward them, skidding to a halt as he reached Tracy's side. "Beauty just got the purple ribbon for biggest hog in Bliss!" he breathlessly announced.

Tracy hadn't even known that Beauty had left the ranch. "That's great."

"It's all because of you." Rusty gave her the same awed look he'd bestowed upon her when she'd told him about her dad working at the reptile house of the zoo. "Because of all that food you made that we couldn't eat and had to feed to Beauty."

Tracy couldn't help laughing at the news. "Well, I'm glad someone benefited from my cooking experiments."

ZANE HAD WATCHED Tracy make one conquest after another during the day's celebrations. He couldn't help but be impressed by the way she managed to fit in. Yet there was no mistaking her city-bred blond hair, with her ponytail swinging as she bobbed through the crowds, on her way to judge the jam contest or to toss a horseshoe. She fit in and stood out at the same time.

But the standing out wasn't in a bad way. She no longer had "tenderfoot" written all over her, as she had that night she'd shown up damp and dripping on his front doorstep. She was no longer hopeless in the kitchen, even if she did still have a few mishaps now and then. And he had to secretly confess to himself that he was getting hooked on the fancy juices she made with that juice extractor of hers. The other morning he'd actually had a papaya-orange smoothie.

If someone had told him a month ago that he'd be sitting down to wild fruit drinks in the morning and coming home to twin time at night, to kids who, while not model kids, had certainly shed some of their hell-on-wheels ways—heck, he'd have never believed it. But she'd done that. Changed things.

And he wasn't sure he liked it. He felt more comfortable when she was a fish out of water, when it was obvious that she couldn't cope on the ranch, that she didn't belong.

He reminded himself that she'd be leaving at the end of the summer, that the changes in her were temporary. She was still an advertising executive just pretending to be a housekeeper. How much longer would she enjoy the make-believe before heading back to the bright lights of Chicago? What could Bliss offer a woman like her?

Sure she ordered her clothes and books off the Internet and had them delivered to the ranch, but the time would come when she'd want to walk into a real store. And while she had gotten that fancy catalog to carry his dad's barbecue sauce, that was small potatoes compared to the big ad accounts she'd talked about being in charge of in Chicago.

The time would come when she'd want to see a play or go to the museum. When she'd want to be part of a city crowd, not a Bliss crowd. He'd hated the crowds in Seattle, but some folks said they loved them, loved the energy. He could see Tracy being that kind of person.

You needed to be quiet in your own soul to like it out here.

And then there was the fact that she was seeing the area during the summer, when the weather was on its best behavior, if there was such a thing. The sky had been known to spit hail and sleet even in July. But the winters here were real bears.

"Can we go to the carnival, Pa?" Lucky tugged on his hand to ask.

"Hmm?"

"The carnival. I want to ride the merry-go-round."

"That's for sissies," Rusty scoffed. "I want to go in the haunted house."

Last year Rusty hadn't slept by himself for a month after taking the haunted house ride. While Zane loved his son, the little fella had tossed in his sleep like a hound with fleas.

"How about the Ferris wheel instead?" Zane suggested.

He rode with Rusty in one car while Tracy and Lucky got in the next one. Buck was afraid of heights, so he stayed on the ground and waved up at them.

As they went on to tour the fairgrounds, Lucky caught sight of a stuffed animal she just had to have. It was a giant purple bear, almost the size of the twins, on the back shelf of the Ponderosa Pines Shooting Gallery.

"Oh, Pa," Lucky sighed, "if you could get that for me I'd never ask for anything ever again in my whole life."

"Get that in writing," Buck wryly suggested.

If his little girl wanted a giant teddy bear, by golly Zane would get it for her. Without further ado, he put his money down and picked up the rifle. Right off he hit two of the moving duck targets. Only three more to go. Ping. Ping. Only one left now.... He missed it.

"Here, let me try," he heard Tracy say.

"You'd just be wasting your money," he told her.

She just smiled at him. "Why don't you let me be the judge of that."

"I'M TELLING YOU it was just a lucky shot," Tracy said.

"I love my bear." Lucky was beaming as she hung onto the bear for dear life. It was indeed almost as big as she was. "Thank you, Tracy."

"You're welcome, sweetie."

Lucky didn't even grimace at the endearment. She was too busy beaming from ear to ear.

Which left it up to Rusty to defend her reputation. "She's not a sweetie, she's a peanut. And a hellion."

"Are you sure you didn't want me to try and win that giant fire truck for you?" Tracy asked him.

"No. Besides, you said it was just a lucky shot."

"Where did you learn to shoot like that?" Zane finally demanded.

She shrugged. "My dad took me to the shooting range whenever he had time. He wasn't a hunter, he loved animals too much for that. But he enjoyed hitting a bull's-eye."

"That must hurt the bull," Rusty said.

"It's just the name for the center of a target," Tracy hurriedly explained. "It's not a real bull's eye."

"Why didn't you tell me you could shoot like that?" Zane said.

"You mean you couldn't tell I was a marksman by the way I handled the cookie shooter or the salad shooter?" she teased him.

"The first time you used the salad thing you shot lettuce all over the walls. And your cookie dough was so thick that you burned out the cookie shooter."

"At least the juice extractor still works."

"Thank heavens."

"I've gotten you hooked on papaya-orange smoothies, haven't I? Come on," she jabbed him with a friendly elbow. "Confess."

"No cowboy is gonna confess to liking papaya."

"You mean it would ruin that bronc-riding image of yours?" Before going to the carnival, they'd attended the Annual Bliss Rodeo, which actually consisted of local ranchers and cowboys showing off their skills for a pot of four hundred dollars donated by Bliss merchants.

"I wasn't in the bronc-riding contest," Zane corrected her. "I was in the calf-roping section."

"I sure hope you didn't hurt that poor little thing."

"Is that why you were standing up and cheering loud?" Rusty asked. "Because you thought Pa was hurting the calf?"

Zane shot her one of those under-the-brim-of-his-hat looks, the kind that made her heart jump just like those broncs at the rodeo. "So you were standing up and cheering, huh?"

"For the calf."

"For the calf, huh?"

"Absolutely." That was her story and she was sticking to it.

But when his blue eyes caught hold of hers, she couldn't look away. Her breath caught in her throat as sexual awareness unfurled deep within her.

"Come on, we don't want to miss the fireworks!" Buck said, interrupting the moment.

Tracy felt like she'd already experienced the fireworks, the internal kind that always meant trouble was ahead.

A WEEK LATER, Rusty still hadn't regained his usual good humor. Ever since Tracy had won the bear—which Lucky had named Fuzzy, much to Rusty's disgust—he'd been acting strangely.

She was preparing a huge bowl of fresh green beans for dinner when she looked through the window over the sink and saw Rusty out in the yard beyond the big cottonwood. He appeared to be lassoing a fence post. He did not look like a happy camper.

Leaving the vegetables in the sink, she wiped her

hands on the kitchen towel before going outside and joining him. "What are you doing?"

"Nothin'," he muttered, clearly not welcoming her company. But something inside of her sensed that despite his behavior, he was just about bursting to tell someone what his problem was.

"Is there something you'd like to talk about?" she asked.

Sure enough, he turned on her, his blue eyes—darker than his sister's—flared as the words spilled out. "You're turnin' Lucky into a *girl*." He said that last word with utter disgust.

"You've got something against girls?" She'd already heard this from Lucky but she wanted to hear Rusty's perspective on the subject.

"They're dumb. We used to hang out all the time, now Lucky is acting dumb."

Ah, so the problem was that Rusty was feeling threatened by the changes in Lucky and feeling left out by the closeness developing between Lucky and Tracy. Hey, she was getting pretty good at deciphering this kid stuff. She paused to mentally pat herself on the back before assuring Rusty, "Lucky may be acting more like a girl, but that doesn't mean that she's dumb or that the two of you won't be as close as you've always been."

"She named her bear Fuzzy. And she brushes her hair all the time now."

"And she can still out-lasso you." At Rusty's surprised look, she said, "Buck told me so."

"I'm getting better. That's why I'm practicing."

"Need any help?" Tracy asked, not really thinking he'd actually take her up on her offer. Silly her.

"Yeah!" His eyes lit up. "I need to rope something moving. Like you."

Tracy wasn't sure she liked the sound of that.

"It's not hard," Rusty added. "All you have to do is walk around, and I'll just float the rope over you, like this. Wait, I need to be taller." He stood on a nearby bale of hay. "There. Now walk, but not too far."

On the first few attempts, Rusty tossed the rope next to her or in front of her. She was amazed that a seven-and-a-half-year-old could do this well. Buck had told her that they'd started swinging string and imitating their father when they were "first able to travel on their hind feet."

She'd often noticed Zane with a coiled rope in his hand as he strode toward the barn or worked with the horses in the corral. Sometimes he'd slap the rope against his thigh to get a horse's attention. It certainly got her attention.

Plop. Yet again, Rusty's child-sized rope fell in the dust a few feet in front of her.

"Here, what if I just stood here and put my arms out." She showed him what she meant, going into a position that would do a scarecrow proud. "Could you aim for my arm?"

Biting his lip in concentration, Rusty gathered his rope and tried again. Bingo! The rope fell into place around her arm.

"Try moving again," Rusty asked.

She did, more slowly this time, even turning around

so that her back was to him. "You've gotten real close," she encouraged him. "And that last shot, or whatever you call it, was a bull's-eye."

The rope whispered over her head and settled around her shoulders. Startled, she lowered her arms and the rope slid lower, to her waist before resting on her hips.

"Wrong terminology," Zane murmured from behind her.

Only then did she realize that he'd been the one who'd lassoed her, not Rusty. She was now connected to him by the rope.

He gently tugged her closer. "An old cowboy once said that ropes, like guns, are dangerous. Guns go off, but ropes go on."

"I've already had some experience in this household with ropes going on me," she reminded him.

She could tell by the look in his eyes that he was remembering that time, when she'd been tied to the bed and he'd had to free her, his hands branding her for all time.

"Are you gonna help me practice ropin'?" Rusty eagerly asked his father.

"Sure thing."

The only sure thing as far as Tracy was concerned was that she wasn't sticking around out here to have Zane tie her up in knots any more that she already was.

"You're on your own, cowboys," she told them, freeing herself from the lasso and walking back to the ranch house.

ON THURSDAY, TRACY was determined to give the living room the thorough cleaning it deserved. No more twenty-five-watt bulbs to hide dust balls. Slipping the Cherry Poppin' Daddies cassette in her portable player, she adjusted the compact headphones and set to work.

First she had to shove the furniture out of the way. It took some elbow grease, but she managed to get the couch and chairs against the walls so that she could vacuum the carpeting without obstacles.

The swing music just made it too tempting to dance while vacuuming. Her right hand may have been on the cleaning upright, but her left hand and foot were jiving. Every so often, she'd pause and make a crazy leg move before circling the vacuum as if it were her partner.

When the twins suddenly appeared in front of her, she yelped in surprise and tugged the headphones off her head.

"What are you doing?" Lucky asked.

"I was vacuuming...and swing dancing." Something about the intrigued look in Lucky's eyes made her add, "Here, I'll show you."

Tracy took the Cherry Poppin' Daddies cassette

from her portable player, popped it into the stereo system in the living room, cued it to music of the hit opening number "Zoot Suit Riot" and then hit the repeat button.

Turning back to Lucky, she said, "Give me your hand."

A minute later, Lucky and Tracy were swinging around the room—the little girl mimicking Tracy's moves with enthusiasm. When Tracy completed a crazy leg move, kicking her left leg as high as she could to the side of Lucky, the little girl did the same. Meanwhile, Rusty had taken the turned-off vacuum as his partner.

When Lucky went into energetic moves of her own, Tracy took Rusty's hand and swung him.

"What the Sam Hill is going on here?" Buck demanded as he joined them in the living room. He'd been in the den working on ranch paperwork.

"We's dancin'!" Lucky breathlessly shouted back.

"Swing dancin'," Rusty added.

"Then let me show you youngsters how it's done." Buck took to the makeshift dance floor like a pro, grabbing Tracy as his partner. With one arm around her back and the other holding her hand, he showed her jitterbug moves she'd only seen in the movies. He ended by rolling her over his back so that she went head over heels before landing on her feet.

"Me next!" Lucky squealed.

"No, me!" Rusty shouted.

With the twins Buck improvised by swinging them to each side of him, their feet off the floor as they giggled with delight to the blaring music.

"Enough," Buck finally gasped before collapsing in his duct-taped recliner.

Tracy barely had enough energy left to turn off the cassette player before it replayed "Zoot Suit Riot" for the twentieth time. She made it to the couch before she, too, collapsed in breathless laughter.

"Where'd you learn to dance like that, Grandpa?" Lucky said.

"And how come you never taught us before?" Rusty asked.

"Didn't know you young'uns would be interested." Leaning forward, Buck propped his elbows on his knees and shook his head. "Whew! I haven't jitterbugged since your grandmother and I were newlyweds. Appears to me that's about how old this carpet is, too." He squinted down at it. "Am I going blind or is the light getting bad in here?"

Feeling guilty, Tracy confessed. "I changed the bulbs to a lower wattage."

"I can see why, looking at this rug. It's in bad shape."

This was her chance, and Tracy grabbed it. "Is the hardwood floor beneath it in good shape?"

"As far as I know."

"I was thinking we could take up this rug and let the hardwood floor shine. I think it would make this room look great. Open it up."

"Fine. Let's get to it."

His response took her by surprise. "You mean now?"

"You had some other time in mind?"

She did some rapid mental calculations. She could

use the cold leftover pork roast from last night's dinner to make hearty sandwiches for the men at lunch. A store-bought peach pie would finish off the meal. All in all, pretty much a self-serve meal, which gave her time to work on tearing up the carpeting before Buck changed his mind. "Let's do it now."

"Might as well put that music back on the tape player while we work."

And so it was that they tore up the carpet to the swinging sound of the Cherry Poppin' Daddies.

When Zane came in for lunch, he passed by the living room on his way to get something from the den. Standing in the doorway and staring at them in astonishment, he said, "Anyone care to explain why the living room carpet is all torn up?"

"Pa, Tracy taught us how to swing dance today!" Lucky said.

"And for that you had to tear up the carpet?"

Putting her hands on her hips, Tracy just stood there and grinned at him. "Darn right we did."

"Was this your idea?" Zane asked Buck.

"Only if you think it's a good one," his father replied with a chortle.

"I'm not sure what I think," Zane muttered before heading for the den.

"There's a lot of that going around," Buck called after him. His meaningful glance in Tracy's direction had her wondering if Buck had noticed the chemistry between his son and her.

She found out two weeks later. It had taken that long to complete the living-room project. The room was now taking shape just as she'd envisioned it.

She'd confiscated a Navajo rug from a storage room upstairs and laid it down on the oak floor, which glowed with a patina only age could produce. A throw featuring horses in browns and blacks hid most of the duct tape on Buck's recliner.

Today she was checking out the den to see if anything from there could be used in the newly redone living room.

The largest piece of furniture was the desk, which was an L-shaped design. On top of it was a computer with a monitor and printer. Seeing her curious look, Buck said, "That machine sure comes in handy for keeping ranch records, calving, hay production and accounting, that sort of stuff. I told Zane right fast that getting it was one of the smartest things he ever did."

"Next thing you know, you'll be cruising the Internet."

Buck just snorted and went on to proudly point out the stuffed armadillo his great-great grandfather had brought up from Texas.

The stuffed armadillo could stay where it was. Averting her eyes from it, she instead focused on the various items on the wall. There was Zane's college degree and Reno's as well. Family photos, both old and new, adorned one wall. And there was a set of lovely framed cross-stitch pieces on the far wall.

Stepping closer, she realized they weren't the traditional sayings but were instead Cockeyed Curly's poems.

"Don't tell me Curly was an accomplished cross-stitcher as well as a poet and thief?" she said.

"My grandmother did those up. The words are from Curly."

She read one aloud.

"Don't never confuse me with Robin Hood.
I took from the rich as best I could.
But where it goes is just to me.
The poor can do their own robbery."

Another was just two lines:

I'm Curly the robbin' poet.
Now we both know it.

"You never told me how your visit with your son Cord went. Did you have time to look for the treasure map or was that just a ruse to get the twins to go with you?"

"Don't rightly know what a ruse is," Buck replied, "but the truth of the matter is that I didn't have time to do any map searching. The kids got antsy, so I couldn't look through the old trunks I got stored up there."

"The twins? Antsy? I find that hard to believe," she murmured with a bat of her lashes.

Buck chortled just as she knew he would.

"Now that I've got you in a good mood, how about letting me move this wrought-iron floor lamp into the living room."

"Sure you don't want the armadillo?"

"I wouldn't dream of moving it," she demurred.

"Not when it's been providing such good luck right from where it's at."

"How about this here sign." He pointed to the carved western pine.

"Cowboy's Logic—Be Sure to Taste Your Words Before You Spit Them Out," she read aloud. "Hmm, your son might have need of it in here. No, I'll just take this."

She grabbed hold of the floor lamp and took it to the living room before Buck could offer to do it for her.

"There." She stepped back to admire the room. "Do you think Zane will like it?"

Buck narrowed his eyes to give her an intense look. "Appears my oldest son of a buck has made quite an impression on you."

"He's my boss."

"He's more than that." Seeing her glare, Buck held out his hands in a conciliatory way. "Now don't go gettin' all defensive with me. I know how she-folk are. Don't like admittin' what's in their hearts any more than we do. But I ain't blind, although I thought I was going that way when you changed the bulbs in here. Glad you put them bright ones back in. Now where was I...oh, yes. We were discussing how Zane is a tad slicker shy when it comes to city gals."

She blinked at him. "Slicker shy?"

"Cowboy term. Some horses shy at the rustle of a slicker."

She knew from reading Western romances that a slicker was a type of long oilskin raincoat worn out on the range. She didn't know what that had to do with her.

Buck seemed eager to explain. "See, the same way some horses shy away at certain things or sounds, some people do the same thing."

"I already know Zane's opinion of women from the big city," Tracy said. "He's made himself very clear on that subject."

"Seems to me he may be saying one thing and doing another. I've seen the way you two look at each other. Like a pair of lovesick calves."

She laughed at his words. "You're exaggerating. I just want him to think well of me, that's all. I don't like people thinking I'm incompetent."

Even so, she was the first to admit she hadn't become a Martha Stewart clone overnight. While she had finally mastered the intricacies of fabric softeners so that the towels no longer felt like sandpaper, just yesterday she'd forgotten to plug in the Crock-Pot and dinner had been almost two hours late. But at least the roast and vegetables had been edible once they'd finally cooked.

Murph'n'Earl had been the ones to alert her to the advantages of using a slow cooker like a Crock-Pot. It seems that Murph's first wife had been a good cook, but a little lacking in the faithfulness department.

Not that either cowhand talked about his past much, or anything else for that matter. Mostly they just ate their meals in silence, only resorting to shuffling their feet and bending their hats when called upon to speak.

Not that they wore their hats while eating. They

were always careful to remove them in her presence, which is when the hat-bending began in earnest.

More at ease with the art of conversation were both Susan Grey and Annie Benson, who had phoned her after the Fourth of July celebration and offered their own easy recipes for her to try.

She'd even had a breakthrough about her own goals in her career of advertising. And it was linked to, of all things, Rusty's dislike of broccoli.

When Rusty told her that he wouldn't eat the vegetable despite never having tasted it, she considered using blue food coloring to turn broccoli into ''a blue life form from the planet Zargot.'' She even went so far as to put the blue-dyed broccoli in a bottle with a Planet Zargot label she'd done up on her laptop and portable printer before deciding that she'd be betraying Rusty's trust by deceiving him.

And that's when it hit her that she wanted to work on selling only products that she really believed in, like Buck's Barbecue Sauce. Not products that she had to deceive the consumer into buying.

As for Rusty, Tracy had received a recipe for roasted red pepper soup from Annie that he loved. And he gobbled fresh green beans like there was no tomorrow. So there was no need to sell him on broccoli.

The sound of Buck's voice interrupted her train of thought. Derailed it actually. ''I'm not saying you're incompetent, I'm saying you may be infatuated. There's a difference.''

''I am *not* infatuated!''

Her anger had him backing up a step or two. ''Now

don't go getting on your high horse, I'm just trying to help out here.''

"Then help me move this lamp over to the other side of the couch."

For once Buck did as he was told.

SHE FIRST NOTICED the button missing from Zane's shirt when he sat down for the midday meal the next day. It was one of the few shirts he owned that didn't have pearlized snaps. He was probably wearing it because she was a little behind in the washing as a result of revamping the living room.

"You've got a loose button," she told him. "I'll fix it."

"I don't have time," he began, but she already had a needle and thread in her hand.

"No, don't take your shirt off," she said. She certainly didn't need him standing bare-chested in her kitchen. Okay, so it was his kitchen. Even so, she didn't want him half-undressed. Okay, so she did want him half-undressed. She wanted him totally undressed.

Stop that! she ordered herself. *Just do your job. Sew on his darn button and impress the heck out of him with your stitching skills.*

"The button is near the bottom of your shirt. Just tug it out of your jeans and I'll sew it while it's on you." When he did as she requested, she started babbling nervously. "I'm not as good with a needle as your great-grandmother was. I saw her cross-stitching in the den. Pretty impressive." Head down, she kept her attention focused on the needle and thread—in and out, in and out. The one time she did look up, she almost smacked the top of her head against his chin.

For his part, Zane wasn't saying much. But she could feel his body heat emanating toward her, beckoning her closer. Her fingers trembled. Must be because she was trying to sew so fast.

"There." She finished off by wrapping the thread around the button several times. It was only then that she realized what she'd done. "Oops."

"I don't like a woman with a needle in her hand saying oops," Zane said.

"It appears that your shirt has somehow gotten sewn to mine."

"Somehow?" he repeated. "I know exactly how. You're driving me plumb loco!"

"Hey," she shot back, "it was an honest mistake..."

The rest of her words were smothered by his lips as he lowered his head to kiss her. As before in the barn, there was no tentative fumbling, no awkwardness. There was only immediate heat and instant hunger.

He repeated that flick of his tongue across the roof of her mouth in a way she found incredibly seductive. His work-roughened hands cupped her face, holding her in place. She was vaguely aware that she still held a sharp needle in one hand, but that left her other hand free to tug him closer. She did so.

Ah, that was better. A thread wouldn't fit between

them now, so tightly was her body pressed against his.

It took the sound of a booming voice from across the room to send them apart.

"Son of a buck!"

10

TRACY HAD PULLED AWAY from Zane so quickly that she ripped off the button she'd just sewn on to his shirt. Not only that, but the material on her shirt ripped as well, creating a rather large hole in the blue chambray material. Another outfit down the drain.

She should have been embarrassed to have been caught in a compromising position with Zane. But she was too distracted by the realization that Zane was not as indifferent to her as he'd said. Despite all his claims to the contrary, there was no mistaking the way he'd kissed her.

He'd kissed her like a man who needed her the way he needed air to breathe and water to drink. As if she were necessary for his existence. As if he couldn't go a millisecond longer without tasting her mouth and caressing her lips.

He'd told her she was driving him plumb loco. No man had ever said that to her before. And she could commiserate, because he had the same effect on her.

Zane's expression now wasn't giving anything away. Buck, on the other hand, looked like he'd eaten one of her inedible meals and was about to choke on it.

Somebody had to break the silence, so she did. ''I

was just sewing a button back on Zane's shirt.'' Not the most brilliant of openings, and thank heavens Buck made no comment. He might have wondered how locking their lips together got a button sewn back on. ''Everything is…uhm…fine now,'' she added, her voice clearly distracted.

Better than fine. Despite getting caught, she couldn't help the way her heart was soaring. She wasn't the only one wrapped up in this wild attraction—Zane was as much a victim of it as she was. It felt so good knowing this was a two-way street. She wasn't the only one in love.…

Her eyes opened wide. In love? Was that what this was all about?

It would explain a lot.

In love. With Zane. She tested the concept. It was terrifying and exciting.

She needed some time to herself to get her thoughts together. ''I'll leave you two alone,'' she murmured.

As soon as Tracy left the room, Buck lit into Zane. ''Are you loco, son?''

''Probably,'' Zane muttered, tucking his loose shirt back into the waistband of his jeans.

''That little gal is falling for you like a heifer in a mud puddle.''

''That little gal is city born and bred,'' Zane scoffed. ''No way she's like a heifer in a mud puddle. More like a fancy butterfly, here while things are good and gone when they aren't.''

''What you know about she-folks would fit in the ear of a gnat,'' Buck retorted. ''Ain't no way she's a butterfly. A butterfly would have hightailed it back to Chicago that first day. Or the next, when the twins tied her to the bed. Or the next, when King was on the toilet. Or…''

Zane held his hands out in a reluctant concession. ''Okay, so she's kept her promise and stayed. But it's only for the summer.''

''She's no delicate flower. That woman can hold her own out here. She's got a temper that would turn a blizzard around and send it home with a suntan. Yet she's real gentle and patientlike with the kids. And she's turned this place into a home, in case you hadn't noticed.''

''I noticed,'' Zane said gruffly.

''I figured you did.'' Buck fixed him with a piercing look. ''That why you were kissing her?''

Zane shrugged. ''Like you said, it was a plumb loco thing to do.''

''Only if you're regretting it.''

The only thing Zane regretted was being this attracted to a woman who was sure to leave. It was like lying down in a stampede and asking to be trampled by a herd of cattle. But he couldn't honestly say that he regretted kissing her. Not when it had felt so good. Better than good. He wasn't a poetic man or he'd come up with some kind of description. Only thing he knew was that a kiss had never affected him this way before. But that didn't change the facts. ''She's not our kind.''

''And what kind might that be?'' Buck demanded.

''From around here.''

"Pam was from around here," Buck pointed out. "That didn't seem to help matters none."

"Pam was a *city* girl." Zane made sure to place the emphasis where he did.

Buck snorted, clearly not impressed with Zane's logic. "Pam's problems came from her character, not from her geography."

"I'm telling you, you don't have to defend Tracy this way." Zane was getting aggravated by his father's attitude. The way he saw it, he was the injured party here, the one perched on the horns of a dilemma. And as any cowboy could tell you, being stuck on a pair of horns is a mighty uncomfortable place to be. "She's well able to look after herself. As for me, after my first marriage, I'm love-proof." Saying the words were meant to make him feel better. "My heart belongs to my kids."

Buck fixed him with another steely-eyed look, the kind he'd often given him as a kid when he'd known Zane was about to do something stupid. "She's taken to this ranch like a horse takes to corn. You'd be a fool to let her go."

"She's not going anyplace until the kids start school. Then she'll head back to her old life and I'll…"

"Be back where you were when this started," Buck interrupted him to say. "Knee-deep in cow patties. Take them blinders off, boy. They're affecting your vision. No need to be slicker shy around this filly. I'm telling you, she's a keeper."

"I TOLD YOU he'd be a keeper," Maeve was telling Tracy over the phone.

"What do you mean?" Tracy had retreated to her room and done what she always did whenever she had a personal crisis. She called her aunt, this time using her cell phone. There was no telling when the twins or, heaven forbid, Zane, might pick up the extension on the ranch phone. So Tracy always used her own phone for personal calls.

"I mean that I could tell by the way Herbie talked about Zane that he'd be perfect for you. I can't wait to meet him. Have you two set a date yet?"

"Whoa!" Tracy exclaimed.

"How cute," Maeve murmured in delight. "You're even sounding like a cowgirl."

"Zane doesn't think so." Tracy started pacing. "I think I love him anyway."

Tracy winced and held the phone away as Maeve squealed. "I knew it! I could tell you were falling for him."

"And I think he may be falling for me, but he's not happy about it."

"What man is? They're never happy when their hearts get lassoed."

"Now you're starting to sound like a cowgirl."

"Herbie and I have been talking about coming out there for a visit."

Tracy could just imagine the mayhem of adding her aunt to the mix. That's all she'd need, Maeve hugging Zane and asking him if he'd set a date yet. "I don't think that would be a good idea. Not yet, anyway. Things are still too much up in the air." Tracy plopped onto the bed. "I can't believe I've fallen in love so quickly."

"Quickly is a relative term," her aunt retorted. "I knew I loved Herbie the very first moment I saw him. You, on the other hand, have been on that ranch for two months now. And it's not like you were truly in love with Dennis. You told me so yourself."

"I know. And Zane is nothing like Dennis. Do you think Zane could really grow to love me?" she asked, almost afraid to say the words aloud.

"If he's half as smart as Herbie says that Buck says he is, then he'd have to love you. He certainly doesn't seem like the kind of man to kiss a woman he doesn't have feelings for."

"That's true. And I've already got the man hooked on papaya-orange drinks. I'm the only one who knows how to use the juice extractor to make them."

"He'd be lost without you."

Tracy laughed at the concept. "So all I have to do is sit back and wait for him to realize that I'm invaluable, huh?"

"That's right."

"As Buck would say, that's about as likely as pigs flying."

TWO DAYS LATER Zane was stunned to walk into the house and find his father upstairs packing up the twins. "What are you doing?"

"Taking the twins to see the state fair," Buck replied as if this was an everyday occurrence.

"But that's clear down in Pueblo."

Buck nodded. "Which is why we're staying a few days."

Zane trailed his family down the stairs and out to

the front porch, grappling to keep up with this new wrinkle in his life. "I'll come with you."

Buck shook his head even as he loaded the twins and their bags in the truck. "You've got to stay here at the ranch and keep an eye on things."

"Murph'n'Earl…"

"Can't do everything that needs to be done by themselves," Buck interrupted him to point out. "It's only a few nights. Is there some reason why you're suddenly so nervous you'd make a rat in a snake's den look comfortable?"

Zane shifted from one foot to another before catching himself. Heck, he was acting like a fool teenager. He had to come up with some logical explanation, so he grabbed hold of this one. "The twins have never been away from me overnight."

"About time they were then," Buck retorted, clearly not moved by Zane's reasoning. "They're excited over the prospect of going to the fair. Don't ruin it for them just because you're scared."

Zane threw back his shoulders and glared at his father. "I'm not scared."

"Fine." Buck patted him on the back with enough force to make Zane step back a pace or two. "Then we'll see you in a few days."

The twins hugged him and waved out the truck window, but Zane could tell that they were thrilled at the idea of going on a trip with their grandfather.

So why was he standing there feeling like he'd just been deserted in a blizzard and kicked in the heart by a mule.

"What are you looking at?" Zane growled at

Murph'n'Earl, who were standing nearby, eyeing him with knowing grins. "We've got fences to check. Let's get to work."

"WHERE IS EVERYBODY?" Tracy asked as she and Zane sat down to dinner.

Zane glared at her as if she'd just committed a capital offense instead of having asked a simple question. "You mean to tell me that you only now noticed that the twins and my father are gone?"

"Of course not," she said, stung by his implication that she wasn't paying attention to the twins. "Buck told me they were going to the state fair. I asked if I could go with them."

"Wanted to get back to a big city, huh?"

Ignoring his taunting words, she just finished her explanation. "Buck said that I was needed here more."

"You were disappointed at not going to Pueblo."

"I'll go another time."

She seemed mighty unconcerned about things. Why wasn't she itching to head off to Pueblo? Maybe it wasn't a big enough city for her.

It hadn't escaped his notice that she didn't spend her days off exploring any of the bigger cities in the area. Not even when he'd given her an entire weekend off.

No, she'd spent the time surfing the Internet on that little computer of hers, looking for more places to distribute and sell Buck's Barbecue Sauce. Or she'd read the twins a book or cajole Buck into writing down some of his Cockeyed Curly stories. Or she'd go riding with him or work on the garden she'd planted with the kids.

She'd done just about everything but what he expected her to do. And he suspected she was doing it deliberately. Just to aggravate him. Or to prove him wrong.

Still deep in his heart, he was finding that excuse more and more lame. But he wasn't about to give it up without a fight.

After helping himself to a large serving of Tater Tots, he resumed his questioning. "So you must be missing your job back in Chicago?"

"No."

"No?" he repeated, clearly surprised by her simple denial.

"I've decided that this job could be just as rewarding as the one I had back in Chicago."

He frowned. "How do you figure that?"

"Because what I'm doing here is making a difference. Do you deny that?" she challenged him.

"No comment," he muttered.

"You never did tell me where Murph'n'Earl are," she reminded him while passing him the bowl of peas.

"They went into Kendall for the evening."

"So we're alone?"

"Something wrong with that?" Now he was the one who challenged her.

"Not as far as I'm concerned," she replied, deliberately keeping her voice light and unconcerned. "How about you?"

"Fine by me, too."

She nodded. "Good. Glad to hear it. Here, have some more steak."

"This actually tastes pretty good," he confessed.

"Why sir—" she waved her hand in front of her face as if she were doing a Scarlett O'Hara impersonation "—you're going to make me swoon with all your fancy compliments."

He narrowed his eyes at her. "That your way of saying I'm a rough ol' cowboy and not a silver-tongued sweet-talker?"

"I don't think anyone could ever accuse you of being a sweet-talker," she assured him with a grin.

For some reason her words irritated him. It had never bothered him before that Reno was the charmer in the family but now he found that he wanted to…how had she once put it? He wanted to wow her with his words. "Oh, I don't know. If I had the proper inspiration, say like your hair, I might be able to surprise you with my lyrical ways."

She looked at him. When had this conversation turned seductive? There was no mistaking the warmth in his voice or the intensity of his gaze. It was one of those full-impact, sin-city looks from eyes so blue they put the sky to shame. Now she was the one getting lyrical.

Looking down, she nervously tugged down the hem of her white T-shirt and wished she was wearing something more…alluring than jeans and a T-shirt. She couldn't remember that last time she'd worn a dress. At least her top didn't have any stains on it from cooking dinner.

"When you're outside your hair is like liquid sunshine," he suddenly said. "The sun hits it and makes these little streaks of gold stand out. There are times when you look too good to be true."

"I am true," she whispered.

"Prove it."

"How?"

He shook his head as if already regretting his words. "Forget I said that."

"The same way I was supposed to forget that kiss we shared out in the barn?" she said.

"Forgettin' seems harder where you're concerned," he admitted before shoving back his chair and leaving the table. "I'd better go check on the horses."

He'd never done that in the evening before. "Check on the horses?" she repeated, still astonished by the way he'd turned that seductive voice of his on and off. "What for? What do you think they're going to do?"

"I'm more afraid of what I might do," he muttered before jamming his hat on his head and taking off.

It didn't surprise her that she didn't see him again for the rest of the evening. So, he was hiding out in the barn. Fine. Let him. She wasn't going to chase after him.

She went to her own room and brooded. She felt such a strong sense of belonging here on the ranch with Zane and his family that she'd actually allowed herself to start daydreaming about a possible future with him. Why was it so hard for him to believe she could be happy here?

Okay, so he was slicker shy. So was she. But there

were times when you had to take the bull by the horns
and…kiss him? What would Zane do if he came back
from the barn to find her in his bed?

She'd been in his bedroom before, when putting
away his clean washing. She'd just been in there yesterday. She knew everything from the green color
scheme to the way he neatly stacked his loose change
on top of his dresser. She'd washed his underwear for
heaven's sakes. In the same load with her own. And
both had managed to survive.

So what would he do if he found her in his bed?
Kick her out or welcome her with open arms?

If she was a gutsy girl she'd find out. Instead she
applied an avocado face mask and considered her op-
tions. A knock on her door caught her by surprise—
green goop covered her face and fingertips.

"Who is it?" she croaked. Dumb question. There
were only two of them in the house.

"It's Zane." His voice sounded just as froggy as
hers did. "I wanted to…never mind."

She heard the sound of his boots ringing against
the hardwood floor as he headed back to the main
part of the house and away from her room.

What had he been about to say? Why had he chick-
ened out? Maybe he just wanted her to make him a
midnight snack, even though it was only nine at night.
Or maybe he planned on making her his midnight
snack.

Either way, she had to find out. So she quickly
rinsed the face mask away and tried to decide what
to wear. At the moment she was dressed in her night-

gown and ivory satin robe. It wasn't as if he hadn't seen her in it before. Several times.

Securing the belt around her waist, she paused long enough to splash on some cologne before heading out on her fact-finding mission. Only problem was that Zane was nowhere to be found. At least not on the main floor.

Maybe he'd gone back to the barn. Or maybe he'd gone upstairs to bed. She'd promised Rusty and Lucky she'd check in on their pets and feed them tonight. Which meant she should go upstairs anyway and do that.

Precious, already curled up and snoozing, didn't need dinner, but King did. Tracy had brought some shredded lettuce up with her, which the iguana ate with appreciation. Joe, the mouse, however, was missing. The door to his cage was slightly ajar, which meant he'd made a break for it.

Then she saw the mouse, perched on the bookcase above Rusty's bed. Laughing down at her. Just as Randy, the horse, had in the barn a few weeks earlier.

She was tired of being laughed at. It was the last straw.

Marching over, she grabbed the mouse in one hand and read it the riot act. "Listen, buddy, you've been making me nervous long enough, checking under my bed every night to make sure you're not hiding out there. And all because some bully traumatized me with a mouse when I was a little kid. Okay, the truth is that I'm never going to love mice, but I refuse to have you turn me into a quivering idiot. Are we clear on that?" The mouse wiggled its little whiskers at her and appeared to nod its head. "Good. I'm glad we both agree on that. Now you get back in your cage and behave yourself."

Two seconds later the mouse was back where it belonged and Tracy felt on top of the world. She'd done it! She'd confronted one of her worse fears. She'd met the mouse and beat it, figuratively speaking. If she could do that, she could do anything!

Like confront Zane. Feeling gutsy and confident, she headed right for his bedroom, where she pounded on the door.

She began speaking the instant he opened it. "You came to my room a few minutes ago. What did you want?" she demanded almost belligerently.

"You."

His blunt declaration took the wind right out of her sails. "Oh," she sort of hiccuped.

"Yeah, oh."

Not wanting to misunderstand him, she carefully said, "You mean you wanted me to do something for you?"

His smile was positively wicked. "Yes, ma'am, you could say that."

She was getting impatient with him again. "Then why don't you say it?"

"I want you in my bed."

"I want the same thing," she admitted. "So what's stopping us?"

"A whole passel of things, none of which seem to matter right now."

"Which leaves us where?" she asked.

"Here." He leaned down and kissed her. Gently.

Giving her time to back away. Letting her know the final decision was hers. Come or go. Stay or leave. Her choice.

"Yes," she whispered against his mouth, deepening their kiss.

Once again, the heat was instant. It was as if their previous kisses hadn't been interrupted, as if they'd picked up right where they'd left off—wanting each other with a hunger that was elemental and went clear through to the soul.

Zane made short work of undoing her robe, peeling it back to reveal the nightgown she wore beneath it. He glided his hands over her satin-covered form with both reverence and ravaging in mind. When he bent his head to kiss the curve of her breast, she threaded her fingers through his dark hair.

She could feel him smile. Her own smile turned dreamy as he practiced his tongue-tasting ways on her, lapping along the lacy edge of her nightgown before slipping his hand beneath the material to free her breast. The cool night air was a direct contrast to the wet warmth of his mouth against her bare skin. He brushed his thumb across her nipple with a velvety touch, before covering it with his lips.

Undeniable flames of desire flared deep within her body as her need for him grew with every passing second.

When he suddenly pulled away and put her nightgown back in place, she felt the loss intensely, so intensely she ached from it.

"If you change your mind now, I'll kill you," she warned him, her eyes glittering with feminine passion.

"I'm not changing my mind," he assured her, his own gaze just as heated. "I just don't aim on taking you right here against the door frame. And that's what might have happened if we didn't slow down a tad. We've got all night."

"We do?"

He nodded. "I thought a highfalutin advertising woman like you would have figured that out some time ago. This is why my father left us alone."

"So we could..."

"Get acquainted."

She smiled. "I guess you wouldn't have much trouble selling me on the idea of getting better acquainted with you."

"You're the one who is the expert on selling."

"Maybe I should teach you a thing or two about the dynamics of selling. The first step is getting your audience's attention." Her smile was pure temptation filled with naughty enjoyment as she undid the bow holding her wraparound nightgown in place, then whipped it open to flash her bare breasts at him before covering them again so quickly he might have dreamed the whole thing. "The second step is arousing interest." This time she removed her nightgown and robe from one shoulder and gave him the kind of come-hither over-the-shoulder look he'd been dreaming of. "Next step is creating desire."

"You've been doing that since the second you showed up on my doorstep," he huskily confessed, drawing her into his arms.

"Same here." She set to work on undoing the snaps on his shirt, each pop indicating a cause for celebrating, which she did by kissing the newly exposed skin.

"What's the next step?" His voice rumbled beneath her lips.

She smiled against his chest before looking up at him. "Producing action."

"I think I can manage that just fine."

"I think we both can."

Words were forsaken for action after that, as Zane kissed her and walked her toward his bed. Her long hair fell around her shoulders as he undid her hair clasp. He seemed fascinated with her hair, running his fingers through the long strands.

She focused her attention on getting him naked as quickly as possible. It seemed only fair since he now seemed intent on doing the same to her. Besides, he had more clothes on.

She removed his shirt and tossed it over her shoulder, placing tiny kisses along his bare collarbone as she did so.

He'd already removed his leather belt with the shiny silver buckle.

While he nibbled on her ear and whispered words of encouragement, she set to work on the fastening of his button-fly jeans. The sight of her slim fingers against his tanned abdomen was incredibly erotic and empowering. She felt his body quiver as she undid the first metal rivet.

The backs of her fingers were against his skin as she moved on to the next, one hand inside his jeans and the other outside—which meant the fingers of her left hand got to enjoy the warmth he was emanating while the fingers of her right hand brushed against denim and metal. Until she got lower. Then her hands were brushing against the ridge of his arousal.

Pushing her hands aside, he undid the single remaining button himself and tugged off the jeans. His underwear just happened to go with them.

He was just as she'd imagined he'd be. Maybe better. Definitely better.

While she paused to admire him, Zane took the opportunity to rid her of her robe and nightgown. Now she was as naked as he was.

Slinging her arms around his neck, she kissed him. He took her down with him as he fell onto the mattress. It was firm. Like him.

No, he wasn't just firm, she decided. He was hard, all heat and steely need. She explored him with awe and appreciation, her fingertips not missing a thing.

"Wait," he gasped. "Protection." He fumbled in the bedside table, his eyes on her bare body as he yanked what was required from the drawer, holding it up triumphantly.

"Nice bubble gum," Tracy said.

"What?" He looked and, sure enough, he held a packet of the twins' favorite brand of bubble gum in his hand instead of the condom he'd been looking for.

"What exactly do you aim on doing with that?" she asked with naughty interest. "I should warn you that I was an excellent bubble blower in my youth. It's all in the tongue, you know? Shall I show you?"

He groaned, his body already on fire for her. Now she fanned the flames.

By the time he finally found the condom and rolled

it on, he'd made sure that he wasn't the only one trembling with need.

He came to her in one powerful surge, filling her completely. The friction of his thrusts created a ripple of undulating pleasure that grew to monumental proportions until she shouted his name as her world expanded and contracted with the ultimate satisfaction.

It was only later that she realized that she'd told him she loved him, not only with her body but with words.

TRACY WAS AWAKENED by the sound of someone pounding on the front door. Since her body was still wrapped around Zane's, she knew it wasn't him pounding.

"Who is it?" she asked groggily. She hadn't gotten much sleep last night. Not after they'd made love two more times.

"You stay here. I'll go see." He stepped out of bed, giving her a nice but all too brief glimpse of his sexy backside.

"Your father and the twins aren't due back yet, are they?"

"They wouldn't knock before entering," he reminded her as he tugged on his jeans.

"Maybe it's Murph'n'Earl wanting their breakfast."

"If it is I'll get rid of them," he promised her with a quick kiss.

He left the door open as he hurried downstairs. "Keep your pants on," he shouted as the impatient pounding on the front door continued. "I'm coming."

Because Zane's bedroom was located at the top of the staircase, she could hear what was going on as he opened the door.

"Who are you?" she heard Zane ask.

Then she heard a voice from her past, a voice she never dreamed she'd hear out here in Colorado. "My name is Dennis. Dennis Waverly. I'm here for my fiancée, Tracy Campbell."

11

Tracy leapt from the bed as if shot out of a cannon. What was Dennis doing here? How had he found her? She certainly hadn't told him where she was going.

She had to get dressed and find out what was going on.

The problem was that the only clothing she had up here was her satin nightgown and robe. Or she could raid Zane's closet. She yanked one of his shirts out and tugged it on before adding—what? His jeans were miles too big for her. She found a pair of long johns she then rolled up around her waist. Big shirts and leggings were in, right?

She hurried downstairs to find that Zane had let Dennis into the front hall. She'd half been hoping he'd have tossed Dennis off his property by now. But it was cowardly of her to want Zane to fight her battles for her. She was a gutsy woman who'd gone nose to nose with a mouse. She could handle Dennis.

"What are you doing here?" she demanded, her tone cool.

"Keisha told me where you were. Said you were working on a new account out here. Barbecue sauce, I think she said."

Tracy knew darn well that Keisha wouldn't have been so forthcoming if Dennis hadn't pushed her. She wondered what he'd promised Keisha to get her to talk.

"I'm here to tell you that I want you back," Dennis said with that dramatic flair she'd once found so romantic and now just found ridiculous. "And I'll do whatever it takes to win your love again."

Tracy was so stunned she could only stare at Dennis in amazement. What planet was he on? Did he really think for one instant that there was any chance of her coming back to him?

Or was something else going on here?

Wait a minute. A few things Keisha had mentioned casually in her e-mails started slipping into place. Something about business at Dennis's ad agency suffering since Tracy had quit. No doubt that was what was really behind Dennis's appearance here along with his declaration of love.

Before she could speak, however, Zane said, "I'll leave the two of you alone."

She didn't like the sound of that at all. Or the way Zane had said it. As if it had nothing to do with him. As if she was of no importance to him.

Maybe he just felt awkward.

"There's no need for you to do that," she quickly assured Zane. "Anything Dennis has to say can be said in front of you. I have no secrets from you."

"You two should be alone," Zane stubbornly insisted. "To decide how you're going to work this out." He hadn't said *if* but *how*. His tone and his attitude made it clear that he thought she would be returning to Dennis and the life she had in Chicago.

Tracy was furious. How could Zane think that after the night they'd just shared? She'd even told him she loved him. Did he think so little of her?

Did he think that she jumped into bed with every cowboy she met?

She was so angry she could hardly think straight. Enraged, she advanced on both Zane and Dennis, intent on giving them both a piece of her mind. And she didn't aim on being quiet about it. Oh, no, she was mad enough to scream from the rooftop, and the decibel level of her voice reflected that fact.

First she focused her attention on the man from her past.

"Dennis, I'll make this brief. Go jump in Lake Michigan and get out of my life. We're history. It's over, kaput, ain't gonna happen, not ever in this lifetime or the next."

She barely registered his stunned look before turning her full fury on the man from her present—Zane. "As for you," she shouted, her voice getting even louder. "You are a total coward who's afraid of loving again." She punctuated each word with an angry jab of her finger to Zane's bare chest. "Just because you had one bad experience. You think you're the only one who's ever made a mistake? I made a mistake with Dennis. But I've moved on. Not you. No, sirree. The great Zane Best knows better. But the bottom line is that you're afraid of believing I really do love you with all my heart even though I'm an idiot for doing so. Neither one of you is worth the powder to blow you up!''

As she yelled at them, both Dennis and Zane quickly backed away from her, their hands outstretched in male confusion as if to ward her off, until they'd backed right out the still-open front door.

It was only when the door slammed in his face that Zane realized that Tracy had just thrown him out of his own house.

His first thought was that Buck was right. Tracy did have a temper that could turn a blizzard around and send it home with a suntan. Then it hit him that she'd said she loved him, not in the midst of a passion-induced haze but in a moment of feminine outrage. When she'd said the words last night while they'd made love, he'd been afraid to believe her. But now, how could he doubt her? She'd been fierce in her declaration, unwavering in her intent, which at the moment had been to get rid of him.

She'd nailed his fears to the wall by accusing him of thinking her feelings for him were fleeting. He'd assumed that she'd prefer her old life in the city to the new one she'd made with him and his family out here on the ranch. He'd been wrong. About a lot of things.

Tracy was no butterfly. No fleeting breeze. She was a keeper. She was nothing like his ex-wife.

Pam had been all surface shine, like fool's gold. But Tracy's emotions ran deep and true, like a vein of the kind of gold men would risk their lives for.

He loved her. And he aimed on fighting for her.

Turning to Dennis, Zane growled, ''Beat it. We still

hang two-timing jerks out here in Colorado. You've got one minute to get off my property. And don't ever come back.''

Zane must have looked convincingly dangerous because after a few sputters, Dennis turned tail and drove off in a rush, his BMW leaving a cloud of dust.

One problem dealt with. Now he just had to make up with Tracy.

He started by trying the door. She'd locked it. His door hadn't been locked in years. And never against him.

He gently knocked on it, figuring he had some ground to make up. "Tracy, honey, let me in. We need to talk.''

He was hoping his first use of an endearment with her would soften her somewhat. His hope was in vain. She refused to answer him.

"Come on, honey,'' he said in his best coaxing voice. "Let me in. I know I made a few mistakes. Okay, some big mistakes. Like assuming that you'd prefer your old life in the city to the new one you've made out here. Clearly you took offense at that.'' One way of describing her fiery temper tantrum. "But honey, I believe you now. I believe that you do truly love it out here. And I believe that you love me. Tracy, honey, are you listenin' to me?'' He moved closer so that his lips were practically smack up against the wood of the door. "I'm telling you somethin' important here, honey. I'm telling you that I love you. So let me in, honey. Let me into your heart and I swear I won't hurt you again. Come on, sweetheart.'' If honey didn't work, maybe sweetheart would. No. Maybe another endearment, then. "Darling? Sweet cakes?" Still no answer. Shifting his head, he put his ears instead of his lips to the door. There was nothing to indicate she was on the other side—no telltale breathing or crying or yelling.

It was only then that he belatedly realized two things. First off, mad as she was, Tracy had probably stomped back upstairs and was no longer within hearing distance—which made him feel like an idiot.

But not as much an idiot as the second discovery, which was that Murph'n'Earl were standing not twenty feet behind him. Maybe they hadn't heard.

No such luck.

"Darling?" Murph said, his voice choked with laughter as he hung onto his sidekick's shoulders to stay upright.

"Sweet cakes?" Earl replied, his shoulders shaking.

Both ranch hands were smacking their hats against their knees as they were just about bent double with their enjoyment of the moment, tears of mirth running down their weathered cheeks.

Zane didn't take the time to reprimand them. Not that they'd listen to him anyway. He had bigger fish to fry. He needed to get back in his own house. He tried the windows on the main floor. All locked. Tracy was nothing if not efficient.

There was another way...one he hasn't used since he was a teenager—up the large cottonwood tree in the back. Unless Tracy had left the back door unlocked? He raced around back, but that door was also dead-bolted and the windows downstairs locked. Which left him with the tree.

If he thought he could make the climb without an audience he was mistaken. Murph'n'Earl followed him around the ranch house and had plunked themselves down on the back stoop as if waiting for the show to begin.

"Don't you two have something else to do?" Zane said.

"Nope," they replied in unison.

"There's horses out in the barn waiting to be fed."

"Done."

"What about that length of fencing out by Rock Creek that needs fixing?"

"Later."

He was wasting time arguing with them. Not that Tracy was likely to go anywhere, locked up as she was in his house. But she might take it into her mind to pack up and leave, mad as she was. And he didn't want to have to hightail after her. So it was either make a fool of himself now or do it later, farther away.

He preferred being on home territory. So he moved closer to the tree, looking for a handy branch to pull himself up with. He hadn't climbed this tree in what…twenty years?

"Your pa cut down that low branch a few years back," Murph told him. "Just in case you were wondering."

"Great," Zane muttered, wondering how bad his luck could get.

"You need us to give you a hand up?" Earl offered.

It went against the grain to ask for, or even accept, their help after they'd just laughed themselves silly at him, but given the situation Zane didn't have much of a choice. His grunt was meant to be a yes and was taken as such.

"I'm taller so I should be the one to give him a leg up," Murph said.

"I'm stronger," Earl maintained. "That means I should be the one."

"I don't care which of you gives me a leg up," Zane impatiently interrupted them. "But let's get a move on here before I turn fifty."

In the end it was Earl who joined his fingers together for Zane to step into, but it was Murph's taller shoulders that he stepped onto for a minute before grabbing a thick branch and swinging himself onto it.

From there Zane managed to move higher to another branch and another, until he was almost at the window of the guest room. He moved out along the branch.

"Take care," Earl called up. "That branch is thinner than you think it is, and you're heavier."

No sooner had the ranch hand spoken than the branch beneath Zane's bare feet broke with a crack, leaving him dangling from the limb. It took him a moment or two to haul himself back up to a safer position.

When had he gotten so old that tree climbing took his breath away?

Moving more cautiously now, he inched his way

back out on this branch, which was thicker than its predecessor. Reaching out as far as he could, his fingers brushed the window frame. The window wasn't locked. It opened easily.

The same couldn't be said for his entry through it. Oh it was easy enough to get his shoulders through, but then a belt loop on his jeans got caught on something, leaving him dangling like a beached fish, half in and half out the window.

He could hear Murph'n'Earl laughing themselves silly down below. He could also hear something else. The sound of a shower running. So that's where Tracy was. In her bathroom downstairs.

The blood rushed to his head as he reached around and tried to undo the belt loop from whatever it was caught on. Nothing worked. No matter how he wiggled he couldn't get free. He had to work fast. He sure as hell didn't want Tracy catching him this way.

There were times a cowboy had to do what a cowboy had to do. Zane had done up his jeans in a hurry, only fastening the top button. Once he got that undone, he wiggled out of his jeans, leaving them behind as he went hunting for the love of his life.

She was still in the shower. He planned on joining her. Pulling back the shower curtain, he said, "So you really do love me, huh?"

12

Tracy's startled scream echoed off the bathroom's ceramic-tile walls, nearly deafening both her and Zane.

She'd decided to take a quick shower to cool down after her fight with him. She certainly hadn't expected him to join her there! Not after she'd locked him out.

But she'd only locked the outside doors. Not the inside ones. Like the bathroom door. Tactical error.

"What are you doing here?" she demanded, as if it was of no importance that she and he were both naked.

"Joining you." He stepped into the tub and leaned forward to lick the droplets of water from her shoulder.

Tracy refused to be swayed by his persuasive mouth. "Stop that and get out of my shower!"

His "umph" was the only response to her elbowing him in the stomach.

"Did I forget to tell you that I love you, too?" he murmured in her ear.

She stopped her protests long enough for him to kiss his way down the column of her throat. He held the golden rope of her long wet hair in one hand, lifting it out of the way to place a string of kisses along her nape.

To his surprise, Tracy wasn't easily convinced of his feelings for her. "So you love me, huh? Big deal. You don't *want* to love me. You don't think I'm the right woman for you. You think I'm the kind of woman who would go from your bed back to Dennis."

The next thing he knew he had a faceful of cold water, as she reached down to twirl the faucet before hopping out of the tub.

His yowl of surprise gave her some satisfaction. He really had his nerve. Thinking he could kiss her into submission. And okay, so she did weaken for a moment when he'd finally said the words she'd been longing to hear, when he'd finally said that he loved her. But it wasn't enough. He still had plenty of making up to do, before there could be any making out.

Marching into the bedroom, she toweled off and deliberately put on a citified outfit of black-linen slacks and a tailored lime-green blouse. She twisted her wet hair on top of her head and held it in place with a banana clip.

By this time, Zane came out of the bathroom, with a towel wrapped around his waist.

"Anybody ever tell you that you've got a temper that could turn a blizzard around and send it home with a suntan? I know I've got some explaining to do but I need you to calm down and listen to me."

She gave him a haughty look. "I'm listening."

He sighed, as if talking was the last thing he wanted to do next to being tied to an anthill. But his rugged face wore an expression of stubborn determination that Tracy recognized. This rancher was on a mission and heaven help the person who tried to sway him from it. "My ex-wife, Pam, left when the twins were only a year old, just starting to talk and walk. Well, actually they went right to the running stage, rather than walking," he admitted with a wry smile that warmed Tracy's insides. "I had to put up those kiddy gates all over the house. Ended up breaking my toe by climbing over one of them. It was mighty embarrassing. After climbing over fences and gates all my life, I get tripped up by a little kiddy gate. But I'm getting off the subject here."

"Which is?" Her voice was husky, her resolution already wavering just a tad.

"Why it took me a mite bit longer to realize that I love you than it should have. Pam was a city girl from Denver who headed for the bright lights of Las Vegas when she found life on the ranch downright boring. After she left, I vowed that the next woman I let into my life would be one born and bred for ranch life."

"Like the cattle are, you mean," she sarcastically tacked on, her aggravation rapidly returning.

"I was trying not to make the same mistake twice."

She narrowed her eyes and shot him a warning look. "I have to tell you that you're not endearing yourself to me by referring to me as a mistake."

"You're not a mistake. You're my destiny."

With those words he scored an emotional bull's-eye with her. Her breath caught in her throat and her heart pounded. And the look in Zane's eyes…it was enough to make her kneecaps melt.

Zane hadn't wanted to love her, true enough. But then she hadn't come west looking for love, either. He came with emotional baggage and so did she. But the bottom line was that he loved her and she loved him.

As if sensing she was weakening, Zane reached out to cup her cheek in his hand. "I was wrong about you," he admitted gruffly. "You're the strongest woman I've ever known and you'd succeed at whatever you set your mind to. I have no doubt of that. I'm just grateful you set your mind on loving me."

Was he just saying what she wanted to hear? Could she believe? "I don't know."

He placed his finger over her lips, stopping her words. "I admit that you're not getting much of a bargain here. I'm never going to be the kind of man to make pretty speeches. The prettiest speech I ever made you missed out on because you weren't at the front door when I made it. But I do love you. And I do believe in you."

"Was that so hard to say?" she whispered.

"Well, normally I'd rather eat rattlers than talk about this emotional stuff, but you're worth it."

Throwing her arms around his neck, she kissed him, letting her lips do the talking as he'd so often done with her. He seemed to understand what she was trying to communicate, because he returned her kiss with raw abandon.

He wooed her with erotic flicks of his tongue across

the roof of her mouth in just the way he knew she loved.

His bath towel fell to the floor as he pulled her closer, his thumb brushing her breast through the silky material of her blouse.

She wasn't sure who was leading whom, but when they ended up on her bed Zane surprised her by leaving her there. Was he going back upstairs to get more condoms?

"This time we're going to do this right," he declared.

She arched an eyebrow at him. "Meaning there was something wrong with the way we did things last night? The *several* ways we did things?"

"No." He grabbed the towel and wrapped it around his waist again. "I'm not exactly dressed for this situation, but what the heck." Returning to the bed, he went down on one knee and took her hand. "Tracy Campbell, will you marry me?"

She gulped like a fish out of water.

"You're not going to make me dress up in a suit or something to propose, are you?"

His put-upon tone of voice made her smile. "Your birthday suit is fine," she replied with a saucy grin. "I must say that your proposal of marriage has caught me off guard, Mr. Best. And that manly chest of yours is a mighty big distraction. How did you get those scratches?" She frowned in concern before blushing, wondering if she'd marked him while they'd made love last night.

"I got these from climbing the cottonwood tree to get in here," he told her.

"You poor baby," she crooned. "Let me make it better." Leaning forward, she kissed the scrape closest to her before licking her way to his nipple.

"Do you aim on answering my proposal or just driving me to distraction?" he asked with male stoicism.

"The answer is yes. Yes, I plan on answering your proposal. Yes, I plan on driving you to distraction or plumb loco as you so often put it. And yes, I will marry you."

With a cowboy howl of victory, Zane leapt to his feet and grabbed her in his arms. This time when they fell to the bed they stayed there and made love with a newfound tenderness, as well as the familiar passion and heat of two souls destined to be together.

ZANE DID EVENTUALLY have to get out of bed several hours later to take care of some chores that couldn't be put off. A ranch didn't close for weekends or holidays or joyous occasions. There were still animals to be watered and fed. But he only did the bare necessities before returning to her.

Zane told her that Murph'n'Earl were keeping a low profile and had left a big note in the barn saying they'd gone off to fix those fences over by Rock Creek. Which meant he and Tracy should have the rest of the afternoon and evening to themselves.

Tracy cooked her special Shrimp de Jonghe dinner for him and Zane made a point to be suitably impressed. He showed her just how much by carrying her back to bed and making love to her.

Afterward, wrapped in each other's arms, the setting sun bathed them in its warmth. And in that moment, Tracy felt such a sense of inner peace.

A second later it was shattered by the sound of the front door banging open and the booming sound of Buck's voice. "We're ba...ack!"

Tracy gave Zane a panicked look. His expression wasn't much calmer.

"I thought they weren't due back until tomorrow," she said even as she dove for the closet and some clean clothes.

"That's what he told me." Zane was yanking on his jeans and tugging a shirt on as he spoke.

How had her underwear gotten on top of the lamp? she wondered. Oh yeah, now she remembered. She tried not to blush.

Buck had already caught her kissing Zane, but catching her in bed with him was another matter entirely, even if they were now an engaged couple.

"You ready?" Zane asked, hurriedly jamming his shirt in his jeans.

She nodded, wondering if anyone would be able to tell that she had her T-shirt on backward.

"Hey, this is a surprise," Zane said as he met his family in the kitchen.

"The kids got homesick halfway down to Pueblo," Buck said. "So we overnighted and came on back."

"We missed you, Pa," Lucky said.

"I missed you too, peanut. And I've got some news for you."

"Is Joe okay?" she asked nervously.

He ruffled her hair and gave her a reassuring smile.

"Your pets are all fine. This is about Tracy and me. We're engaged."

"Engaged in what?" Buck asked suspiciously.

"Engaged to be married," Zane retorted.

"Does that mean Tracy is staying here?" Rusty asked. "For good?"

"For good, for bad and for all the times in between," Tracy replied, nervous of the twins' reaction. While they'd certainly warmed to her, and she loved them to bits, she wasn't sure what their reaction would be to this news.

She quickly found out. With a miniature version of their father's cowboy howl of victory, both Lucky and Rusty launched themselves at her to engulf her in hugs.

"I guess that means it's okay with you two," Zane noted wryly.

Turning to face his dad, Rusty said, "She's not bad for a girl."

"Yeah, that's how I feel about her, too," Zane said with a slow smile.

"I guess I won't even ask why there's a pair of jeans hanging out the upstairs back window," Buck said. "Instead I'll just say that I'm pleased you two finally came to your senses. And I'll add that I've got a bit of good news myself, thanks to missy here." He nodded his head toward Tracy. "She sent out a letter and box of samples to that major chain of Western supermarkets. Well, I stopped by the post office in town to pick up the mail and, well, to make a long story short—"

"Which would be a first for you," Zane teased him.

"I got a letter from them saying..." Buck paused to snap his suspenders as he puffed out his chest with pride before continuing, "They want to carry Buck's Barbecue Sauce in their stores."

His news caused another round of cowboy howls of victory, with the twins jumping up and down and asking for a puppy now that they were going to be rich because Grandpa was going to be famous, just like the Kentucky Fried Chicken guy. Then the jumping stopped and the search began as Lucky screeched that Joe, the mouse, was loose again and Precious was after him.

In the ensuing bedlam, Zane carefully made his way over to Tracy's side to put his arm around her.

"See what you've let yourself in for?" he asked her over the rowdy din.

"I see," she said, leaning her head against his shoulder and smiling at her newfound family. "And I can't wait," she added before reaching up to kiss him.

The search for love and Cockeyed Curly's legendary treasure continues with Cord Best's story. THE COWBOY FINDS A BRIDE, Harlequin Duets #17 January 2000.
For a sneak preview turn the page...

1

"I DON'T TRUST HER. She's up to something." Cord Best shoved a hand through his long dark hair and glared at his older brother, Zane.

"Who are we talking about?" Zane inquired absently, his attention on the spreadsheet of cattle production displayed on the computer in front of him.

"Hailey Hughes. I'm telling you, she has ulterior motives. Coming back here to Bliss and asking all kinds of questions about Cockeyed Curly's lost gold." Cord started pacing the small confines of the den, the only room in the ranch house not yet transformed by Zane's new wife, Tracy. "She's definitely up to something. I can't help but be suspicious of why she wants that kind of information."

"You can't help being suspicious, period," Zane retorted. "Especially where Hailey is concerned. The truth is that she's come home for the summer. She's a history professor at the University of Colorado. Anyway, she's come home to research a book on Cockeyed Curly's treasure."

"There is no treasure. Just like there's no Easter Bun... Oof!" Cord grunted as Zane elbowed him in the stomach.

"The twins see all and hear all," Zane reminded him with a meaningful nod at the open doorway.

"Fight, fight!" Rusty, Zane's small son, yelled as he ran into the den from the hallway where he'd been hiding.

"Son of a buck," Cord's dad exclaimed as he hurried into the room after Rusty. He looked at his two grown sons disapprovingly. "Aren't you two old enough to settle your differences peaceful-like?"

"We were talking about Hailey Hughes," Cord said, knowing his dad would understand.

Sure enough, Buck's expression darkened. "Tadpole Hughes's daughter?"

"I don't believe that's his given name," Zane replied dryly.

"It's the name I've given him. Lucky for him it's not worse." Buck's voice reflected his agitation. "What can you call a low-down gizzard-sucking coyote who steals the best fish from your own river?"

"I know, I know," Rusty inserted, eagerly jumping up and down. "You can call them a ba..."

Zane covered his son's mouth with his hand before reminding his father, "Troublesome Creek borders their land as well as ours."

"Bah," Buck scoffed.

"Hailey is coming back to research one of your favorite topics—Cockeyed Curly," Zane said in a clear attempt to distract his dad.

Buck's blue eyes narrowed as he thought back. "She's coming home? She always was a cute little thing as I recall."

"Cute, hah! She was hell on wheels," Cord vehemently declared. "She left a permanent mark on me." He held out his hand where, if you looked very carefully, a faint scar was still evident.

Buck and Rusty both squinted to take a look. Buck shook his head. "Hard to tell with all those other nicks and dings you got on your hands."

"Comes from working with wood." Cord shrugged. "One of the dangers of the trade."

"Carpenters work with wood. You, boy, have a God-given talent." Buck thumped him on the back in a paternal show of pride.

"Yeah, well, talent or not I'm not looking forward to running into Hailey again," Cord said. "She made my life miserable, making a nuisance of herself by trailing after me like a lovesick calf for years. You remember how she used to dog me, no matter how I tried to get rid of her. She had this crush on me the size of Texas." Seeing Zane's frantic hand movements, Cord said, "There's no use denying it, I'm not exaggerating. She was a hellion who wouldn't leave me alone, literally gluing my butt to my seat in high school. Even in the summer, I couldn't turn around without bumping into her..." Finally recognizing his brother's expression, Cord said in a resigned voice, "She's standing right behind me, now, isn't she."

"Yes, she is," a woman's clear voice replied. "And she assures you that you have nothing to fear from little ol' me." Her tart voice dripped with sarcasm.

"Son of a buck," Buck exclaimed, looking as if butter wouldn't melt in his mouth. "You boys sure need some training in how to act when there's a lady around, even if she is an offspring of our no-good coyote of a neighbor, Tadpole Hughes.''

Hailey sighed. ''I can tell this isn't going to be easy, is it?''

''Nothing worthwhile is,'' Buck assured her with a grin.

MARISSA
HALL

An Affair
of Convenience

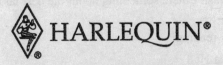

HARLEQUIN®

TORONTO • NEW YORK • LONDON
AMSTERDAM • PARIS • SYDNEY • HAMBURG
STOCKHOLM • ATHENS • TOKYO • MILAN • MADRID
PRAGUE • WARSAW • BUDAPEST • AUCKLAND

Dear Reader,

Have you ever concocted the perfect plan? You know
what I mean: You decide you'll just get that one
particular job, then you'll head up that high-profile
project, bringing it in under budget and on schedule,
of course! That will naturally lead to another
promotion and, before you know it, you're the head
honcho.

At least, that's the way the plan goes.

Or maybe you'll just clean out that front hall closet,
the one you have to lean against to shut the door.
Then, while you're at it, you might as well get rid of
the kitchen floor's waxy yellow buildup, rewire your
house and convert your attic to a charming vacation
getaway complete with Jacuzzi and exercise room for
less than $50.

I got to thinking about plans—and reality—and I
realized that for most of us, real life has a nasty way
of interfering with our ambitions. So that's why I
had my hero and heroine construct their own plans to
build perfect lives, get their perfect jobs and conduct a
perfect affair. As a writer, all that perfection is just too
good a target to pass up.

And wasn't there something about the best laid
plans...

Happy reading!

Marissa Hall

To Joyce Winter,
the big sister I always wanted

1

MALLORY REISSEN fiddled for the fourth time with the glass of ice water by her plate. Why had she given in to Mark's demands and agreed to this Sunday brunch?

It wasn't the restaurant. She'd frequented La Grande Passion's Sunday buffet on a regular basis since she'd moved into a nearby condo complex three years ago.

It wasn't the weather. She and her date sat in a small nook on the restaurant's terrace in bright San Diego spring sunshine. At the other table in the nook, intent on their own conversation, sat her handsome neighbor Cliff Young and his current girlfriend.

It wasn't even the company. Mark was an attractive, entertaining man—most of the time.

When he wasn't haranguing her about her work habits.

"Mallory, you've got to put things in perspective. You're never on time for any of our dates. And that's not counting that you break half of them because your boss wants you to do a 'little something' extra.'' A flush tinged Mark's face, giving it a pettish, unattractive quality.

"I was on time today, wasn't I?"

"Yes," he snapped. "The first time ever. Should I give you a medal?"

She put down her fork and tried to ignore the tightening of her stomach. God, she hated this. How many times had she gone through the same argument with other escorts? Fifty? A hundred?

"No," she said. "A simple recognition that I'm not always—"

He didn't let her finish. "The only reason you were on time today was because I told you that we were through if you weren't!"

"Hush! This is a public restaurant." Too late. Mallory's gaze had already been snared briefly by Cliff's at the next table. His date sat with her back to Mallory and Mark's table, and Cliff was facing them.

"Do you think I care?" Mark said without lowering his voice. "I'm a good catch. I could have practically any woman in San Diego, and you're too busy fussing with your cameras and makeup to notice."

Mallory sighed. "Mark," she said as gently as she could manage, "as a television news anchor, cameras and makeup are part of my business. It's what I do." She touched the pristine pink linen napkin to her lips to hide their wry twist. She'd heard this complaint a hundred times, too. "You knew about my job before you asked me out the first time."

"Yes, but I didn't know you'd made your job into some kind of obsession. And a full-time one at that."

Damn. Men always wanted more from her than she could give. Didn't any man understand that a woman in the television-news business had to work twice as hard, be twice as good, to command respect?

To be a success, to become someone even her parents would admit had done well, she had to break out of the local news market onto the national scene. That big break hovered just around the corner. She could feel it. She'd already received a few feelers from one of the networks. Nothing substantial, of course, but still…

But to grab that opportunity when it finally presented itself, she had to prove herself better than all those other local newspeople.

She had to be the best.

And being the best meant always being ready to cover a breaking news story, wherever and whenever it happened. That always-on-call status sometimes—often—meant broken dates, late arrivals, damaged egos whenever she tried to have a relationship with a man.

None of them ever understood how important it was to her to be a success. None ever realized that any personal relationship—even a lover—must always take second place to her career. And rightfully so. The only way she knew to get ahead was to put job and career at the very top of her priority list.

Those priorities had worked so far, though she had left a string of broken relationships and lost friendships scattered behind her.

Frustrated, concerned she would say something to Mark that would sever the few threads remaining in their friendship, she rose and manufactured a smile. "I'm going to get a plate from the fruit table."

She lingered at the artistic display of exotic fruits to avoid returning to the argument Mark seemed determined to pick. She reached for a luscious strawberry, but the tongs she held were trembling so much she nearly dropped the berry.

A warm masculine hand closed over hers, steadied the tongs, and helped her put the berry on her plate. Startled, she looked over her shoulder, prepared to jerk away, only to relax when she realized the hand belonged to Cliff.

"Thanks." She reached for another strawberry along with a dollop of sweetened whipped cream— her fatal weakness—and again his hand kept hers from fumbling.

He took the tongs and lifted two or three succulent berries to her plate. "Enough?"

"Yes." More grateful than she felt comfortable admitting, she studied the display of fruit, mainly to keep from having to meet his gaze. She didn't want more to eat—she knew she would have a hard time swallowing the fruit already on her plate.

"Trouble with your date?" Cliff asked in an undertone.

She started to lie, then stopped herself. What was the point? Cliff had to have overheard much of her argument with Mark. Besides, in the three years they'd lived next door to each other, she'd come to count on him as a casual but very real friend. She had shared more in-depth conversations with him than with anyone else she could name.

Something about Cliff inspired confidence. It was one reason he was a terrific lawyer, she supposed. But long ago she'd learned to stifle the occasional pang of attraction that surfaced and to concentrate on building a platonic friendship with him.

He seemed to be doing the same, never giving even the slightest hint that he wanted anything more personal from her.

"Yeah," she admitted, dragging her mind away from Cliff and back to their conversation. "Mark's not very happy with me right now."

"Why? Have you been two-timing him?" He put the question so smoothly that it took her a moment to take offense.

"Of course not!" She turned to look at him fully.

"I barely have time for one relationship. When would I find the time for another?"

He shrugged, and plucked a juicy green kiwi slice for his own plate. "Women cheat all the time."

"Not me." Mallory glanced over her shoulder. From this angle she could see his date's face. She thought she recognized her as an actress currently starring in a production downtown at Spreckel's Theater. "If you ask me, your friend doesn't look too happy, either."

Cliff grimaced and added a spoonful of raspberries to his plate. A questioning brow asked if she wanted some too, and she nodded automatically.

"She's not. In fact, I think Suzanne and your guy could well be singing the same song."

"I don't understand."

"Wasn't Mike—"

"Mark."

"Oh. Well, wasn't Mark complaining that you spend too much time working? That you break dates because of work commitments? That you don't spend enough time with him? That you willingly sacrifice your social life if something needs to be done at work?"

Mallory's jaw dropped. Hastily, she shut it again. "How did you know?"

He hunched a shoulder to subtly indicate his date,

who was now tapping her fingers on the tabletop. "Sounds just like what Suzanne says to me."

Their eyes met in mutual understanding. Mallory knew that Cliff was one of San Diego's hottest defense attorneys. He had once confided over coffee that he planned to be the youngest partner ever in his law firm, the most prestigious in San Diego. She knew enough of his schedule to understand that sixty-to-eighty-hour workweeks were typical for him.

Just as they were for her.

"I'm sorry," she said softly.

"It happens." He glanced over at their tables as he snared a couple of muffins. "I guess we've both stalled too long."

Mallory turned and saw Mark swallow the last of his champagne cocktail, get to his feet, and stalk off. As he passed the fruit table, his glare should have incinerated her on the spot, though he didn't say a word.

Right behind him came Suzanne. She sashayed up to Cliff, ran her crimson-tipped fingers along his jaw, and gave him what had to be a stinging pat.

"See you, Cliff," she said. "Next time you want to get together, give me a call. If I'm not doing anything that night—" her tone indicated that counting coat hangers in her closet would be preferable "—maybe we can see each other."

She sauntered away, snaring every masculine glance in the room.

Mallory looked down at her plate of fruit and over to their two empty tables, then glanced up at Cliff. "What do you want to bet both our respective dates stuck us with the checks?"

CLIFF SMILED, relieved to see the hint of laughter lurking in Mallory's eyes. While Suzanne had been jabbing his ego with her subtly snide barbs, he'd found himself straining to overhear as much as he could of the conversation at the next table. The tension between Mallory and Mark could have supported a span of the Coronado Bridge.

Although he'd never tried to date Mallory himself, her relaxed manner and sympathetic smile made him count her as one of his few friends. He rarely allowed people close enough to be called friends.

The lure of that friendship was strong enough that he'd deliberately trained himself not to think of her in a romantic way. It wasn't that he wasn't attracted to her—he was. But he didn't want to ruin the one so-far-successful relationship he'd ever forged with a woman.

He walked with Mallory back to their seats. Sure enough, each table had an unpaid check for two outrageously expensive buffet brunches. He set his plate of fruit and muffins on his table, thought better of it, and carried it and his check to Mallory's table.

"We might as well finish the meal together, don't you think?"

"Well...I'm probably not very good company right now."

"Haven't you ever heard that misery loves company?" Without waiting for a response, he slid into the chair across from her. "Besides, I'm sure the restaurant would appreciate having an open table. Didn't you notice the line of people waiting to be seated?"

She fingered her fork but made no move to pick it up. "We could just leave. Then they'd have both tables for other parties."

"And waste a brunch that's going to cost each of us well over fifty bucks? Are you kidding?" Cliff wasn't really joking. Although he could spend money with the best of them, he made sure he got good value for his dollars. When you grew up thrift-shop poor, you didn't waste your pennies. Or in this case, you didn't waste your twenty-dollar bills.

With a smile that spoke eloquently of Mallory's reviving spirits, she said, "You're right. Let's at least get a good meal out of this disaster."

After a few moments, Cliff picked up an enormous blueberry muffin and buttered it. "Was it such a disaster for you?"

Mallory cocked her head in a characteristic position

he'd seen her assume many times on the nightly news. A surprised note entered her voice. "You know, I don't think so. Mark obviously didn't understand me very well." She paused. "What about Suzanne and you?"

He shrugged. "Same thing." He put down the muffin and leaned forward, striking his best Henry Higgins pose. "Tell me, Mallory, why *can't* a woman be more like a man?"

"What? I don't know what you mean."

"This whole thing with Suzanne. I've been through it a dozen times. I invite a woman out for a date. We have a pretty good time. Then, sooner or later, I have to work late on the night she wants to go to the opera. Or I can't take her to some party because I've got a court date I have to prepare for." He leaned back, his point made. "Women always try to trap a man into doing something that jeopardizes his job."

"Women? What about men? Do you know the number of times I've had to cancel a date because of a breaking story, only to have my escort give me hell for not adapting to his schedule? Or how many times men have backed off as soon as they realize that I don't work a simple nine-to-five shift?" Mallory's cheeks glowed as she warmed to her theme.

She glared at him, food forgotten, and he glared right back. Dammit, he was just trying to point out...

A laugh surfaced and he relaxed against the back

of his chair. "You know what we're saying? We're two of a kind, you and I. We're both paying the price."

Her smile glimmered then faded. "Yeah. Neither of us is any good at relationships I guess."

"It's not us, Mallory. It's just that everyone else has unreasonable expectations. We work long, hard hours. We have to be dedicated to our jobs if we want to get ahead. We're not the ones with the problem. It's everyone else." He took a huge, satisfying bite of his buttered muffin.

She swallowed the last of her strawberries. "So you're implying that we both have to put personal relationships on hold until after we're established in our careers. You're going to make partner within a few years and I'm going to be at one of the networks. Until then, we just have to cool it."

Cliff frowned. He couldn't see any flaw in her reasoning, but that didn't mean he had to like her conclusions. "But I like going out with women. I like being around them. I like dating. I like—"

"Sex?" she asked sweetly. "Are you saying you can't go without it?"

Pugnaciously, he stuck his chin out. "I happen to like women. So sue me."

Her smile faded. "It sounds like you just need to have an affair with someone."

"Like who? I'm telling you, every time I begin to

think about getting involved with a woman, she pulls the same old your-work-means-more-to-you-than-I-do crap. I haven't even made it to first base with anyone in ages." Suddenly aware that he'd admitted more than he'd intended, he shut his mouth.

Sneaking a peek across the table, he saw a genuine smile flirting along the edge of her mouth.

"Mallory Reissen," he said accusingly, "if you don't make it big-time as an interviewer, it's not for lack of talent. How the hell did you get me to admit so much about my love life?"

"Or lack thereof?" Her smile transformed into a smirk. Definitely.

"Or lack thereof." Funny, he didn't even mind her knowing. A suspicion snuck into his head. "And I'll bet your love life isn't any more, uh, satisfying, is it?"

Her eyes met his and the smirk faded. "No. Men don't like to hang around the edges of a woman's life. They want to be front-and-center all the time. I can't give them that, so..."

"Front-and-center? That would drive me crazy. I don't need—or want!—a woman center stage in my life. All I want is an occasional comfortable evening with a woman who understands that my work is very important to me. Is that so much to ask?" He paused, then admitted, "With maybe some really great sex thrown in. Just to keep things interesting, you know?"

She cocked her head again. "If I ever find a man willing to take less than a full-time commitment from me, I'll be sure to tell you all about it."

He finished his muffin in silence while she polished off the last of her raspberries. He didn't really want to wait for years to share intimacy with a woman. He didn't want to make a major commitment, either, of course. But that didn't mean he had to live like a monk.

Did it?

Mallory interrupted his morose thoughts. "You know, there's a solution to all this. We merely have to find partners who understand going in that all we really want is a pleasant, healthy physical relationship. Neither of us wants a family right now. We don't want someone to cling. We just want someone we can, um…"

"Have sex with on the odd occasion?" he inserted silkily.

She tipped her chin upward. "Yes. That's exactly what I mean. We just want an affair that's got some good, clean sex—and there's nothing 'odd' about it. What's so bad about that?"

He smiled and snagged a lonely slice of papaya off her plate. "Nothing. All you have to do is tell me how we go about finding such amenable partners."

"Well, we could advertise, I suppose." She propped her elbow on the table and put her chin in her hand. "Isn't that the growing thing in the nineties? Going the personal-ad route?"

"That's dangerous. Especially for you. All kinds of crazies answer those ads, and with you being a public figure and all—it's just not safe." He repressed a shudder at the thought of what might happen if some nut found her.

"Well, what do you suggest?"

He considered her question carefully. No doubt about it, they were both in the same pickle. "Maybe we could...help each other out," he said slowly, feeling his way.

"Help each other? How?"

"Well, you understand women better than I do. And I probably understand men a little better than you. What makes us tick, and all that."

"So?"

The hint of a plan nudged forward. "Maybe you could help me find a woman who wouldn't be such a clinging vine. And I'd help you find a man who wouldn't mind your working late."

His idea had merit, he decided. It was a good plan. Surely she would be able to tell him which women he could count on to understand his situation. She could make up a list of potential candidates. Then he could talk to them, see them, and decide which one would do. And he could do the same for her. He probably knew half a dozen men who would be pleased to take her out any time she was available.

His plan was perfect. It was simple. It was logical. It was surefire.

"It would never work." Mallory's blunt comment punctured his rising spirits.

"Why not? It seems simple enough to me."

She gestured impatiently. "Because it won't, that's all. Women fool other women as easily as they fool men. And with you as the prize..."

His ears almost physically pricked up at that. "What about me as the prize? What's wrong with me?"

"Nothing. That's the point. Women would crawl all over you—or me—to get into your bed. You're young. You're making good money and will be making even more in the future. You're good-looking. You're sexy. What's not to like?"

"You think I'm sexy?" Why had that one phrase stuck in his head? He tried and failed to burst the bubble of attraction that surfaced.

"Of course I do! Who wouldn't? That's my whole point." She brushed a strand of hair back behind her shoulder. He'd always liked the fine golden strands, especially when she wore it down. On most of her television broadcasts, she tamed it into some kind of sleek bun.

"I don't get it." Not for the first time, he imagined

that smooth blond hair running through his fingers—then shook the thought away. She was his *friend,* dammit. Not some babe to hit on. "What's so bad about being sexy?"

"Nothing—except that it makes it all but impossible to figure out who's sincere and who will decide after the fact that she wants more."

He considered that point. Yeah, he could understand that women might line up to leap into bed with him. Of course, he hadn't ever noticed them doing it in the past, but it could happen.

Sure it could.

Of course, the same was true of her. She had the looks—striking cheekbones, translucent skin, great curves. She had a sex appeal that could lure men with a smile. Yeah, his problem in identifying candidates for her wasn't a matter of coming up with a long enough list of possibilities. Instead, he'd be hard-pressed to prune the list to manageable proportions.

And guys did lie to other guys, too.

He pondered the unexpected complexities of his potential task. The click of Mallory's champagne goblet meeting the table interrupted his thoughts.

She took a deep breath. "Rather than look for other partners for each other, why don't you and I have an affair?"

2

ONCE THE WORDS popped out, Mallory wished for nothing more than to pull them back. How had she found the nerve to suggest that she and Cliff have an affair—together! She opened her mouth to deny she'd made the suggestion, but it was too late.

"You mean, you—and me?" he asked.

His words took a bite out of her ego. "You don't have to sound so astonished. I mean, some people consider me—"

He waved her to silence. "Yes, of course. But I never thought about you and me, uh, like that."

"If you're not interested, we could go back to considering your plan."

"No! I mean, it's not that I don't want to. I'm just kind of surprised you suggested it."

She leaned forward, pushing her plate to one side. "Look, Cliff, we know each other reasonably well."

"Yes, I guess we do."

"And what we know, we like."

"Uh-huh." His face adopted a definite wary look.

"Neither of us wants ties or commitments right now—we can't afford them if we're going to build our careers."

He nodded with certainty. "That's for sure."

"And both of us are prime targets for people who want to latch on to our success. At least, I know I am, and I'd be willing to bet you are too. Right?" She waited for him to challenge her assumption.

"Yes," he admitted. "Suzanne constantly asked me how much I made, and if I represent any of the Hollywood types that hang around in La Jolla."

Mallory allowed herself just a trace of satisfaction. "That's what I thought. The point is, we both know we're safe from that kind of thing with each other. I don't need you to advance my career, and you don't need me."

"That's true, too."

His hand captured hers and a trickle of heat warmed her skin. Startled, she pulled her hand away. This was no time for distractions.

"The key thing is that you want a partner to enjoy an occasional evening with—without having to worry that she's going to cling and demand too much of your attention. I want the same thing." She shrugged and smiled. "Sounds to me like we're made for each other."

He drummed his fingers against the table. "You've got a point. Maybe we are."

"Best of all, we live next door to each other. We don't even have to bother with the usual dating stuff. When we want to get together, all we have to do is go next door."

"Another excellent point."

Was she making sense? She thought so, but couldn't be sure. Still, there was one last thing she had to be clear about....

"I just had my physical last month." She didn't let the blush searing her neck interfere with her blunt announcement. "I'm, uh, perfectly healthy."

To her relief, he took no offense. "Me, too. Mine was just a couple of weeks ago. And I'm very careful about sex. I always have been." A boyish grin lightened his serious expression. "Wanna swap medical histories?"

His humor eased her embarrassment. "I don't think so," she said. "I trust you."

He clasped her hand again and this time she didn't pull away. "That's what we're really talking about here, isn't it? Trusting each other not to make demands neither of us is capable of meeting?"

"Uh-huh." She rotated her palm so her fingers interlaced with his. "Trust. Respect for each other's career. And a little old-fashioned sex."

"Not too old-fashioned, I hope!" His boyish grin was back and she smiled in response.

Still, as they raised their glasses in a mutual toast

to their pact, for some odd reason she felt a stab of concern as she looked into his eyes.

What had she done?

She put down her glass and gathered her courage to keep her voice calm and level. "So we're in agreement?"

"Yes." His smile was half predatory and half reassuring—and totally seductive. "We're going to have an affair that's guaranteed not to interfere with our careers. None of this love-and-happily-ever-after business. Just two people out to have a good time together with no strings."

"Right." Why did it sound so cold when he summed it up that way? She certainly hadn't felt cold when she'd proposed it.

"One thing, Mallory."

"What's that?"

The dark, seductive tone had left his voice, making it deep and utterly serious. "If you want out of our agreement at any time, just say so. You don't even have to give me a reason. Just tell me it's over and that will end it."

The gray of his eyes sharpened to silver. It was obvious that this stipulation was very important to him. She didn't know if he'd been burned with other girlfriends who'd clung too long or if something else triggered it. Either way, he wanted a way out of the relationship.

An escape route.

She didn't want to agree to his implied request for the same assurance. For some reason she couldn't quite define, the thought of articulating the easy-out nature of their agreement made her shift uneasily. It made everything seem so…sordid. Her throat closed, and she swallowed hard to clear it. His gaze held hers with its utter sincerity. He didn't look as if he thought she'd proposed anything unsavory.

Her agreement popped out before she could stop it. "That's fine. And the same for you. If you want to leave anytime—" her voice caught and she had to swallow hard to continue "—just tell me. No problem."

What have I done? What have I done?

He visibly relaxed. "Good. Then I guess we really do have an agreement."

"Should we put it in writing?" she asked, trying to keep the cynical note out of her voice. "After all, you being an attorney and all…"

He cocked his head and tapped his cheek with one finger. "No," he said slowly. "We're not contemplating any commingling of funds or assets, so I don't think it's necessary."

He'd actually considered it! How could he!

She almost stabbed him with her fork before she saw a suspicious twinkle in his eye. "You're teasing me, you rat."

Suddenly, she felt a lot better about their new arrangement. His humor reminded her that she could have fun with Cliff—and fun was something her life sorely lacked. Fun, sex, companionship—what more did she need?

Nothing, she told herself firmly. *I don't have time for more.*

"I was just kidding you a little bit." He tipped up her chin and gave a wicked grin. "Couldn't you tell?"

"I can now. And I warn you. You won't catch me off guard so easily again."

"No? You sure of that?" His eyes teased her unmercifully.

"I'm sure," she promised. "But you might want to watch out yourself."

While their banter continued, Mallory realized she was genuinely enjoying herself, more than she could remember doing for years. His teasing-flirting-enticing manner reminded her of exactly why she'd conceived of their plan in the first place.

Surprisingly, she couldn't wait to find out if the other benefits of their arrangement would be equally enjoyable.

She put her napkin beside her plate and shoved her chair back from the table. Now, with excitement fizzing in her veins like the bubbles in her champagne, she could hardly wait to get him to herself. "Why don't we leave now? We can go home and…"

But nothing would let her finish that thought with his eyes on her. Eyes that held an unmistakably salacious gleam.

"Good idea," he drawled. "By all means, let's go home and…"

YET, DESPITE her earlier eagerness, when they walked out of the restaurant, Mallory's doubts resurfaced. She would never have believed a five-minute car ride could generate so much tension. Neither she nor Cliff said a word as he expertly backed his gold Lexus sedan out of its parking space, turned onto the street, then almost immediately turned into the condominium parking lot.

During that brief time she envisioned a hundred ways to handle the situation.

My bed or yours? No. Too blunt.

In the mood for a little whoopee? Too dated.

Cliff, you're very sexy. How about coming over to my place and I'll show you how much? Too overt.

Wanna get naked? Too raw.

Dozens more comments flitted through her mind, but none appropriate for a woman who had just asked a man to have a sex-only, no-strings affair. Nothing in her life had prepared her for a situation quite like this.

With a start she realized that Cliff had pulled the car into his garage and turned off the engine.

"Having second thoughts?"

She shivered. She'd known the man for three years, so how come his voice suddenly sent goose bumps up and down her spine? From somewhere deep inside her, she dredged up enough courage to meet his eyes. "No. No second thoughts."

Liar!

No, I'm not, she assured her screaming conscience. I'm having twelfth or thirteenth thoughts. My second thoughts came and went minutes ago.

"I'm glad." His hand touched hers for a moment, then he opened the car door and got out. Too soon, he walked around the front of the car and opened her door.

Silently she accompanied him to the front door of his town house. It looked like a mirror image of her own. *Get a grip, kiddo. You wanted exactly this. So why are you so nervous?*

Because it's different! She wanted to scream the words. She wanted to make a run for the sanctuary of her home. She wanted to forget she'd ever mentioned such a stupid idea. She wanted to lean against Cliff and have him tell her everything would be all right.

She wanted...

The door stood open, and he stood aside, waiting for her to enter. "Do you want to come in now?"

Was that break in his voice from nerves too?

For the first time since they'd left the restaurant, she took a good look at him. His hair, a deep glowing auburn in the sunlight, had an unusual disheveled look. A fine quiver tickled one cheek and his Adam's apple bobbed as he swallowed deeply. No question about it, he was as nervous as she!

The realization calmed her, and she tried to reassure him with her best smile. "Sure."

He ushered her into the living room that bore a surreal, reversed resemblance to hers. But while her unit's decor featured elegant eighteenth-century cherry furniture, Cliff's had modern brass and glass mixed with two huge burgundy-leather sofas and modern art prints on the bleached-oak paneled walls.

"A glass of wine?" His voice had a slight catch that betrayed his nervousness.

She took a deep breath and walked close to him, breathing in the spicy aroma of man and aftershave. "Don't bother, Cliff. This isn't about seduction, you know."

"It's not?" He had to swallow before the words came out. She noticed, however, that his hands had come to rest on her hips.

"No." She raised her hands to unbutton his designer knit shirt. "It's about each of us getting what we want from the other."

His hands moved restlessly over her tailored slacks. "And what is it you want from me?"

Any trace of nervousness had utterly vanished from his voice, leaving a dark seduction that rippled through her. It set her heart thumping and froze her hands at their task. She breathed deeply and her head swam from the rich luxury of his scent. Her hands went to work, tunneling under his shirt to the warm muscles of his back.

"I just want you," she told him. And she did. She wanted his charm. She wanted his teasing. She wanted his humor. She wanted his companionship.

Most of all, right now she wanted his lean, hard body.

He smiled. "And I want you." Gently he lowered his head until his lips barely touched hers. Breathing the words into her mouth, he added, "More than anything, I want you."

His lips finally descended fully on hers in a gentle kiss that nonetheless carried the fire of passion. That first touch was both tentative and assured, the kiss of a man who knows he has the time to taste and the inclination to savor.

Mallory let herself relax against him. Her arms tightened around his back, moving restlessly against his sinewy strength. She breathed in his intense,

manly scent, part spicy cologne, but mostly pure
Cliff. Giddy, she savored the combination of sensations.

Their mouths touched, separated, touched again.
Each contact lasted a fraction longer. Each separation
was incrementally briefer. His hands roved over her
back until one lodged at her nape, holding her head
at the perfect angle to deepen the kiss.

Only when she gasped for air did he release her,
pressing his forehead against hers. Even while concentrating on regaining her breath, she noted that his
lungs strained as hard as hers. She moved one hand
from his back and around his side until it hovered
over his heart. The thumping beat beneath her palm
confirmed his excitement.

"You pack a wallop, Mallory," he whispered. His
mouth tenderly explored her temple and the corners
of her eyes. "How come you never told me about
this before?"

She froze. "This?"

"Your heat. Your fire. Your passion."

She relaxed and let her hand do its own exploring.
He had the most marvelous chest! "Maybe you never
asked me?"

"Can't imagine why not. Can you?" A thread of
humor laced his voice. "I mean, here I've been, cold
and lonely right next door to you. And you, hard-
hearted woman that you are, never said a word about

being hot enough to warm the coldest nights and the loneliest bachelor.''

He accompanied his accusation with at least a dozen more of those tender, tempting kisses. She tilted her chin to give him better access to a particularly sensitive spot. ''I confess, Counselor. Guilty as charged.'' His tongue generated a spear of heat blazing through her, making her voice breathy. ''I throw myself on the mercy of the court.''

He paused just long enough to send her an approving smile. ''Perfect response, Ms. Reissen. And definitely a fascinating idea. The prospect of you throwing yourself on top of me leaves me barely able to stand upright.''

Mallory's wandering fingers burrowed through the silky hair on his chest and found the raised pebble of his nipple. Her lips curved in triumph when his breath caught.

''You think I'm properly contrite for my crime, Counselor?''

He sent her a mock frown. ''Maybe not. I think I need to see more of your willingness to atone for your felonious ways.''

''You mean—'' She didn't have to ask him to clarify his pronouncement. He was already busy unbuttoning her silk blouse and spreading it with a jerky movement. Her bra received equally brief attention before its front clasp released and the two sides spread apart.

He stared at her uncovered breasts for a long moment, before raising his eyes to meet hers. His voice deepened to a husky note. "I mean you're the most beautiful thing I've ever seen."

Her mouth dropped open in surprise. Unlike their earlier banter, she couldn't find the slightest hint of humor in his quiet words.

"Cliff…"

"Mallory," he mocked gently, "didn't you expect a compliment or two along the way?"

She smiled with seductive intent, her hands busily tackling his belt buckle. "I hadn't thought about it, I guess. But it's very nice, Counselor. Smooth. I think I'm beginning to understand why you hotshot lawyers are so slick."

"You do, hmm?" His words were muffled because his mouth nibbled her ear, sending quivers through her. He whispered directly into her ear, "Wanna find out how come they call me the office hotshot?"

His erotic promise turned her spine to a river of fire and conjured images that burned her breath in her lungs. He pushed her blouse and bra off her shoulders, letting the garments fall to the floor. While her hands surged through the dusting of hair on his chest, his palms covered her breasts and pebbled nipples. He bent and closed his lips over one breast.

Mallory's breath stopped, though her heart thundered. Every sense concentrated on the liquid flame of his mouth against her flesh. Blood rang in her ears, a musical, insistent tone that echoed over and over and...

"Cliff—" She struggled to get the word out through lungs that barely remembered how to function. "Cliff...wait."

"Hmm?" His mouth released her nipple and drifted over the fullness of her breast toward the other aching mound. "Just a minute."

The ringing hadn't stopped. "Cliff. Wait." With every bit of strength she could muster, she pulled his head away from her. The frustration glittering in his eyes almost made her groan, but she persisted. "My pager. It's beeping."

It took a moment, but she saw the arousal fade in his face and awareness replace it. He loosened his grip on her enough to allow her to step away. It wasn't easy when every atom in her wanted to step closer, but she managed.

And with that slight distance, sanity returned. She scooped up her blouse and pulled it around her, not bothering with the bra, which she stuffed into the pocket of her pants. She took one shaky breath, then another, before reaching for her purse to retrieve the persistent device. A familiar number displayed on the screen. "It's—" she cleared her throat of the final traces of passion "—my boss. I have to call him."

Cliff waved her toward the phone on the table. His eyes still held lingering flickers of arousal, but he said nothing while she absently buttoned her blouse.

With the closing of each button, Mallory felt more in control, more professional. By the time Stanley Rosen, the station's news director, answered the phone, she could speak with her usual crisp tones.

Less than two minutes later, she hung up and turned to face Cliff. He, too, had repaired his appearance, stuffing his shirt back into his pants and rebuttoning it. "I take it you have to leave?" he asked before she could say anything.

"Yes." Just looking at him heated her blood—but she had no time for that now. "There's a major story breaking at Camp Pendleton. Stan wants me to come in and anchor the coverage."

If she were with Mark, she knew he'd be protesting that the marine base north of the city always had some "breaking story" or another. But Cliff merely nodded. "I understand. Do you need me to do anything for you?"

She wanted to feel happy that he was letting her go to work so easily. She ought to feel happy. But disappointment lingered. "I'm sorry about…this." She gestured vaguely to indicate the passion that had exploded between them and the interruption that had killed it too soon. "We'll have to start our, um, association later."

He reached her side before she realized he'd moved. "Don't worry. We'll pick up where we left off another time."

Despite her own hormones singing in her veins, she smiled at him. "And will you remember where we were before the interruption?" she asked softly.

He gave her one hard, lingering kiss before escorting her to the front door. "Count on it."

She left quickly, refusing to look back at the temptation of his farewell.

HOURS LATER, Cliff still blinked in wonder that Mallory Reissen had actually propositioned him!

With his sensual plans for the day ruined, he had decided to make use of the afternoon as he did most Sundays—by working. He'd changed into his favorite grungy sweats and parked himself on the couch in his living room, with a stack of paperwork covering the coffee table in front of him and Mozart filling the air.

As he mulled over the complex briefs needed for a client meeting the next day, he had to admit that she'd definitely come up with the best solution to both their problems. She'd looked serious, a little earnest, even...sweet while she calmly and logically explained why some hot nights in the sack together would solve both their problems.

He shook his head. He found it hard to imagine he'd ever thought of Mallory as "sweet," but there it was. Her hopeful-but-please-don't-notice expression reminded him of sneaking kisses from Barbara Sue Denton behind the bleachers at a pep rally.

Of course that was before Barbara Sue's parents convinced her that dating a kid from the wrong side of town was only one step away from being with a leper.

He hadn't thought of Barbara Sue in years. Last he heard, she'd been married and divorced twice and was on the prowl for husband number three. He spared a moment of silent thanks that said husband would never be him, then returned his attention to his paperwork.

Despite his concentration, his soon-to-be-consummated affair with Mallory sparked a glimmer of anticipation and tightened the fit of his normally loose sweats. Kissing her had been an exercise in pleasure he hadn't anticipated. Not even the charming, half-shy uncertainty in her eyes when he'd bared her breasts compared to the luxury of her kiss.

He regretted the untimely interruption from her beeper—a lot. He wished she'd been able to stay, though he understood the demands of her career had left her no choice. If she had stayed, he knew he'd have had her upstairs and naked in his oversized bed within minutes. The details of what he planned to do to her, with her, for her, simmered in his mind.

It was going to take him hours and hours to go through every step of that envisioned scene. Then he would start all over again.

Yes, he thought as he shifted once more to accommodate the hardness that showed little sign of abating, sex with Mallory was going to be spectacular.

Their affair could well incinerate them both with passion, but he had no compunction about diving headlong into the flames. He wanted her more than he could ever remember wanting another woman.

And he intended to have her—very soon.

3

ON FRIDAY NIGHT, Mallory dabbed a final puff of powder on her nose, grabbed her purse, and started for the door of her office. She had talked to Cliff this afternoon when he called to arrange a late dinner—late because she couldn't leave work until after she'd anchored the six-thirty evening news, which usually meant leaving the station somewhere around seven-thirty. They planned to grab a quick meal, then go home and finally get their fledgling affair off the ground.

She could hardly wait. After the untimely interruption on Sunday afternoon, the prospect of starting an affair with Cliff offered an even more enticing reward for surviving a long workweek.

A quick glance at her watch showed the minute hand creeping ever closer to the twelve. She was late, of course. Why was she never able to get out of the station at a reasonable time?

Firmly putting her work out of her mind, she was flicking off the office lights when the electronic chirp of her telephone halted her in the doorway. She stopped, debating whether to go back and answer it or just let whoever was at the other end assume that she'd already left for the day.

A second chirp, then a third convinced her. With a disgruntled sigh, she flipped the lights back on and returned to her desk. Without sitting down, she picked up the phone.

"Mallory Reissen here." At this time of night she didn't care if her voice was a little curt.

"Mallory, glad I caught you." The voice of her agent boomed through the receiver, so she pulled it away from her ear. "I wasn't sure you'd still be at the station. Should've known you were too dedicated to have left already."

She grimaced, glancing again at her watch. Cliff would be looking for her at the restaurant very soon. "What is it, Lenny? I was just on the way out the door."

Another hearty chuckle blasted her ear. "Well, you know that tape I sent to the network guys last month?"

"What about it?" Suddenly she was *very* interested in what her agent had to say. Thoughts of the date with Cliff faded.

Lenny summed it up in two words. "They're interested."

Her breath caught, and she collapsed into her chair. "Tell me this isn't a joke."

"No joke, kid. They haven't made a final decision, of course. But you've definitely made it onto their short list. They told me that much already."

Visions of success danced before her eyes. She had to take three deep breaths before she could get any words out. Dozens of inarticulate questions buzzed around her head, but the only one she could think to ask was, "Did they tell you anything more about the project?"

"Not really. But they did dangle one carrot."

Lenny always had a sense of the dramatic. He was going to make her ask.

"What carrot?"

"Are you sitting down?"

"Yes," she said impatiently. "What carrot?"

"It's for prime time."

Long moments passed. For once in her life Mallory could think of absolutely nothing to say. "I don't believe it," she finally whispered. "Prime time. Are you *sure?*"

"Scout's honor, kid." Again Lenny chuckled. "Looks like we're headed for the big time."

"But they haven't made up their minds yet, right?"

"That's right. They'll be talking to you and two or three other candidates over the next few weeks.

It's up to you to convince them that you're not just someone on their short list—you're the only person on their final list."

"I can do that," she vowed.

Twenty minutes later, having rehashed the entire situation with Lenny several times before hanging up, she finally arrived at the small Thai restaurant where she had arranged to meet Cliff. Despite being a solid half hour late, she practically floated to the table on winged feet. The words "network prime time" filled her head almost to the exclusion of anything else.

As she sat down at the table where he waited, she apologized for her tardiness.

"Don't worry about it," he said, handing her a menu. "I was a little late myself. I take it things got a little crazy at work?"

She nodded. "I'll tell you about it later. Have you ordered?"

"Nope. I was waiting for you."

To her relief he didn't show the slightest sign of disgruntlement. This arrangement really was going to work out, she thought while she scanned the menu. He understood when business interfered with their plans and made her a little late for social stuff. The thought cheered her even more.

They ordered a simple meal of pad Thai rice noodles with shrimp and settled back to talk. Mallory explained about the last-minute delay leaving the station and he congratulated her on her opportunity.

"Of course, it's way too early to celebrate. It could be months before they actually make up their minds. And these new projects can be cancelled before they even get on the air." She tried to inject a note of realism to keep herself from getting too excited too early.

"Yes, but things do look good."

"That they do." Putting down her chopsticks, she lifted her glass of wine in a silent toast.

This was one of the best parts of their infant relationship, she realized as they enjoyed their dinner. She could talk to him about her work without worrying that he would think her overly ambitious or unfeminine. His congratulations on her successes tasted sweeter than any dessert. She tried to remember when any man had displayed such a reaction to a professional coup. She couldn't think of a single occasion since she'd begun to make her mark at the station.

She smiled at him over a cup of steaming ginger tea. "I've really been looking forward to tonight," she confessed. "I'm sorry things didn't work out on Sunday, but it's going to be even better now. We— I really have something to celebrate."

Cliff shifted in his seat. "Yes. Well."

But she interrupted him. "But we've been talking

about me all through the meal. What about you? How's your work going?''

With precise care he positioned his cup on the table and didn't meet her eyes. "Busy, of course."

"I know what you mean," she said when he failed to expand on that comment. Something was bothering him, but what? "Is anything wrong at work?"

He smiled too quickly. "Of course not."

She believed that just about as much as she expected the sun to rise over the Pacific some morning real soon. On the other hand, she didn't want to pry if he didn't want to talk. "Maybe we should go home," she suggested. *And maybe you'll feel more like talking once we have some privacy.*

"Uh, that's the problem, Mallory."

She froze, her chair half-shoved back from the table. "Problem?" Had he changed his mind about their agreement? Was this dinner together merely a way of telling her he didn't want a relationship with her after all?

Or was he a lot angrier about her lateness this evening than he'd let on?

"Cliff, if this is about my being late," she said carefully, "we did agree that—"

His surprised look cut her off. "Why would I be mad about that? I know your job entails unexpected demands."

"Oh." She paused, still balanced on the edge of

her chair, afraid to either continue or abort the movement. "So what's the problem?"

He took her hand. The warmth of his palm against hers melted the frozen lump inside her and let her relax again against her chair. "I just feel like I got you out here under false pretences. I know I implied we'd go home from here and...well, anyway, I'm afraid that's not going to be possible tonight."

"Why not?" Whatever his message, she didn't understand it.

His words came out in a rush. "Mallory, I have to go back to work tonight after we leave here."

"On a Friday night?" she asked blankly.

"Yes." His gaze searched her face while he explained. "The firm is going to take on a major case—the Bartlett murder trial—and the client is coming to the office tomorrow morning to talk about it with us. I've got to review everything for the meeting. I'm up for a position on the defense team—and if I get it, I'll be the only nonpartner included."

Fiona Bartlett was a much-married socialite who had—according to the press accounts—shot her fourth husband when she caught him in bed with another woman. The husband and his lover were killed, and Fiona allegedly wiped the gun, cleaned up, and left the house to go to their Palm Springs home. When the police arrived there to notify her of her husband's demise, she had put on an impressive show of histrionics. Ten days later, after a highly publicized investigation, she had been charged with two counts of first-degree murder.

The case promised to be nothing less than a circus. Women's groups claimed that if Fiona indeed had done the crime, it was because her husband abused her and drove her to murder. The prosecutor insisted Fiona planned the entire thing with cold-blooded calculation. Fiona professed her innocence and great love for the slain husband everyone knew she planned to divorce.

Meanwhile, the public gobbled up every salacious detail of the Bartletts' opulent, sensual life-style. In fact, Mallory's news reports offered updates on the case nearly every day.

Immediately she understood the implications of his words, and her palm gripped his fiercely. "Cliff, this could be an incredible break for you. Surely the senior attorneys must think very highly of you to consider including you on a case like this!"

As if he suddenly realized that she was congratulating him, not condemning him for a disappointing evening, he relaxed and let a huge grin surface. "I've been told that my participation in a successful resolution of this case would definitely result in 'positive appreciation from the powers that be.' I think that means a partnership could well be in the works."

She couldn't resist planting a smacking kiss on his cheek. "Wonderful! I'm so pleased for you."

"But I'm afraid we're going to have to put off our evening together until another time." Genuine regret shone in his eyes, which went a long way toward soothing any frustration that lingered.

She waved the comment away. "Of course. You're right. You have to go back to work and prepare for the meeting tomorrow."

They left the restaurant and Cliff walked her to her car. When she had opened the driver's door, his hand stopped her from getting in. "You know, I really hated having to tell you our evening had to be canceled. What a relief to know you understand."

Mallory turned to face him, only to find herself all but surrounded by his arms and the open car door. "I do understand, Cliff. It's a tremendous opportunity for you. And I'm glad you're not angry about my being late tonight."

He tipped his head, considering. "Well, about that...don't you think I should get some kind of reward for being so sympathetic?"

Even in the distorted illumination of the parking lot lights, she could see the gleam of sensual teasing in his eyes. "What did you have in mind?" The breathiness in her voice surprised her.

"Maybe...a kiss?" His mouth lowered, just a whisper away from hers.

She hesitated a moment to savor the anticipation, then lifted her face just enough to make contact. Her lips molded to his and clung, focusing her attention on the moist warmth radiating from him.

Her arms slipped around his neck. With an equally smooth motion, his arms moved around her waist and pulled her into the curve of his body. Automatically she fit herself against him, savoring his heat and strength.

He lifted one hand and used a thumb to nudge her mouth open, and his tongue took immediate advantage of the opening, swooping inside her mouth in a territorial claim she had no wish to deny. Her tongue dueled with his.

By the time he broke the contact just enough to rest his forehead against hers, both were almost breathless.

"Wow," Cliff whispered.

"Wow, yourself." Her hands loosened, to slide to his shoulders. "Why didn't you tell me about your earthshaking skills?"

"Me? I thought it was you."

With a compliment like that, how could she resist? She stretched on tiptoe to kiss him again. She'd always believed good behavior should be rewarded, she thought hazily while his lips captured hers and took charge of their kiss. And this was reward enough—or almost enough.

This time it took the raucous blare of a horn to separate them.

Reluctantly stepping away from her, Cliff's hands lingered on her waist before dropping to his side.

Mallory tipped her head and peered up at him. A few deep breaths steadied her voice. She hoped. "You've got to go back to work. Remember?"

"Yeah." He didn't move.

"Work? The meeting tomorrow? Remember?" If he didn't move, she knew she couldn't. Not while he was standing there looking as sinfully tempting as a box of Godiva chocolates.

Finally he shook his head and took another step away. "You're dangerous, woman. You know that?"

"I could say the same about you."

He traced a shaky finger down her cheek. Automatically she tilted her head into the slight pressure. "I'm likely to be tied up all day tomorrow. What do you think about continuing this sometime Sunday?"

"I think that's a wonderful idea." At last free of the spell he wove so effortlessly, she slid into her car. Her keys rattled loudly as she blindly stuffed the right one into the ignition. Habit was a wonderful thing sometimes. "Go to work, Cliff. I'll see you Sunday afternoon."

But as she drove away she could see him standing in the parking lot watching her leave.

HOURS LATER, Mallory still hadn't gotten to sleep. Fantasies of being with Cliff invaded every speck of consciousness. Every time she dropped off to sleep, heated dreams of the two of them, entwined in ecstatic explorations, reappeared. Her sheets twisted into knots and her stomach churned from the need writhing inside her.

When the telephone trilled at 3:27, she was wide awake, staring at the black ceiling. Hastily, she grabbed the receiver. Was Cliff home? Was he burning for her as she was for him?

"Hello?" She winced at her own eagerness.

"Hi, Mallory. It's Mother."

Mallory's desire dissolved like the morning fog under a July sun. Another glance at the illuminated clock in her bedroom confirmed the time. She was probably the only person in America whose mother would call her in the middle of the night.

"Hi, Mother. How are you so early in the morning?"

"Fine, dear. Uh, early?"

"Yes. *Early.* It's three-thirty out here."

"But it's six-thirty here and you're three hours ahead, right?"

Mallory gave up. For a woman with a Ph.D. and an acclaimed academic career, her mother never could keep straight the time difference between the

East Coast and the West. "That's all right. Is anything wrong?"

"Oh, no. I just heard from your father. Enjoying himself immensely. He's in the middle of that concert tour. Eastern Europe, I believe. The Europeans so *appreciate* classical music, you know."

"That's nice. Did he ask you to contact me?" Mallory couldn't help the stiffness that iced her voice. Her parents maintained an apparently happy two-career marriage in which neither partner spent more than a few weeks a year in the same city as the other. It worked well for them, but not as well for Mallory. After her grandmother died when Mallory was twelve, she was brought up by expensive nannies and spent much of her time in boarding schools.

"Of course, dear. He is always very interested in how you are doing."

I've heard that lie my whole life. "I'm fine. Was there something you needed?"

"Well, yes, there was."

Disappointment tightened Mallory's stomach before she deliberately forced it to relax. She should be used to this by now. "What can I do for you, Mother?"

"I'm going to be on the West Coast in a couple of weeks. I'm meeting with Jonassen up at Stanford to prepare for this summer's dig. I thought you and

I might get together for a lunch or something while I'm out there.''

"Mother, Stanford is in the Bay Area. It's six hundred miles from San Diego."

"Oh."

Damn her for sounding disappointed! Of course Mallory gave in. Again. "I'll see what I can do, all right?"

"That's fine, dear. I was cleaning out some of your grandmother's things and found a few items to give you. I thought it would be just a little cold to put them in a box and mail them."

Cold, Mallory could deal with. A token maternal visit chilled her more than polite formality at arm's length.

"I see." Mallory scribbled down the dates and times of her mother's trip and promised again to try to arrange to meet with her while she was here.

Conversation over, Mallory tried to recapture the dreams that had kept her company all night long. Better the physical frustration of wanting Cliff and not having him than dealing with the lifelong frustration of wanting a parent who simply couldn't be bothered.

CLIFF FRETTED with anticipation until Sunday afternoon finally arrived. By the time he opened the door to Mallory's knock, he could barely restrain himself to a single, sizzling kiss. "The barbecue's hot. The salmon steaks are marinating in the fridge. Let's go to bed."

She actually giggled. "What kind of a greeting is that?"

Leading her out to the patio at the back of his condo, he said, "An honest one?" He gave his best Snidely Whiplash leer.

She settled comfortably into a padded patio chair, propped her feet on a convenient stool, and waved him to his cooking duties with a grand gesture. "Don't distract me, slave. I've survived a very hard week, and I am here to be waited upon."

Obediently, he opened the gas grill. "Well, I've certainly raised waiting to a fine art after this week."

"As in waiting for me?"

He snatched a quick nibble behind her ear as he handed her a glass of iced sangria and a huge bowl of salad fixings. "Of course, I mean you. But while you're waiting to be fed, could you toss the salad?"

She smiled and agreed, but he noticed a fine tremor in her hands as she took the bowl.

While he fussed with the grill, they chatted about their work. But silently, he pondered the quiver he'd seen. Now that he looked at her, he noticed the dark circles under her eyes—artfully disguised by makeup, but present nevertheless. What the hell was wrong?

When he caught her stifling a third yawn, he said, "You have had a long week, haven't you? Anything wrong?"

She shook her head. "I just haven't been sleeping well."

What's wrong, Mallory? Why aren't you sleeping? Everything inside him wanted to ask the question, but he hesitated. Would such a question be considered unwanted interference? Too intrusive? If she was simply working too many hours to have time for sleep, would she assume he was criticizing her?

A sudden glimpse of the pitfalls of their career-friendly agreement kept him silent. No doubt as they settled into their new relationship, such issues would disappear, he assured himself as he turned the salmon on the grill. They would find a way to work things out.

The doorbell interrupted his silent, unconvincing argument. "I'll be right back," he promised with a smile. "Keep an eye on the salmon for me, all right?"

Long strides took him to the front door. He had every intention of ejecting his untimely caller—posthaste. But once he opened the front door a crack, a size-twelve, sneaker-clad foot jammed it the rest of the way open. Then the foot was followed by a tall, muscular frame and a shock of black hair.

"Lemme in, Cliff."

"You already seem to *be* in. It's nice to see you. Are you ready to leave yet?" Subtlety accomplished nothing with Todd Sinewski, Cliff knew. His best friend, accountant, and sometime handball buddy simply didn't recognize the concept. It merely rolled off his hide like water off a suntan-oil-slicked beach bunny.

"Aw, c'mon, buddy. I got problems."

"Too bad. Maybe you can solve them somewhere else."

"Nah. You've got a way with babes. Tell me what I'm doing wrong."

Before Cliff could refuse, Todd launched into a detailed account of his latest dating fiasco. He never paused for breath as he described every aspect of his unhappy situation. Only when he finally ran down did Cliff get a chance to insert a word.

"Have you ever considered that asking a nineties woman if she'll do your laundry might be considered just a tad, uh, retro?" Cliff asked.

Todd nodded. "I was afraid of that. But it was an emergency. I swear."

Cliff lifted one eyebrow in silent query.

"It was," Todd insisted. "A grateful client gave me tickets to the Lakers game and I had to go up to L.A.—the Chicago Bulls were in town."

Cliff whistled in appreciation. Yeah, Lakers tickets

for a game of that magnitude were more precious than gold.

"And I had a big client consultation the next morning—and no clean shirts! I mean, what was I *supposed* to do?"

Cliff hardened his heart against the man-to-man appeal. "Your laundry?"

He glanced over his shoulder toward the silent patio. His masculine instinct for self-preservation told him he might find himself on shaky ground unless he got back to Mallory. He took Todd by the arm and aimed him toward the door.

"Look, Todd, it's too bad your girlfriend doesn't appreciate the necessity of going to an important basketball game—but you've got to handle your trauma by yourself. I'm busy right now." He gave a meaningful nod toward the patio.

His friend dug in his heels for a moment, then relaxed and—finally—began to cooperate in his eviction. Todd lowered his voice to a booming whisper that no doubt carried halfway down the block. "Jeez, I'm sorry, Cliff. You've got a girl here, don't you?"

Cliff nodded, still urging more progress toward the front door. "Yes. Goodbye."

"'Bye." Todd finally exited, then poked his head back in before Cliff could slam the door. "Does your babe do laundry? If so, I've got a pile at home—"

Cliff pushed Todd's head out and slammed the

door shut. What a disaster! Still, he'd managed to get rid of his buddy in only—he checked his watch—seventeen minutes, a new record. With steps that grew jauntier by the second, he walked back to the patio, only to stop short at the threshold.

Two perfectly tossed salads, glistening with dressing, sat in splendor on the table, while the cooked salmon kept warm off to one side of the grill. But it wasn't the teasing aroma of marinated fish or raspberry vinaigrette that stopped him in his tracks. It was the even more tempting sight of Mallory, curled up in a lounge chair like a contented kitten, her head nestled in one hand, her legs drawn up in a sexy curve....

And her eyes closed in deep sleep.

4

DISAPPOINTMENT BURNED like acid in Cliff's veins. He took one slow step onto the patio, then stopped again. Should he wake her? Or let her sleep?

Wake her up! Wake her up! You've been waiting for this for days. It's time to get this affair going.

But his nobler half had a different argument. *Yes, but she was so tired earlier. She even admitted she hasn't been sleeping well. It'd be cruel to wake her now that she's finally resting.*

While the debate raged within him, he softly moved to the gas grill and turned it off. He eyed the salads waiting on the patio table. Maybe he should take them inside to the refrigerator? They could be brought out again later when...if...

"Your visitor gone?" Mallory's voice, always slightly husky, now was more of a contented purr.

"You're awake?" His knees almost buckled. He'd spent hours this past week imagining the sound of her voice when she first woke, but the reality was like the velvet rasp of a kitten's tongue against his ear. Soothing. Tickling. And arousing, definitely arousing.

She smiled. "Awake and hungry," she confirmed. "Where are you taking those salads?"

"Nowhere. Not if you're ready to eat." He plunked the plates back onto the table, moved her glass of sangria to her place setting, and gave her a hand up, almost in the same motion. "I'll get the salmon."

But though the meal went down smoothly and the conversation was amiable, Cliff couldn't figur how to make the transition from friendly cha to ardent loving. It wasn't a problem he'd often had, he admitted silently. Usually he had no difficulty on his dates with women. But Mallory was, well, different. Why, exactly, he couldn't quite explain, even to himself. But she just was.

You don't want to rush her. You don't want her to think you're only after her body. Well, maybe, he admitted silently. But it wasn't as if he *didn't* want her body—as soon as possible. It was just that…hell, he didn't have any idea. Never mind that tingle of desire fizzing through his veins, never mind their no-frills agreement, he had too much respect for Mallory—and himself—to rush her into bed.

"D'you mind?"

Mallory's question jerked him out of his mental floundering. "I'm sorry. What did you say?"

"Is it okay if I do a bit of sunbathing while we're out here? My patio is impossible." She gestured at the huge eucalyptus tree that loomed over the end of the condo building. Its shadow darkened the patio of Mallory's next-door unit, though it barely affected his.

"Sure. That's fine." What male in his right mind would ever tell a gorgeous woman not to wear a skimpy bathing suit in front of him? Not he, that was for sure.

"Thanks. I wore my suit in hopes you'd say that." Before he could draw two breaths she'd slipped out of her shorts and jersey top to reveal an attractive but fairly conservative bikini. She adjusted the lounge chair flat, pulled a bottle of sunscreen from her bag, and tossed it to him. "Would you do my back?"

He forgot to draw a third breath. *You're not going to rush her. You're not going to rush her.* The mantra bongoed through his brain while he slowly uncapped the sunscreen. *This scenario could have come straight from a 1960s beach movie. She could be Annette, everyone's sweetheart. You could be...*

Nuts. That's what he could be. Certifiably, undeniably, crackers.

Sitting beside her on the lounge chair, he warmed some of the oil in his palm, then slowly smoothed it over skin as smooth as butter. The instant wriggle of contentment he felt under his hands sparked an answering swirl of arousal through him.

You're not going to rush her. You're not going to rush her.

Frowning, he tried to keep his mind strictly on the task at hand. He cupped his hands around those long, long legs and stroked the oil into her skin from ankles to hips. When his hands strayed into her inner thighs, he thought he heard a moan.

"Did I rub too hard?" His hands froze into position, nestled intimately between her upper thighs.

"No." Her voice was slightly muffled. "I just got a kink in my neck."

"Let me see." He moved his hands away from the far-too-dangerous territory at the top of her legs. He worked on the muscles at her shoulder and nape. "Your muscles are so tense I could bounce quarters off them."

She purred something that might have been an agreement.

He put real effort into working out her kinks, enjoying the slick blend of skin and coconut lotion. As he moved further down her back, he hesitated at the back closing of her bikini top. "Uh, do you mind?" *Dolt! What happened to your cool, man?*

But Mallory looked over her shoulder at him and gave him a slow, sleepy smile. "Go ahead."

His fingers fumbled the closure—when did he lose

every trace of finesse?—but eventually he got it open and spread the straps wide. Now he had free range of her body from head to toe, save only for the small swath of material over her hips. He shifted uncomfortably to accommodate his growing arousal. His kneading motions only reminded him of the silky steel of her muscles and the feminine lushness of her curves. When his hands moved around her to cup the side swell of her breasts and refused to move away, he'd had enough.

"Mallory. I—we—"

With the sinuous motion of a mermaid, she rolled over. Her arms twined around his neck, tugging him closer. "I wondered how long you'd hold out."

"You *planned* this?" His mock outrage probably didn't have much impact when his lips nuzzled her breast.

"Sure." Her hands busily unbuttoned his shirt. "Well, sort of. You certainly seemed to be taking a long time to get anywhere." She grinned. "You look kind of cute when you're just a teensy bit embarrassed. Did you know that?"

Heat warmed the back of his neck. "I was not— am not—embarrassed. I just didn't—don't—want to rush you into anything."

With her fingers spearing through his hair and outlining the rims of his ears, he was sure she'd feel the steam sizzling off him and recognize his claim for the lie it was. But she just nodded. "It's okay, you know. About being embarrassed. I was, too."

"Sure you were. You were so embarrassed you told me to take off your bikini top."

It might have been a flush that tinted her cheeks pink. Or maybe it was just a trick of the sun. But her sudden stillness in his arms wasn't an illusion. "Do you want to know the truth?"

Did he? He had enough experience with women to know that truth-telling could get a man into a lot of trouble. Warily, he nodded. "I guess."

She took a deep breath and her tongue left a shiny track across sun-kissed lips. The action almost derailed Cliff's train of thought. "The truth is, while I was waiting for you to come back I started worrying about…us. And how hard it was going to be to just, well, do it. With no preliminaries or anything. And I thought that maybe you might feel the same way, so if I took things into my own hands—"

A sappy grin was spreading across his face and he couldn't do a thing to stop it. His hands moved down to cover her breasts. "Or rather, if I took things into *my* hands?"

"Yes." But the word was more gasped than articulated. "Anyway, you got the point."

His fingers plucked a crowning nipple. "And the point being?"

Her own sudden sappy grin was almost as wide as

his felt. Her hands dropped from his ears and busily explored his chest. "The point being that you lawyers talk everything to death. You're all talk, no action."

"No action, huh? I'll show you 'no action.'" With a mock growl, he levered her over his shoulder in a fireman's carry and toted her inside to the comfortable couch in the living room.

Within seconds, he'd stripped off her bikini bottom and his own clothes, pausing only long enough to pull a condom from his pants pocket before rolling on top of her.

She was giggling so hard and her back and legs were so slippery with sunscreen lotion that it was hard to hold on to her, but he managed to lever himself into position above her.

"What were you saying about no-action lawyers?" His implied threat was muffled by her sizzling kiss. This woman could kiss like no woman he'd ever met before. Why hadn't he realized before that she was so incredible, fabulous, magnificent...

Words failed him as he simply reveled in the experience. Only when he grew dizzy did he break away from the kiss and nudge himself more intimately between her legs.

Her hips tilted up to accommodate his forward thrust. God, she felt wonderful! Hot and tight, like sinking into a pool of wet velvet, only softer. With a surge, he pushed into her as deep as he could manage. "God, Mallory, you're—"

From the patio a strident electronic beep demanded attention. He froze.

"—being paged." He raised his head to stare at her face. "Do you want to stop?"

"No!" She shifted her hips, and used her hands to pull him inside her even deeper. "Don't stop!"

"But—"

"Don't stop!"

But his mind never quite left that insistent chirping from the patio. As if in a bizarre race, he felt himself going faster and faster, trying to outrun that persistent call. When he finally spasmed, he realized that though he'd found his release, Mallory hadn't.

He paused only a moment to catch his breath before rolling off her. "Mallory, I'm sorry."

But she had already grabbed his shirt from the floor, wrapped it around herself, and headed for the patio. When she returned a moment later, she carried her clothes and that damned beeper. He could really learn to hate that tyrannical little device.

"I'm sorry," he said again. It was hard to apologize for something he'd really enjoyed, though he wished she'd enjoyed it as much as he had. "I know it wasn't as good for you—"

She waved his feeble excuses aside without waiting to hear them. "Don't worry about it. I've got to run. There's a big story breaking downtown. I'll call you later, okay?''

Absently, she pulled on her clothes, gave him a quick kiss, and headed for the door before he could do more than pull on his cutoffs. He trailed her, trying to sort out his jumbled feelings. But with another quick kiss and an apologetic smile, she was out the door before he could even begin to make sense of his roiling emotions.

He mooched around his condo, clearing away the remnants of their meal, and tried to make sense of his snarled emotions. He seldom spent time in introspection, but he finally collapsed with a can of beer on the couch—a couch that still exuded an intoxicating blend of coconut and Mallory—and tried to concentrate on the situation.

What the hell *did* he feel about what had happened, anyway? Relief she wasn't mad at his failure to satisfy her? Yes. Disappointment? Sure. He'd always liked cuddling after sex. Maybe a little bit of resentment that she could dismiss him so easily?

No way! He understood her commitment to her job. He had the same commitment to his. They'd settled that from the first. He was just…concerned, yes, that must be it. He was worried that she was off to some dangerous assignment—maybe a drug bust or the SWAT team capture of some mad serial killer?—where no one would protect her. He blithely dismissed the technicians and crew that would no doubt be beside her every step of the way, and he just as easily put aside his ignorance of the kind of story she was covering. None of that mattered. He wanted her here, with him, not off doing something dangerous.

But she doesn't want to be here with you. At least not right this moment.

Hmm. A good point. And why should she? So far, their attempts to start an affair with "great sex and no commitments" had achieved the "no commitments" part and even the "sex" part—but "great"? Well, for him, maybe, or at least "good." But for her? Hardly.

Fair was fair. That *had* to change.

He brooded long into the fading afternoon, mapping out a plan designed to guarantee that the next time he got Mallory Reissen alone, she was going to end up more sexually satisfied than any woman in history.

He would guarantee it.

MALLORY DROVE downtown to cover the governor's impromptu visit to San Diego, lending only half her attention to the road. The rest was firmly centered on a certain condo in La Jolla where she'd left her new lover behind.

Lover. Somehow, the word didn't quite describe

her relationship with Cliff. Associate? Colleague? Date? Boyfriend? She grimaced and shifted lanes to pass a car. None of those fit, either.

Maybe after he thinks about this afternoon, he'll be your ex-lover.

There was always that possibility. Darn it! They'd been friends ever since he'd moved into the condo next to hers. One less-than-perfect sexual encounter shouldn't change that. Sure, he knew she hadn't climaxed. Men didn't like knowing that, in her experience. They wanted to be considered the best thing in the sack since penny candy. But this afternoon, with her mind fretting over the insistent pager, her embarrassment at making the first move, even the natural awkwardness of a first time together, she simply hadn't been able to relax enough.

Suddenly a new question loomed. Did he realize that her nerves were to blame for their less-than-world-shattering lovemaking? Cliff was a really nice guy—she knew that—after all, that's why she'd proposed their affair in the first place. He was one of the good guys. He could be trusted, not just with her body, but her feelings, too. She trusted him not to expect too much, just as he trusted her not to read too much into his lovemaking.

Still, maybe he was beating up on himself for something that wasn't his fault.

Would he understand that things would probably be a lot better next time?

Would there be *a next time?*

She turned onto the freeway exit ramp and pondered that question. Next time, she'd make sure things went well, she promised herself. She'd make up for today's nervousness and too-quick departure. She'd be sweet, charming, and make sure he knew she didn't blame him for anything.

Yes, that was it. She'd be sweet, charming, gracious—and she'd climax so obviously that he could be in no doubt of his prowess as a lover.

She guaranteed it.

BUT SHE HADN'T counted on "next time" happening on a day that combined all the delights of Friday the thirteenth, an IRS audit, and a *really* bad hair day.

"Hi, Mallory." Cliff straightened as she approached where he leaned against his car in the condominium parking lot. He gave her a warm peck on the cheek. "I'm glad you decided you could come out and play tonight."

"It's been a tough day," she said, reluctant to move. She'd arrived home twenty minutes ago, with just enough time to change clothes before meeting him. It was "hump-day"—Wednesday—after a half week that already seemed as long as a month. The aspirin she'd gulped hadn't yet touched her throbbing head, a new perm and unusual humidity had her looking like the Bride of Frankenstein, and she'd had separate fights with both the news producer and the station makeup artist. Not to mention having an incipient case of PMS that promised to be a lulu.

Still, when Cliff had called earlier to say he was taking the entire evening off and couldn't she come with him for a late dinner, she couldn't find a way to say no. She wanted to be with him, lousy mood, lingering headache, cramping stomach and all. While exhausted disgruntlement scratched sex from her personal agenda for this particular evening, she knew she could count on Cliff for a sympathetic ear and a relaxing good time. Besides, when she'd delicately pointed out that she wasn't in the mood for a sleepover, he'd insisted that didn't matter. Still, she owed him the opportunity to back out of a date that could go nowhere.

"Are you sure you want to be around me?" she asked him. "I'm pretty grumpy when I'm tired. And this has been an incredibly hellish day. Maybe I should settle for a mug of Ovaltine and an early night."

"Oh, I'm sure," he said, opening the car door. "I intend to make up for last Sunday by whisking you away from all your troubles. In fact, I think I can promise you an evening you'll never forget."

Tempted, she wavered, then conceded with a little

sigh. Maybe by the time he brought her home she'd be unwound enough to get some sleep. She surreptitiously flicked her pager to "off" as she stepped into the car. She needed an uninterrupted night, and this time, by George, she was going to get it. "You did say we were going somewhere not too dressy, didn't you?" She gestured at her designer jeans and simple short-sleeved cotton-ramie sweater.

"You look perfect."

"And I'll never forget this evening?" She fastened the seat belt. "Sounds like a lot for you to live up to."

"Don't worry." He closed the door and walked around to the driver's side. "I think I can impress you. I've been working hard and I'm in the mood to have a little fun. You game?"

Mallory nodded, leaned against the seat back and closed her eyes, not bothering to pay attention to where Cliff drove them. She wasn't sure she cared where they went. She wasn't all that hungry—the knot of tension that lodged just under her breastbone ensured she'd eat little, anyway.

The whole week had been a disaster, starting with Sunday's unsatisfactory tryst and capped by her agent's call that morning telling her the network honchos had put off her job interview for another two weeks. Lenny had even agreed with her morose assessment that it probably meant they had someone else in mind and might never even get around to talking to her. With her hopes of a huge career advancement fading, she retreated again into her dour gloom. She simply wasn't in the mood for dinner at some upscale restaurant where she'd be expected to be "on" all evening.

She could envision the meal already. Cliff was trying to impress her, he'd said. That probably meant a trendy restaurant where the service staff had names like Tiffany or Darryl and the noise factor was loud enough to make sure no meaningful conversation could possibly take place. The menu would feature only the most fashionable ingredients—was this month's favorite the chiles that gave her gas, the cilantro that left a nasty taste in her mouth, or the exotic fungus that reminded her of some alien lifeform? Whichever, everyone would be so busy posturing to impress those around them that no one would pay the slightest attention to anyone else.

She'd seen it all a hundred times. Resigned, Mallory mentally condemned herself to another inedible meal that cost five times as much as it should. She wondered if she had enough antacid in her medicine chest to make it through the inevitable night of heartburn.

Just once, she thought wistfully, just once I'd like to go somewhere...different.

HE TOOK HER TO a bowling alley.

When Cliff opened the door to the moderately busy lanes and escorted Mallory inside, he took a deep breath. Familiar odors of hot grease from the snack bar, sweaty rental shoes and chalk from the battered pool table in the far alcove assaulted his nostrils, bringing on a wave of bittersweet nostalgia. The hum of conversation, the clatter of pins falling, and the rumble of the pin-spotting machines strummed his ears like his favorite song from high school.

He'd spent many a pleasant hour hanging out here when he was about thirteen. While his mother flipped burgers in the snack bar, he'd become unofficial after school pinspotter for the owner, taking his pay in free games and meals instead of money.

His mother had hung on to that job for more than a year—one of her longest stints anywhere—and Cliff remembered the place with more fondness than most of the joints she'd slaved in. Besides, Bertie, the alley owner, had taken one look at Felicia Young's half-wild kid and opened his heart to him. Cliff knew that without Bertie's intervention he could well have ended up in some street gang instead of an expensive condo.

Hell, he'd even brought Rebecca Salinger, his first sweetheart in junior high, here on their first date. And snatched a kiss in the hard plastic seats of the next-to-last lane. The distant memory of that innocent embrace evoked a recollection of far more heated kisses with Mallory. This time, he vowed again silently, she'd find satisfaction from more than his kisses.

"Let's get you some bowling shoes," he said, guiding her to the desk. "What size do you wear?"

"Cliff, I don't think—"

"Yo, Cliff! How ya been? Been a while, hasn't it?" Bertie said. The butterball man's gap-toothed grin warmed Cliff like a wood fire in winter.

"Hi, Bertie. Ready to go grunioning again?" On Cliff's last visit Bertie had closed the lanes early, then he and Cliff had headed for the beaches of La Jolla to watch the grunions do their spawning dance in the moonlight.

"Maybe. Or maybe you've got better company." Bertie gave Mallory an openly salacious wink. "What size shoe do you take, darlin'?"

"I'm not—"

Overriding her protests, Cliff said, "Give her a size seven, I think. And I'll take elevens."

"I'm not—"

Lowering his head so his mouth was right beside her ear, he whispered, "Sure you are. Remember? When I asked where you wanted to eat you told me to pick someplace I wanted to go. Well, this is it."

She turned her head, tickling his chin with a few stray hairs and leaving her cheek only millimeters from his mouth. God, how he wanted to close that distance!

"You know I didn't mean—"

"Bowling? It'll do you good. Besides, it's fun, good exercise, and I want to do it." Deliberately, he closed the span between their flesh until barely a whisper separated them. "Don't worry. I won't laugh, no matter how bad you are. All you have to do is give me an adoring smile every time I make a strike."

His ploy worked. He saw her competitive spirit surge in the glare she gave him. "I see," she said ominously. Her lips parted in what probably looked like a smile to anyone watching, but which he knew bore more similarity to the snarling challenge of a lioness.

Hastily, he drew back his head. Just in case. "Good," he said and handed her the shoes, then showed her where to choose a ball.

But it was no accident that he led the way to the battered next-to-last lane hardly anyone used these days. The one directly under the fluorescent tube that for twenty years or more had flickered stubbornly between full illumination and occasional sudden darkness. The lane with the crack in the seat that made only half of it usable, forcing a comfortable squeeze if two people sat in it at the same time.

It was the perfect spot to ensure an illusion of privacy with the woman he intended to seduce.

GIVE AN ADORING SMILE? Sure she would, Mallory thought. Right after hell froze over.

"Didn't you mention food?" she said as soon as she'd dumped her purse on the appalling flamingo-pink seat. A few lanes away, balls rumbled down the hardwood floor and pins chattered in defeat. "My stomach's so hollow I may start chewing on a bowling pin."

"Never let it be said that I disappointed a lady. What do you want on your dog?"

"You're buying me a whole hot dog? What a prince."

"Well," he rubbed his chin with stone-faced glee, "it's either that or the *chiles rellenos* or bean burritos, and I can't recommend them. They give me gas."

Maybe she *wasn't* the only person in America who couldn't eat hot chiles. "All right. I'd like mustard, relish, onions, and cheese."

"Onions?"

Sternly she frowned at his devilishly quirked eyebrow. "Lots of onions," she repeated firmly.

"Okay. I guess I'll have onions, too." He sent a too-adorable-to-be-true grin her way. "They say it doesn't matter if both participants eat them."

Before she could do more than frown, he left for the snack bar.

He returned a few minutes later with a tray holding a huge pile of greasy french fries, two wrapped but equally grease-shiny hot dogs with appropriate fixings, and two large beers.

"You realize there's enough cholesterol on that plate to clog the Alaskan pipeline?" Despite her words, she reached for her share of his booty.

"C'mon. How often do you get one of Bertie's gourmet dogs? One meal won't hurt. Indulge yourself." His voice dropped to a tempting snake-in-the-garden murmur. "Sin a little."

Surprisingly, the food was good—no, it was scrumptious. If only she could have ignored the heat he radiated as effortlessly as he breathed, she might even have admitted to enjoying the meal.

She picked up a french fry and had almost popped it into her mouth when Cliff's hand stopped hers.

"Hold it a second."

Automatically she froze, her lips forming an *O* around the end of the fry. Before she could ask what the problem was, he lowered his head and sent his tongue on a steam-heated lick across the corner of her mouth and chin. Instantly her thoughts scattered and toppled like all ten pins in a strike.

He sat back to admire his accomplishment. "There. That's fine."

Though he released her hand, Mallory almost choked before she could get the bite of french fry swallowed. "What was that for?" Not that she cared why, particularly. All she really wanted was to feel his tongue stroking her skin again—and again. Her lousy mood was getting more and more slippery with every moment. Pretty soon, she'd lose her grip on it altogether.

He cranked up her body temperature another notch or two by retracing his tongue's path with a gentle finger. "You had a smear of mustard right here."

"You ever heard of napkins, Young?"

"Napkins? Gee, now there's a concept. I never thought of them." His smile would definitely have tempted Eve to chop down the Tree of Knowledge. "Besides, they're no fun."

"Is that what we're here for? Fun?" Even to herself her words sounded wistful.

"You bet. Didn't I promise you a night you'd never forget?"

Mallory glanced around the slightly seedy bowling alley and suddenly saw the humor in the situation. Her lips curved upward in a rueful smile that broke through her grump, melting it and washing it away. She finished her beer with a long swallow. "I think you've succeeded. I can honestly say that none of my dates has ever—" the beer she swallowed too hastily made her hiccup "—treated me to a lively evening at a bowling alley."

"That's because they lacked imagination. I, on the other hand, have *plenty* of creativity. Not to mention inspiration." Cliff finished his hot dog and took a final gulp of beer before looking at her expectantly. "You ready to let me trounce you bowling?"

"Look, Cliff, I really don't want—"

"That's what you said about your hot dog, and you liked it, didn't you?"

"Yes, but—"

"So let's have some fun."

"I told you…" Darn it all, why couldn't she just enjoy these moments with him? Her problems at work and with the will-o'-the-wisp network career opportunity would still be there tomorrow. Even her headache had temporarily been beaten into submission by the aspirin and her stomach was practically purring in contentment after the deliciously unhealthy meal. Why not seize this evening and wring every bit of pleasure she could from it?

With a sigh, she stood and picked up her ball. "Okay. We'll bowl."

"Great!"

She headed for the proper position and gave him her most challenging look. "But I want you to know I intend to beat the socks off you—and *I'm* keeping score."

Just as she stepped forward to roll a practice ball down the lane, she was thrown off stride by his low-voiced Bogie drawl. "Sweetheart, socks are the least of it. You can get anything you want off me—all you have to do is ask."

When her ball glided ignominiously straight into the gutter, she glared at him. "That wasn't fair! You broke my concentration."

"All's fair. Isn't that what they say?"

Darn it. There was that devilish-choirboy grin again. If he ever figured out she'd forgive him anything for that smile, she'd be dead meat. So he thought all was fair, did he? Well, he didn't know who he was daring with that comment. All was fair in love—and war. She barely restrained the impulse to do her best Groucho Marx imitation and assert, "Of course you know this means war."

Instead, she deliberately waited until he was preparing to bowl his own practice round. In the middle of his first stride she said in a butter-wouldn't-melt voice, "Don't you think that'll be a bit embarrassing with all these people around? I mean—strip bowling?"

He didn't even bother to watch his ball skitter sideways into the gutter. He loomed over her with eyes glittering promises. "Strip bowling?"

"Wasn't that what you were proposing?" she asked innocently. "Sure sounded like it to me."

After a moment studying her he asked, "What happened to that life-is-real-life-is-earnest lady I walked in here with?"

She smiled. "I found Ernest—and strangled him."

He tugged her out of her seat and into his arms as he roared with laughter. "You constantly surprise me."

"Good. So no strip bowling, huh?"

"Oh, no." Satisfaction dripped from his voice. "I'd *never* let a dare like that pass."

She looked around the alley. While it wasn't crowded—no one was closer than five lanes away—the place certainly wasn't private enough for, well, stripping. "But all these people—we'll get arrested!"

"No, we won't. Not if we do it my way."

"Your way?" Her mental alarms shrieked in warning. "What's your way?" Was she really contemplating agreeing to…?

He whispered instructions into her ear, sending tropical shivers down her spine. "We'll do it with our imaginations. With each ball, you get to describe what garment you'll remove from me if you win that frame—and what will be revealed once you remove it."

Her throat tightened into a thick clot of—nerves? *No, you dummy, it's excitement!* "Describe?" she managed to utter.

"In detail. The sound of the garment rustling. How it feels in your hands. Everything you'd experience if you removed it from me yourself. I'm talking color. Texture. Scent. Taste." His lips captured the lobe of her ear. "*Especially* taste."

Her eyelids drifted downward as rivulets of sensation rushed from her earlobe to the core of her body. It was as if his lips had found her heartstrings and plucked them deliberately. Did she dare agree to his outrageous proposal? Yet did she have the will-power to refuse?

Gathering her strength of mind, she pulled her head—and vulnerable ears—away from his mouth. "What do I get if I win?"

"What do you want?"

You! You! You! Her senses screamed their response. But her mind answered for her with the thing she least wanted to win yet knew she most needed after her exhausting workweek. "An early night—alone?"

Disappointment dimmed his gaze, but he nodded acceptance of her request.

"And what will you get if you win?" she asked.

Darn it. That impish choirboy was back. "Why, Mallory," he promised, "*when* I win, I get to go home and do it all over again—in person."

5

SHE SHOULD HAVE WON.

She would have won—if Cliff hadn't cheated. By the tenth frame, she'd managed to acquit herself pretty well. Whether through her descriptive talents or her skill at ignoring his, she'd brought her score to within one pin of Cliff's. He'd already bowled his last ball, ending with what he called a "humiliating" ninety-six score.

"It's the worst I've bowled since I was in fifth grade," he complained. "You're lethal, you know that?"

She smugly refused to admit that her current score of ninety-five was the highest she'd ever bowled in her life. By luck or the intervention of some guardian angel, she'd actually made a tenth-frame spare, knocking down all ten pins in two attempts. It was only her fourth spare of the game, and she had no idea how she'd accomplished it.

Of course, it hadn't been easy. Not when she'd mentally and verbally stripped Cliff of every article of clothing, leaving him dressed only in a pair of tight white undershorts that molded lovingly to his very masculine form. Ten frames: Two shoes. Two socks. A belt. Pants. A watch. A shirt. A T-shirt. The class ring on his finger. Despite their hurried intimacy on Sunday, she simply hadn't the courage to remove—even in imagination—that final, soft cotton covering. Or to let herself describe the delights hidden beneath it.

Her scruples certainly hadn't fazed him. He'd started with her sweater, then her bra. With each following frame, he'd returned to a detailed description of how her breasts swayed and bounced and tasted as he one by one removed her knee-high stockings, shoes, belt, and slacks.

"You have some fetish about breasts, Young?" she'd finally demanded after missing an easy spare because of his eager description of how her nipples tasted.

"Never before," he said, as if seriously considering the matter. "But I think I'm developing one about yours. Did I mention how perfectly they nestle in my palm?"

She threw up her hands and gave up chastising him.

In the ninth frame, she thought she'd faint when he deliberately explained how he would unhook her left earring and exactly where he would tuck it.

Could she hold it in her navel while she rolled the ball? The image left her breathless, and she plonked the ball awkwardly onto the lane.

It knocked over nine pins.

In the tenth frame, he described exactly how he'd rub her breasts against his own bare chest while he used his tongue to undo her right earring. His hands, he said, would be busy rubbing her hips tightly against those straining undershorts. Her mouth would be all over his chest, teasing and licking his nipples while he tugged her ear.

She was a nervous wreck, but converted a difficult seven-ten split into a impossible spare.

But that final-frame spare not only brought her to within a pin of his final score; it also gave her an extra ball to roll. If she knocked down more than one pin, she'd win the game. And it had been five or six frames since her last gutter ball.

"I hope you realize that it's all over for you, Young," she taunted as she took her position. "I'm going to beat you pretty handily."

"Does this mean you're not going to jump my bones tonight and insist on doing all those incredibly delightful things you've been describing to me? Even though I've got you naked?"

"I'm not naked!"

"Not yet," he promised. "But you've got another

ball to roll, and as far as I can see, there's only one more thing for me to remove.''

Unless he meant her nail polish, he could only be talking about her panties. A hot flush bubbled up her neck at the thought of him actually... No! She had to get her mind back on her bowling. If she didn't, she'd dump this ball in the gutter and lose. And then *he'd*...

Her eyes glazed over as she thought about that possibility. But Cliff's triumphant chuckle broke through her contemplation.

''You want to lose to me, don't you? You want me to put my fingers inside those pale pink panties—''

''They're white!'' she blurted before she could stop herself.

''Sorry. I've been picturing them as pale pink, almost the color of your skin. But white is good too. There's a shadow in the front that hints of the curls I'll find when I use my finger—no, my tongue—to ease the elastic down just a bit.'' He shook his head. ''No, that's not how I'll do it. I'll come up behind you and press you back against me. You'll feel how hard I am against your hips. I want in, and you know it. I want in *bad*.''

His voice was husky, soft, barely intelligible. Her back was to him, so he couldn't see the hard points of her breasts revealing how he aroused her. He couldn't know for sure that he was melting her to jelly with his words.

"I'll take my hand and slip it in the front of your panties, so I can play with the curls there. I'll tug them and caress them carefully. Then I'll tip my head over your shoulder so I can look down and see my fingers when they delve lower. Lower. Aaah, you're wet. You want me too, don't you? You shift your legs just far enough apart to make room for my hand. You're ready, aren't you?"

Frozen, she couldn't think what to do, couldn't remember to breathe, couldn't remember why her right arm felt so heavy. Closing her eyes was another mistake. His seductive voice grabbed every iota of her concentration.

"Your hips are straining against me, begging for me to finish it. You're gasping for breath, and your heart is beating so hard you think you're going to faint. I can feel it under my hand. I'm cupping your breast, pulling gently on your nipple."

Desperately, she found the strength to turn her head to look at him. Her vision was fogged but she saw him rise slowly and approach her.

"Need some help, Mallory?"

"Help?" *I need you. I need you to do all those things you've told me about.*

"Help rolling your ball, I mean. You've got one more chance to catch up with me."

He stood on the floor of the seating area, a step below the hardwood ramp where she stood. His eyes were almost level with hers. "Help?" It seemed the only word she could utter. With the exotic images he'd evoked scrolling before her blurred vision, she wasn't quite sure if it was a question or a plea.

He stepped up behind her, passed his left hand around her waist and used his right to guide her right arm. No wonder it felt so heavy. She had a twelve-pound bowling ball stuck at the end of it.

That's right. She was *bowling*.

"If you make a gutter ball," he whispered against her ear, "you'll lose and I'll take you home and do all those things I told you about."

"All—" Her tongue was so thick, she could barely squeeze out the syllable.

His tongue nuzzled her ear. "Uh-huh. *All.* And we haven't even gotten to the part where I take those very sexy, very white panties off you. All you have to do is roll the ball down the gutter and you get exactly what you want from me."

Deliberately, his hand drifted lower, across her abdomen, whispering across the juncture of her thighs, to hover over the place he'd been describing so erotically moments before. Hot wetness flooded through her and she melted back against him. Sure enough, his thick arousal pressed against her hips.

"Remember how I told you I'd do it? My fingers

touching you, my hand holding your breast. Remember?''

Automatically she took a step forward, but he followed with a step of his own.

''All you have to do is roll the ball down the gutter.''

Would that seductive voice never stop? What did he want of her, anyway?

''Just drop the ball down the gutter and I'll take those panties off you for real. I'll spend the night proving how good we can be together. My imagination's been running wild since Sunday, you know. We didn't get the chance to really explore our relationship. Just drop the ball in the gutter and we'll both discover the possibilities. C'mon, Mallory, all you have to do is drop the ball.''

Her mind bowed to the command in his voice. Her fingers relaxed and the ball dropped.

Into the middle of the lane.

Once she'd released the ball, she stepped away from his arms. A measure of sanity returned.

''You cheated!'' she said.

He took a deep breath, straightened slowly and walked stiff-legged back to the scoring area. It hadn't been a total put-on, she realized. The front of his pants tented outward noticeably.

''I never cheat. I don't have to.''

Her composure was seeping back. ''What do you

call putting your hands all over me while I'm trying to roll my ball?''

Humor glinted in his eyes. ''Copping a feel?''

''And trying to persuade me to throw the game by rolling a gutter ball?''

''Good strategy?''

She suddenly realized she hadn't bothered to see how her last ball had done. She swiveled back to face the pins.

It was still staggering down the lane, moving at a tortoise-slow pace. At that barely moving speed, the variations in the lane's planking gave its trajectory a definite side-to-side wobble.

''What do you want to bet it never makes it to the pins? I think I just won.'' Cliff eyed her up and down. ''I can't wait to collect my winnings.''

Steadily, the ball wavered on, slowing down with each revolution. ''C'mon, ball. Knock something over. Even a few pins will do.'' Her fists clenched, she pushed her hip forward to urge the ball on. At least it was staying in the middle of the lane, so if it made it to the pins it would almost certainly knock a few over.

''It'll never make it that far. Trust me. You lost.''

''It'll get there. I know it will.'' The ball barely inched forward, finally approaching the perfect spot for a strike, the pocket between the foremost one-pin and the three-pin just behind and to one side. "Go, baby, go! Knock 'em all down!"

But the ball wheezed to a weary halt, right beside the one-pin, giving it a nudge but not knocking down anything. The pin teetered a bit, and Mallory held her breath. Would it fall?

"The rule says if the ball doesn't make it to the pins, it counts as a gutter ball," Cliff intoned with satisfaction. "You lost."

"No! Look!" With regal slowness, the teetering one-pin finally gave up and toppled to the side, completely missing all the other pins. "I knocked one down!"

She'd tied Cliff with a score of ninety-six.

But she should have won.

MALLORY'S SMILE from her Wednesday-evening bowling adventure lingered for nearly a week. It survived crises at the station, an irritating taping session for promo shots for the upcoming May sweeps campaign, and another dead-of-night phone call from her mother. It even outlasted another network delay in interviewing her for that plum prime-time slot. The promised meeting was now nearly a month away. *If,* that was, they didn't hire someone else without even talking to Mallory.

But her satisfied smile couldn't survive a week of utter neglect from Cliff.

In her spare moments, Mallory went over every detail of that memorable evening—a process that usually resulted in an unplanned cold shower. No doubt about it, Cliff was going to be an unusually creative lover. She would never have dreamed that bowling—*bowling!*—could be so...inspiring. Even though her physical exhaustion insisted that the evening end in separate bedrooms, the memory of Cliff's seductive whispers generated a sensation that in olden times would have been called "palpitations."

Yes, despite their initial misfires, sex with Cliff would be the best she'd ever had, she was sure. A man as innately sensual and intense as he was couldn't be anything except superb in bed—once she managed to get him there. You had to expect these little awkwardnesses when starting a new relationship, she told herself firmly. Nobody's fault, really. That was just life. All she had to do was hang in there until her schedule finally meshed with Cliff's to give them some uninterrupted free time.

So why did she feel so...well, neglected?

She understood that he was working long, hard hours. For Pete's sake, she did the same. So what was wrong with her? Why couldn't she just enjoy what she had without trying to scrape up trouble where there wasn't any—or shouldn't be any?

Nevertheless, when her phone rang at nine o'clock one evening, she leaped for the receiver. "Hi!" she said, sure it *had* to be Cliff calling to tell her to come right over and "get naked."

"Darling! I'm so sorry to call you this late." Her mother's breathless, perpetually-confused-about-life's-details voice greeted her.

"Hello, Mother." *Why wasn't it Cliff calling?* "Don't worry about the time. It's only nine o'clock."

"Nine? But I thought—it's nearly midnight here, and I know you're three hours different, but I just had to get this settled…"

"Never mind, Mother. Was there something wrong?"

"No. Well, yes, dear. In a way. You remember I told you I was coming out to Stanford this spring? Well, it's settled—or rather, I changed my itinerary again. I'll be out there next week. I'd really like to do that lunch we talked about."

Lunch with her mother. Now there was a treat. "I don't know, Mother. It's pretty hard for me to get away during the week—especially when it's so far away. It'll take all day to shuttle up to the Bay Area, have lunch, then take a shuttle back."

"Oh, my dear, didn't I say? It would have to be on a Saturday. I'll be working closely with Peter Jonassen, you know. Such a wonderful researcher. What he found on those digs in Ur…well! Anyway, I'll be tied up until the weekend for sure. Let me see, that would be Saturday, the fourteenth. Is that all right?''

"Well…" Mallory had hoped to convince Cliff to go away with her on that particular weekend. But realistically, he'd probably spend the day working anyway. Why not make her mother happy and go to lunch with her? At the very least, it would be something to do that would keep her mind off Cliff. For a while.

"Sure, Mother. I'll be there. Just tell me where you're staying and I'll rent a car and pick you up.'' Mallory knew her mother had a phobia about driving in an unfamiliar town.

As she scribbled down the address her mother rattled off, Mallory's eyebrow rose. "You're staying with Dr. Jonassen? At his house?''

"Oh, yes, dear," her mother practically chirped. "He's such a nice man. So accommodating. When he found out that your father wouldn't be coming with me, he insisted I stay with him. I'll be much more comfortable there than in some motel, he said, and it'll be easy for him to give me rides wherever I need to go. Isn't that sweet of him?''

Sweet. Mallory rolled her eyes. "Sure, Mother. I'll see you then on the fourteenth." But as she hung up, her pen tapped the paper thoughtfully. Her father was in Europe again, and her mother was flying cross-country to work with a male professor—and staying in the man's house, to boot. Surely her mother wouldn't...couldn't...

No. Her parents' marriage, strange and unsatisfying as it seemed to her, worked well for them. She was just imagining things. This Dr. Jonassen was probably in his late seventies, married, and had seven grandkids.

Never mind that, *why didn't Cliff call?*

AFTER TWO MORE DAYS of waiting fruitlessly, Mallory took advantage of a break at work and picked up her office phone. The door was tightly closed and she had perhaps ten minutes before someone would come knocking and demand her presence. With fingers that trembled unaccountably, she pressed the sequence of digits for Cliff's work phone.

"Young here."

God, it felt so good to hear his voice! "Hi, Cliff. It's me, Mallory." *Please don't let him say, "Mallory who?"*

"Mallory! Damn, but it's good to hear from you! I'm up to my eyeballs in work and this is the first good thing that's happened to me all day."

A sigh of relief trembled through her. "I'm sorry things are so tied up there. Is there anything wrong?"

She heard his chair creak and she imagined him leaning back and putting his feet on something—a wastebasket? A drawer from his desk? "Nah. Just too much work to do in too little time. Uh, say, Mallory..."

He was going to apologize for not calling her. She could hear it in his voice. But the rules they'd established at the beginning of their relationship were suddenly emblazoned in huge Day-Glo orange letters before her eyes. He'd *hate* apologizing for tending to his career ambitions.

Before he could do so, she interrupted. "I'm sorry I've been so busy lately," she lied. "But it's been really hectic here at work. I guess it's a good thing you understand about that."

"No problem," he admitted. Mallory fancied she heard a note of relief in his voice. "I've been swamped, too."

"Well, I just had a really terrific idea."

"Terrific, huh? Does it include bowling?"

She laughed. "Not this time. It's going to take me a while to recover from our last excursion."

"Darn. Bowling with you is really, um, interesting. Did I tell you how much I enjoyed last Wednesday night?"

She hesitated. "Even though we didn't, uh..."

"Even though," he said solemnly. "I just wanted to be with you. Maybe teach you a few bowling tricks of the trade. So to speak."

Some tricks! Hot blood warmed her cheeks, but she disciplined her voice to a more serious note.

"Um, thanks. What I really called about is this. I've been working so hard lately, and I know you have too, that we've hardly had time to, well, be together. If you know what I mean."

His soft chuckle rippled down her spine. "Yeah, I know. And I'm not real happy about that either, as a matter of fact."

"Well, I happen to have been given a certificate for a free stay at the new five-star Maison Shores Resort. Some kind of promotional offer to the media. And I thought if we could get away from it all, even for a night, it might be, um, fun."

"Fun." He echoed the word in a way that sent another thrill down her back. "Better-than-bowling fun? Or did you have something else in mind?"

"*Definitely* better-than-bowling fun. The certificate is for one of their honeymoon cottages." Mallory tried but couldn't keep the hopeful expectation out of her voice.

"Hmm. Let me get my calendar." A rustle of papers sounded in her ear. "How about this weekend?"

Mallory pulled her own organizer toward her. "I can't this weekend. I'm scheduled to do a shoot up in Temecula. Somebody claims they found some Bigfoot footprints in one of the wineries there, and that always gets good airplay. Can we pick a weekday?"

"Well," Cliff suggested, "how about next Thursday? I don't have to be in the office until noon Friday, so we could sleep in.''

"No. Thursday's out. I'm covering the nine o'clock news for the cable news channel that night. How about Tuesday?"

"No way. I've got dinner with the defense team on the Bartlett trial. What about next weekend?"

This was getting ridiculous. "I can't," Mallory said. "I've promised to go up to the Bay Area for lunch with my mother on Saturday."

"Just Saturday?"

"Uh-huh." A thought struck her. "You know, I'm only going up and back on Saturday. It'll be late when I get back, but...how about next Sunday? We could go straight from there to work Monday morning."

A tappity-tap in her ear told her that he was flicking his pen against something hard while thinking about her suggestion. "You know, that might work out fine. I really ought to work on Saturday, anyway. Sunday the fifteenth it is."

Mallory wrote the date in pen in her calendar. This was one event she refused to alter. "I'll go ahead and confirm the reservations," she said, but then didn't quite know what else to say. *Can we get together tonight, too?* Too pushy. *I miss you in bed.* Too needy. *How about a simple, "I miss you"?*

That one took more courage than she had.

Silence thundered on the phone lines. Finally, Cliff said, "I guess I'd better get back to work."

"Yeah. Me, too." But she didn't hang up. "Cliff?"

"Yes?"

"Is it always going to be like this between us? Having to schedule things weeks in advance just to see each other's face?"

She'd blurted out the question before she had time to consider how he might react—or even how she would react. She had the convenient affair she'd wanted—didn't she? No strings to mess up her work schedule. No recriminations. No ugly scenes.

But not much sex, either.

"I don't know, Mallory. I guess we have other priorities right now than each other."

"Of course. You're right. I'm just…tired."

"You'll call me, though, if you ever need me, won't you? For anything?"

Sure. And the next time you have a free moment—say, sometime next October—I'm sure you'll do your best to help. The bitter upwelling took Mallory by surprise. But she stifled the comment before it could spill out. "No problem, Cliff. You too. If you need anything, I mean."

"Yeah. Me too." After the briefest of pauses, Cliff said a simple goodbye and hung up the phone.

But as Mallory slowly lowered the receiver, she

stared bitterly at her jam-packed calendar. How could this affair possibly be considered a convenience when simply finding a mutually agreeable time and place to get together took a logistics specialist?

Still, next Sunday would clear things up between them. She and Cliff would have a wonderful time and they'd both end up feeling better. He hadn't been disappointed in her, nor was he angry or upset. He was simply being himself—an overworked, driven man struggling to rise to the top of his chosen career. His ambition sometimes meant that personal issues and relationships occasionally fell by the wayside in life—for a time, anyway.

But it was just temporary. It didn't mean he didn't care about her or their relationship. It merely meant he was exactly the man she thought he was.

He was, in fact, just like her.

6

A WEEK LATER Cliff smashed the ball against the back wall of the handball court and stepped back so Todd could take a swipe. Though his stroke was as hard as ever, Cliff's heart and soul weren't in the regular Friday afternoon game.

He needed a heart-to-heart with his best friend.

Unfortunately, Todd, perhaps scenting a rare victory, was concentrating more on returning Cliff's killer serves than responding to Cliff's tentative overtures.

"Didja see that? What a great save! I'm finally gonna win one from you, good buddy."

"Sure you will." Cliff sent the ball on another ricochet around the court. "Todd, I wanted to ask you something."

"Pleading for mercy already?" Todd smashed the ball back, but it took an unfortunate bounce off the corner, deadening its flight. "Damn."

Easily, Cliff captured the ball and held on to it.

He'd never get Todd's attention as long as they were playing. "You win," he declared.

"What? What's going on?"

"I'm calling it quits. You win. I lose."

"But, but—"

"Look, Todd, I need to talk to you, okay?"

"Well, sure. But you didn't need to concede the game just to talk."

"Yes, I did," Cliff said grimly. "This is serious."

With a penetrating glance, Todd shut up. They gathered their equipment bags and let themselves out of the court, heading for the locker room.

"What's up, Cliff?" Todd finally asked as they started to undress for the shower.

Now that he had his friend's attention, Cliff hardly knew where to begin. There were some issues he needed to discuss, but client confidentiality was also a problem. He couldn't give even his best buddy any details of the dilemma he faced.

"Is it about that babe you had over at your place a couple of Sundays ago?" Todd asked. "Listen, I'm sorry I interrupted."

"Don't worry. You weren't a problem." No, the only problem with Mallory was himself. Though he'd walked around all week in a near-continual state of frustration, he was starting to worry seriously. He'd hardly been at his finest while racing her pager, and though she'd apparently had a great time bowling, she'd still sent him to his own bed—alone.

You're obsessing about her—and you have other issues to deal with! Cut it out! Resolutely, he started undressing while he focused on his other big problem, the one that had led him to seek Todd's advice.

Todd shoved his handball shorts and T-shirt into his gym bag and grabbed a towel. "Sure sounds like *something's* wrong, buddy. What is it?"

Naked except for the towel wrapped around his waist, Cliff sank onto the bench in front of his locker. "I'm in a situation at work," he said slowly. "I can't be too specific."

"Yeah. Client confidentiality." Todd sat down too. "So what can you tell me?"

Cliff rubbed his hand along his jaw. "The bottom-line issue is that I don't really approve of how one of our cases is being handled."

Actually, he totally disagreed with the defense team's plan. Because so much evidence strongly indicated their client's guilt, the attorneys had come up with a strategy that attacked the personal life of the police detective investigating the case. If they could change the focus of the jury's attention to the policeman's situation instead of the murder case itself, they believed their client might be acquitted.

"One of your cases?" Todd asked.

"Well...not exactly. One of the firm's cases."

Cliff still hoped to be assigned to the Bartlett defense team, but despite his hard work supporting the partners who were the primary attorneys, so far he hadn't officially been named an associate on the case. And though he was uneasy with the defense plans, the case would certainly be a career-maker.

Todd grinned and stood. "If it's not your client, then it's not your problem."

"Yes, but—"

"No buts about it, buddy. I take it that one of the senior partners is running the case?"

"Yes."

"Then all the more reason for you to keep out of it. Never bite the hand that hands out promotions—and partnerships."

Dammit. Cliff knew his friend was right. Sheer common sense told him not to argue with the boss when trying to get that same boss to approve him for a plum position—and eventually name him to a partnership.

Still…he grabbed an antacid from his bag and slowly followed Todd toward the showers. The chalky taste of the tablet concentrated his attention while he pondered what to do. Sunday was only two days away. He would see Mallory then. Maybe she'd have some words of wisdom on this issue. At the very least, getting away with her—even for a day—seemed like a really good idea.

His stomach churning despite the tablet, he showered and dressed, then reluctantly walked from the athletic club back to his office three blocks away. Piles of work awaited him, not to mention another gut-twisting Bartlett strategy meeting. Absently, he pulled out another antacid tablet and chewed it in a preemptive move. His steps dragged, and he realized he was counting the hours until he could escape his no-win situation and be alone with Mallory.

MALLORY SAT ACROSS the damask-draped restaurant table from her fluttery mother and wondered why she'd bothered to fly half the length of the state to meet her. It was always difficult to break through her mother's "the Eminent Dr. Adelaide Reissen" persona to reach the woman underneath, and it was generally such a futile effort, most of the time Mallory didn't bother trying.

So far, the luncheon conversation had centered around her mother's anthropological digs, departmental politics in the small but prestigious New England university where her mother worked, and the truly excellent attributes of Peter Jonassen.

Mallory's initial curiosity about her mother's possible relationship with Professor Jonassen had yielded to an odd combination of certainty that Adelaide indeed was having an affair, and a dispassionate, who-cares attitude that startled her more than any insight into her mother's possible love life. Granted, she was hardly her mother's confidante, and her parent's relationship—or lack of one—was none of her business at this stage in her life. But shouldn't she feel, well, *something?*

She was so engrossed in puzzlement over her own cold-blooded view of the situation that she almost missed Adelaide's abrupt change of subject.

"—but I've been boring you, haven't I, dear? Besides, I'm sure you agree with me about the utter *egotism* of grad students these days. Things were different when I was younger, let me tell you."

Mallory smiled and nodded, the only reaction Adelaide needed. In common with many brilliant people, her mother had little use for opinions differing from her own.

"...I wanted to tell you why I asked to meet you, dear. Of course, it's always a pleasure to lunch with you, but I'm so *busy* these days that... Anyway, I was talking with your father a few weeks ago—did I tell you that his concerts are getting absolutely *brilliant* reviews? Well, he called me from Prague—or was it Belgrade? These international telephone connections are so bad, you know...."

Mallory smiled, nodded, and crumbled another bite of roll. A sip of the crisp Chardonnay helped her focus on her mother's digressions. Adelaide would get to the point eventually.

Mallory's attention drifted again to the subject of her mother's probable affair. Was this the first one? No, surely not. It couldn't be. She was far too casual about it. How had Mallory lived nearly twenty-eight years and not realized that her parents' marriage was so flawed? Or had she subconsciously known all along?

The effort of swallowing a bitter laugh burned her throat. That question was easily answered: What with all those nannies and boarding schools, Mallory had seen so little of her parents while growing up that they could have had regular Tuesday-night orgies and she wouldn't have known anything about it.

One thing was certain, though. Mallory knew that her children, if she ever had any, would be raised by her and not some nanny. And she'd make sure they had a daddy who'd be there for them. Mallory would rather have no family at all than subject her children to the chilly upbringing that she'd experienced.

Was that why she was so unwilling to focus on anything except her career? The thought frightened her. Maybe her career-is-all attitude arose because she was afraid any attempt to combine work and family would leave her family floundering as she had.

Looking back, the only truly family time she could remember from her childhood were the precious weeks of summer vacation visiting her—

"—Grandmother Lawrence, dear. You do remember my telling you about it, I hope?"

Startled by the mention of the very person she'd been thinking of, Mallory blinked, then said, "I'm sorry, Mother. I was woolgathering. What did you say?"

Fingers stained brown from the sun tapped irritably on the table. "I said that when your father called a few weeks ago, he reminded me about your legacy from Grandmother Lawrence. I told you about it, I'm sure."

"Legacy? From Gramma?"

"Yes. When she died you were still a child, of course, so it's been in trust for quite some time. Till your majority of course, and then... It's not much, I'm afraid. At least not financially."

Mallory thought about that for at least fifteen seconds. "Mother, I'm twenty-eight. Shouldn't I have been told about this before now?" She strove to keep her voice patient and low.

But her mother shrugged. "Really, Mallory, it's been well taken care of. Your father and I have made good arrangements. We've both been so busy, you know, and we never quite got around to telling you. It's only that huge old house up in Sunfield. When your grandmother died, we hired a cleaning service to pack up all her things and store them for you, and a management company to rent the place out. They kept good tenants, at least until now.'' She leaned forward and dropped her voice to state-secret levels. ''Now that the senior man of the management firm has retired, I'm afraid the company has really gone downhill.''

''But...''

Her mother steamrolled over her protest. ''The trust was supposed to last until you were of an age to look after it yourself. Well, your father received some notice from the property manager recently, and when we discussed it, we realized that we really should simply turn things over to you and let you handle it. It's been quite a drain on our time all these years, you know.''

Mallory's mouth opened and closed twice. She'd never realized her grandmother had left her property. The house—her house!—was in Sunfield, a little town in the foothills of the Sierras, deep in the heart of California's Gold Country. Slowly, she forced her attention back to her mother's words. But while she accepted a folder of papers and a key ring from her mother, one thought kept drumming through her brain. She owned her grandmother's house! The one place in the world where she had been happy and contented. She *owned* it!

Only when she was waiting for her flight back to San Diego to board did she remember that though she might own a house in the Sierras, her career was likely to whisk her permanently to New York City.

ALL THROUGH THE short drive up the coast to the posh resort on Sunday evening, Cliff wondered how he could ever-so-casually raise the subject of his problems at work. He glanced quickly at Mallory, then returned his gaze to the heavy end-of-weekend traffic. Last-minute delays had ruined their intended midday departure.

"How was your visit with your mother?" *Well, that really got the conversation moving in the direction you wanted, didn't it?* If he hadn't been driving, he'd have slapped his palm against his forehead in frustration.

But Mallory had taken his tentative question as a signal to talk about her trip. She swiveled in her seat, making the silky skirt of her sundress swirl above her knees. "Fine. You know, it was the oddest thing. I couldn't figure out why my mother had been so insistent that I meet her."

Only half listening to her, he nodded. How could he bring up the subject he really wanted to discuss?

Mallory, I've got a problem at work. Nope. Might destroy her faith in him as a go-getting success story.

Got any advice for an up-and-coming attorney? Ditto.

Mallory, can we talk? No way! Too gossip-show.

In fact, every single opening line he came up with seemed to show him in a less than wonderful light. Surely any really competent guy should be able to handle a minor conflict with his boss—right? The acid taste in his mouth burned downward into his stomach. Automatically, he reached for the now ever-present roll of antacid tablets.

Did having an affair of convenience include listening to each other's professional sob stories? Regretfully, he shook his head slightly. Maybe not. Maybe sharing too much with her would only drive her further away. On the other hand, some women loved to think themselves important to a man. Was she one of them? He glanced speculatively at her and gave another tentative nod. She might be one of them....

"Was that a yes or a no?" Mallory's amused tone jerked him out of his reverie.

"What?" Had she asked one of those sneaky *relationship* questions? Hell's bells. What had he missed? He'd learned long ago that the only recourse a man had in such a situation was to apologize quickly—even if he wasn't sure for what. "I'm sorry, Mallory. I was thinking about something else. What did you ask me?"

She patted him on the knee and he stifled a relieved sigh. He'd guessed right. Dealing with women could be tricky, all right.

"You're not listening to me, are you?"

Oh, no. The worst possible accusation! "Of course I am! I've heard every word." What had she said? Beginning to panic, he reran his mental tape of her conversation. "You said something about the reason your mother asked you to meet her for lunch."

"That's right. You see…"

His mind drifted off as she explained about some small legacy her grandmother had left her. Making sure he responded often enough to keep her talking, he retreated again. He really wanted to talk about the situation at work—a lot. He'd love to get her take on what he should do. But the could-he, should-he, would-he doubts were eating at his confidence.

By the time they'd checked into the resort and had been shown to a truly luxurious private cottage, those doubts had grown so large they could have stomped Godzilla into the ground. He shifted his shoulders uncomfortably, trying to ease the knot of muscles that had taken up permanent residence between his shoulder blades. It seemed so tight he doubted a two-week stay in the resort's massage room could loosen it. And that didn't even include the pounding headache that threatened to redefine the word *torture* for him. All symptoms of tension, he knew.

Somewhere on that drive north, he'd given up discussing his work dilemma with Mallory, he realized. Now, all he wanted to do was hide his unusual lack of decisiveness from her. He simply couldn't bring himself to admit his self-doubts and failings to a woman he so deeply admired for her own career skills.

Besides, they hadn't planned this excursion as a way for him to dump his problems on her. No, he was going to prove to her that he could be the sensitive, caring lover she deserved. After their first romantic fiasco and their near miss with the bowling, he had a reputation to live up to—if only one in his own mind.

It had been days since he'd so much as caught a glimpse of her coming and going, and it was more than time they got their long-anticipated affair off the ground. Hadn't he promised to give her the sexual satisfaction she wanted? Ruefully he admitted that if he was feeling deprived, she must be feeling downright neglected.

At the thought, his head throbbed harder and his stomach churned even more. Automatically, he reached for another antacid pill, only to find the roll empty.

"They've done a beautiful job with these cottages, haven't they?" Mallory was still inspecting their accommodations. "Have you noticed the bathroom? It's got a huge Jacuzzi in it."

"That's good."

"I thought I'd put in a wake-up call for tomorrow

morning. I've got to be at the station early. Is six-thirty all right with you?"

"Sure. Uh, Mallory? Wasn't there a small shop by the registration desk?"

"Yes." Her brows arched in surprise. "Why?"

"I forgot something and I don't want to have to run out to a drugstore."

She smiled. "Don't worry." She dug into her small bag, bringing out an unopened box of condoms. An extra-large box, he noticed. "I brought them. I knew you've been very busy this week and thought you might forget."

Cliff sucked in a deep breath. The pressure building inside him cranked up another notch. "That's good. But I ran out of antacids and my stomach is bothering me."

"Oh." Her brow pleated in concern. "You're having a lot of stomach problems, aren't you? Have you had your doctor check for an ulcer?"

He shook his head and backed toward the door. "I'm okay. But work is pretty stressful right now. It sometimes interferes with my digestion. Once this case is over, I'll be fine."

"If you say so," she said doubtfully.

But as Cliff's shaking hands plunked down an exorbitant price for the precious rolls of antacids from the resort gift and sundry store, he worried even more about pleasuring Mallory when his mind and body seemed to be functioning on altogether different tracks.

"OH, GOD, Mallory, I'm sorry." Cliff squirmed in the bed beside her. "This has never happened to me before."

Mallory rolled over and surveyed her embarrassed lover with a speculative expression. She propped her chin on her hands. "Cliff, it's all right. It doesn't matter."

He glared at her. "If you dare say it's no big thing—"

She couldn't help herself. A giggle—it was definitely a giggle—bubbled up. Hastily she primmed her mouth. "I would never say that. But it doesn't matter."

He groaned and put his forearm over his brow. "I'm in bed with one of the most desirable women I've ever met. She's smart. She's charming. She wants me. And I can't..."

"Appreciate your good fortune?"

"I just *can't,* all right?"

Mallory cuddled against him and put her head on his shoulder. Automatically, his arm curved around her side, pulling her closer. "Cliff, I'm the one who should apologize. You've been upset ever since we left home, haven't you?"

A soft grunt acknowledged her point.

"And I just sat in the car and chattered. I hardly let you get a word in edgewise."

Another soft grunt. But she noticed that some of the tension seeped out of his arm.

"Cliff, looking back it's obvious you had something you wanted to talk about. And I never gave you a chance. I'm sorry."

A long moment passed, marked only by the thudding of his heart against her cheek. Finally, he said, "Look, Mallory. Our affair was just for kicks, right? It wasn't meant for me to dump my troubles on you."

She sat up and punched him in the arm just hard enough to get his attention. Sure enough, that concealing forearm dropped, and he sat up and stared at her. "What was that for?"

"How dare you imply that I'm only interested in your body!"

"But that's what we agreed—"

"Maybe so, but I seem to remember someone who went out of his way to go beyond that for me. I remember a guy who listened to me rattle on about my hopes with the network job. A guy who made sure I felt genuinely desired when I got a little nervous the first time he kissed me. A guy who even took me bowling to help me forget a hellacious day. Does that sound like anyone you recognize?"

He blinked. "Well, yeah. I guess."

"So why should you think all that caring should go one direction only? Why should you have to do all that for me, while I do nothing for you?" She paused. "Look, Cliff. Just because we're only having an affair doesn't mean we can't care about each other, does it? Because if it does—if it does, I think I'd rather just have your friendship back again and forget the sex."

He blinked again, then a slow smile dawned. "You really aren't disappointed, are you?"

"Yes, I am. I'm disappointed that you thought you had to ignore your own problems just to keep me happy. I'm disappointed in myself for not being perceptive enough to realize that you're completely stressed out. And, yes, I'm disappointed that we're not going to be able to make love tonight." She leaned closer and cupped his face with her hands. "But there's no way I'm disappointed in *you*. Do you understand?"

"Yes, ma'am. Got it."

"Good." She lay down and pulled him beside her, settling back into a comforting cuddle. "So, why don't you tell me about whatever is making you eat antacids like popcorn? Maybe we can come up with some ideas to help solve the problem."

But though she paid strict attention to his careful explanation of the uncomfortable situation at work, one tiny corner of her mind contemplated what had just happened. Had she really told him she'd rather have his friendship than his lovemaking? And if so, whatever had happened to her determination to have a relationship that was purely physical, with none of the messy complications emotional ties always produced?

And why didn't she care that this affair that was supposed to be so physically satisfying and convenient for them both, had somehow transmuted into a relationship that was neither satisfying nor convenient?

7

CLIFF WOKE TO A feeling of restful contentment and with Mallory's warm body snuggled against him. For the first time in weeks he'd actually slept the night through. They'd talked long into the night—actually, he'd done most of the talking. Without getting into specifics, he'd managed to explain enough of his work dilemma for Mallory to offer some suggestions for how he might cope with it—beginning with scheduling a meeting with his boss as soon as he got back to the office.

To his surprise, he didn't feel upset or threatened by her knowing he was having problems with his career. She'd shared a few of her own harrowing job experiences, even admitting that she'd handled a couple of situations badly in earlier years.

Yup, having a woman he could really talk to as well as make love to was turning out to have all kinds of benefits.

That thought reminded him that they hadn't actually made love last night. He lay very still while he mentally checked himself out. Stomach okay? Not a sign of the churning pain he'd become so familiar with. Arms and legs? Nicely tangled with their female equivalents. Heart? Thumping out a heavy rhythm against the feminine palm draped over his chest. Mood? Relaxed, affectionate, definitely interested.

Horny, even.

As he began to stir and harden, he decided he really preferred early-morning love to the late-night kind, anyway. So what if he hadn't managed to do his part last night? This morning was another day, and based on what he was feeling now, it was time to give them both a little early-morning exercise.

Smiling with lecherous intent, he leaned over Mallory's sleeping face and nibbled delicately at her ear. "Mallory? Honey? You awake?"

"Mmmmph." But she turned toward his seeking lips.

Ever obliging, he changed his focus to her mouth. "Wake up, honey."

This time her response was slightly more verbal. "Don' wanna. Havin' a good dream."

His smile deepened. He bet he knew exactly what she was dreaming about. Especially since her arms had looped around his neck. "You'll miss some good stuff if you don't wake up."

One sleep-glazed eye popped open. "How good?" she asked suspiciously.

"*Really* good."

The other eye opened. "You promise?"

Deliberately, he let his lower body press against her so she could feel his burgeoning erection. "What do you think?"

Sleep melted from her eyes as she smiled contentedly. "I think I wouldn't want to miss anything that good."

Slowly, taking his time, he started to arouse her. It was fun discovering all his favorite places to linger on her body. They all smelled of Mallory's own heady aroma—light, yet musky; sweet, but definitely sensual. His heartbeat kicked into overdrive as he caressed and teased, tickled and soothed. And could there be anything headier than having her respond with equal heat? Or feeling her hands explore his own body? Or tasting her mouth with his? Or hearing her breathy gasps mixed with an urgent ringing. Why, he could almost hear bells...

Bells?

He froze. "Tell me that's not what I think it is."

Solemnly, she stared up at him, disappointment fogging over the arousal in her eyes. After a long moment, awareness kicked in and she groaned. "You did agree that we needed a wake-up call this morning."

The phone kept ringing.

With rueful intent, he said, "The next time I agree to anything so silly, I want you to kick me—hard." He reached over and grabbed the phone.

An obnoxiously sunny voice declared, "Good morning. This is your wake-up call. The time is six-thirty-two."

"Right," he groused. Clattering the phone back onto its rest, he stared at Mallory. "Where do they get these improbably cheerful people, anyway?"

She rolled out of bed, leaving him with only a lingering, wistful memory and the tempting sight of her, wrapped in the sheet, as she headed for the closet to grab some clothes. "I'll be out of the bath as soon as I can. I want to be at the station by eight."

"It'd be quicker if we shared," he offered, still with the faint hope of finishing what he'd started.

She looked at him over her shoulder, looking so adorably tousled that it was all he could do not to sweep her back into bed. "You're joking, right? If we shared, we'd still be here at noon—tomorrow."

Her words soothed his battered ego. The fates were conspiring against them, that was for sure. But with the determination of a man who had almost achieved nirvana, he vowed that this was the last time he would let the outside world interfere with his lovemaking with Mallory.

The very last time.

"WE NEVER SEEM to get a break, do we?" Cliff slickly maneuvered the car around someone determined to drive at sixty-five in the high-speed lane. Everyone else was breaking seventy. Despite their best intentions, it was after seven-thirty and Mallory hadn't yet made it to the station. Early-morning traffic tie-ups on Interstate 5 had sabotaged them. Having finally reached an open stretch of freeway, Cliff was taking advantage of it.

"No, we don't," she said. "Maybe someone's trying to tell us something."

"Like what?"

"Like maybe this affair idea wasn't such a good one." She swiveled in her seat as much as her seat belt would allow. "Cliff, we've been interrupted more times than a late-night movie has commercials. Maybe I was right the first time when I said that we should both just give up on having a relationship with anyone until after we're more established in our careers."

He glanced at her. "But I don't want to wait."

"Neither do I—but aren't you beginning to see a pattern?"

"What I'm seeing is that we need some serious time together. When we're at either of our condos, the phone and our pagers constantly interrupt. When we try to get away for a night, I bring enough of my work pressures with me that it interferes."

"So what's your conclusion, Counselor? That we should give up on each other and find partners without so many career demands?"

"No!" Cliff paused, not exactly sure himself where he was leading. Wherever it was, he was sure it didn't involve giving up Mallory—or having her start a relationship with someone else! Finally, he said slowly, "I think we need to make our relationship a priority, at least until we're comfortable with each other. Maybe go away somewhere without any phones or pagers or wake-up calls."

The look on her face was odd, closed, protecting her thoughts as she mulled over his suggestion. He had no idea what she was thinking. All he could really tell was that he'd surprised her. Hell, for that matter, he'd surprised himself! Never had he expected to tell any woman that being with her was a higher priority than his career.

But I didn't mean we have to upset our priorities forever—only for right now. It's just until we can get this affair off the ground. Once we've established ourselves in our own minds as a couple, we can settle down to a comfortable time together. And our lives— my life—will be back on track.

Yeah, that was it. They only needed perhaps a week or two together, long enough to scratch the itch that was driving him crazy, work that first urgent rush for each other out of their systems so they could concentrate on other, more important things. Once that driving need had been satisfied, he was sure they'd both be contented with occasional meetings when they could synchronize their schedules.

After all, that's the way they'd planned it in the first place. He had a career to manage and she had a network to impress.

He'd almost forgotten that she hadn't responded to his suggestion when she spoke up. "What exactly are you suggesting?"

"Hell, I don't know. Maybe that we need to plan a getaway together—someplace where no one can get to us and we can truly be alone." Inspiration struck. "How about up in Julian?" The small gold-mining community in the mountains about an hour east of San Diego had transformed itself into a tourist mecca, popular for locals who simply wanted to get away from the daily grind for a while.

He still couldn't figure out what she was thinking. She'd make a damned good poker player. "How long are you talking about for this getaway?"

"Two weeks?" he suggested.

"Two weeks? Are you nuts? Sweeps month is coming up in a few weeks. And did you forget that I'm still waiting on the network's decision to schedule an interview with me? There's no way I can get away for that long." She paused. "Maybe I could do another overnight or something, but..."

"Not enough time. Look what happened this time." His vague gesture encompassed their all-too-frustrating stay at the resort. "No, we'd need at least a week together."

She crossed her arms over her chest. "I don't see how I can be out of touch for a whole week."

Cliff reached over and took her hand. "Mallory, don't you think what we have is worth fighting for? Once we're settled in together, it's going to be great. I promise."

Her face softened but her voice didn't give quarter. "Seems to me you promised me something great for this morning, too."

He ignored that. "Give me a weekend. A long weekend together. We'll leave Friday morning, come back Monday morning. No pagers allowed. We won't tell anyone where we're going. It's only for one weekend. You can arrange that much time off, can't you?"

Slowly, she nodded. "A long weekend. I'll clear my calendar starting this Friday, all right?"

Second thoughts reared, reminding Cliff of his own schedule, crammed full of not-to-be-missed appointments. Ruthlessly, he shoved them aside. "Next weekend it is. I'll make reservations and we'll leave bright and early Friday morning. And don't forget we won't be back until late Monday."

Solemnly, they shook hands on their new deal.

THE PHONE IN Mallory's office rang with an insistent chirp. Despite the week's ill-omened start, she'd made it to Thursday without any serious problems. She'd managed to beg off work for Friday and had cleared her schedule. Of course, next week would be a bear because she'd have to cram in all Friday and Monday's appointments too, but she could live with that inconvenience for the sake of finally having Cliff all to herself.

The phone chirped again and Mallory picked it up.

"Mallory! It's me, Lenny."

As if she could ever mistake that booming voice. "Hi, Lenny. Everything going okay with you?"

He chuckled his I-know-something-you-don't chuckle. "Great, in fact. Hey, Mallory, what're you doing tomorrow?"

Oh, no. "Actually, I'm taking the day off." She took a deep breath. "Why?"

"That's wonderful! You always did have the most perfect timing." He paused for effect, making her ask.

"Okay, Lenny. Lay it on me. Why do you care what I do with my Friday?"

"Because, my favorite-client-of-all, tomorrow is the day the network honchos are coming to San Diego to meet with you personally."

"What?" Mallory's breath started coming in brief, gasping pants.

"You heard me. I got a call this morning. All of a sudden they've changed their minds about putting you off and decided they want to see you—now."

"But...but..." Her mind spinning with possibilities, she tried to figure out what this change of plan might mean. "Do you think they're serious about me? Give it to me straight, Lenny. Are they just jerking our chains?"

"Cross my heart and hope to have to eat cold hot dogs, this is the real thing. I think their negotiations with someone else fell through and they've decided to see what they've been missing in you."

"I don't know what to say."

"Just say you'll clear your calendar for tomorrow and be prepared to knock these guys' socks off."

Mallory stared down at her organizer notebook and flipped the pages to reach the one for Friday. Several appointments had been written in, but each had already been rescheduled to various days next week.

"My calendar's already cleared," she said slowly. The words "Julian with Cliff," stared up at her accusingly. When she'd arrived at the office on Monday she'd written them in herself in bright red ink. Usually she noted appointments in pencil, but for this one she'd used ink, convinced that nothing at all could make her change her plans.

"Perfect!" Lenny burbled in her ear. "You're to

meet them at eight o'clock for breakfast at the U.S. Grant Hotel downtown—you know where that is?''

"Lenny—'' Was she really going to—?

"They said you should plan to spend the day with them—and maybe into Saturday, too. This is going to be a real, in-depth discussion of their plans for the show and how you might fit in with what they want.''

"Lenny—''

"Trust me, kiddo, you'll do fine. I want you to wear that black suit you have—you know the one. It's a smasher and it'll show them you're a real classy lady.''

Mallory listened to Lenny rattle on about how to prepare for the meeting. What was she going to do? This was the chance of a lifetime for her. Surely Cliff would understand—wouldn't he? They could go away together another weekend. In fact, if this offer came through, she really would clear a whole week so she could devote herself just to enjoying some private time with him.

And then you'll leave him for the bright lights of New York.

"You got all that, Mallory?'' Lenny's voice showed a trace of anxiety, probably because she hadn't responded.

"Yes.'' She took a deep breath, ready to commit

herself. "Lenny, I'm thrilled that you managed to arrange this for me."

"I know, I know. I'm the best agent you've got, right? But you're okay with this, right?" His anxiety was increasing.

Her hand pressed over her heart, as if to control the thumping there. She opened her mouth to give him the reassurance he needed and the words popped out. "Lenny, I can't meet with them tomorrow."

Ohmigod. Ohmigod. Ohmigod. What did I just say?

Dead silence rang in her ears.

"What did you say?" Obviously, he didn't believe it either.

Now that she'd said it once, it was easier to repeat it. "I said, I can't meet them Friday—or Saturday. I have something else I have to do. It's very important to me."

"More important than getting an anchor spot on a prime-time network-news magazine? What's more important than that?"

Being alone with my lover. "Lenny, I can't explain. You know I wouldn't blow a meeting like this off unless I absolutely had to, don't you? Believe me, this is something I *have* to do."

She knew Lenny well enough to know he was busily twisting paper clips into useless knots. It was his favorite pastime when one of his clients frustrated him with their irrationality.

She heard him take several long, deep breaths. When he spoke, his voice was dark and serious. "Mallory, you're not sick are you? You're not going into the hospital or anything, right?"

His genuine concern for her warmed her cold hands. "No, Lenny, it's nothing like that. But I've already made a commitment for this weekend and I really can't break it. This is such short notice. I mean, Friday is *tomorrow*. Surely these guys will understand that my schedule is already full, and we can get together next week sometime?"

"Mallory, you don't seem to understand. These guys are coming to San Diego to see you. Everyone else they talked to had to go to them." His voice pleaded with her to reconsider. "How often do you get network guys knocking on your door?"

But those bright red words on her calendar wouldn't release her from her commitment to Cliff. She knew he needed the time away with her as much as she did. Sunday night's disaster had been a huge embarrassment for him—for any man—and she blamed herself for much of it. Her lack of sensitivity to his emotional state had only exacerbated his stress. She simply couldn't let him down again.

"Lenny, I can't do it. Call them back and see if they'll reschedule for another time." Rapidly she flipped through her calendar. ''Tell them any other time this month will do—I'll clear my calendar for them if they give me forty-eight hours notice. *But I can't see them this weekend.*''

''But—''

''We're wasting time, Lenny. I'm not going to change my mind. Please, just ask them to reschedule and let me know what they say. Please.''

Her agent was disgruntled, but eventually agreed. Mallory sat for a long time staring at her organizer, wondering what madness had made her sacrifice everything she'd been working toward for the sake of a far-from-simple affair.

8

_____

"ALONE AT LAST." Cliff uttered the heartfelt cliché with a sigh of relief. "You know, there were times I didn't think we'd make it here."

Mallory glanced at him as she dumped her overnight bag on a chair. Cliff had borrowed a small getaway home from a friend. It consisted of only a bedroom, a living area, and a small kitchen, and was nestled in the mountains within a half mile of Julian's short main street. Best of all, it had no phone service, though both the plumbing and electricity were fully operational.

"I know what you mean," she said. "But we're here. Pagerless. Phoneless. And, as far as I know, absolutely no one knows where we are."

He dumped the last of their various bags and provisions on the battered wooden table that served as both kitchen work area and dining table. "Did you have any trouble clearing your schedule?"

Mallory hesitated. She hadn't mentioned her agent's urgent call yesterday to Cliff for reasons she wasn't quite able to articulate, even to herself. "No," she said slowly, "not any more than I expected. How about you?"

He stuffed some perishables into the ancient refrigerator before answering. "Same here." Having successfully completed his task, he turned to her. "So. What would you like to do first?"

Involuntarily, her gaze focused on the doorway that led to the bedroom. She'd already checked it out and discovered the only truly luxurious piece of furniture in the entire cabin—a king-size bed covered with a fluffy comforter and a pile of soft pillows.

When their eyes met again, Cliff knew he'd been right to insist on this private getaway. Slowly, wanting to savor every second, he walked over to her. "It's time, isn't it?"

She never broke his gaze. "Yes," she said softly. "More than time."

But he had one more worry. "Mallory, this is what you want, too—isn't it?"

"Did you think I've changed my mind?" A smile licked the corners of her mouth, tilting it upwards just enough to entice.

"I haven't been sure. So many things have gone wrong between us. I thought maybe you were disappointed, or maybe just—"

"Shhh." Her fingers covered his mouth. "We went through that before."

His hands settled naturally at her waist, like a nesting bird settling into a well-hollowed space. "God knows I don't want to talk about it any more. But I don't want you to feel rushed."

He saw her smile widen first in those bluebell eyes. "I don't feel rushed. If anything, I feel like maybe I was right the first time."

"Right? About what?" He was memorizing her face. The tiny mole beside her left eyebrow, usually covered with makeup. The slightly asymmetrical arch of her eyebrows. The welcome in her smile.

"When I said you lawyers were all talk, no action." She looped her arms around his neck. "Why don't we forget all the what-ifs and maybes and just do what we came here to do?"

And though his arms tightened around her, Cliff couldn't quite let go of his worry. "This is going to be special. I'm going to make it special for you." He intended his words as a vow.

Only when he led her into the curtain-shadowed bedroom did she answer, a response that left him breathless. "Don't you understand, Cliff? It's already special because it's with you."

SHADOWS AND LIGHT permeated the room, glistening briefly on a gracefully feminine arm here, a sensuously tensed shoulder there. Their first moves were slow, tentative. Cliff helped Mallory undress, taking his time, treasuring each revelation. Then Mallory did the same, bestowing lingering caresses on his arms, chest, legs.

By the time they lay on that enormous, voluptuous bed, he'd forgotten why he had fretted so about his ability to please her. She was the most intensely responsive lover he'd ever had. Alone with him, protected from interruptions, she displayed a sensual enjoyment of his lovemaking that was utterly erotic.

He quickly forgot his worry that she would find him—or the circumstances—unsatisfactory yet again. Instead, he concentrated on drawing out both their pleasure, needing more than anything to demonstrate to her how very much he wanted her—and how much he wanted her to want him.

Wanting him didn't seem to be a problem. With her lips kissed to a rosy glow and the gleam of arousal in her eyes, she responded to his every movement. Sometimes she initiated her own arousing caresses, sometimes she followed his sensual lead as they rediscovered the age-old, ever-changing dance of completion. Her lips traced the outline of his body as ardently as his traced hers. Her hands touched and probed and explored with delight, just as he reveled in his explorations of her. Her body melded itself to his with eager passion that wordlessly conveyed her own pleasure.

And when he entered her, he thought he'd come home.

No, it was better than coming home. He lay for long, thundering heartbeats, buried deep inside her, half-afraid any movement would shatter this unbelievable sensation of utter *rightness*. He'd never experienced anything like it. In Mallory's arms he felt truly loved and wanted.

With his heart thumping out a drumbeat of desire, he slowly began to move, guiding Mallory's hips to his rhythm. He watched her face intently, waiting for the first signs of her release. Only when she called his name in a hoarse moan and he felt her quivering response surround him did he allow his own passion to erupt into a climax that splintered him into a million shards, then, somehow, amazingly, made him whole again.

"WAS IT GOOD FOR YOU?" Mallory's husky, teasing words feathered over his shoulder in sleepy humor.

He'd just managed to catch his breath from their latest bout of Olympic-class sex. If this kept up, he'd be dead by Sunday night. Ecstatic, but dead.

"Couldn't you tell?" Idly, he stroked her arm, tracing the muscles from shoulder to wrist. "If it was any better, I'd have died and gone to heaven." He paused. "What about for you?"

She must have sensed that his query wasn't made

in jest, but her voice was laced with satiated humor. "I *did* die and go to heaven. Didn't you see me sprouting my wings?"

"Wings, huh?" He ran his hands over her shoulder blades. He just couldn't stop stroking her skin, as smooth and warm as molasses left out in the sun. "I don't feel any feathers."

"That's because they all fell off when you dragged me back to earth."

"Dragged? I figured it was you dragging me. Weren't those your hands clutching my butt?"

She giggled, letting her breath tickle his cheek. "Caught. I guess I'll have to throw myself on the mercy of the court. Again."

He adopted a judicial frown and nestled her more firmly against him. "Well, Ms. Reissen, since this is your second offense, I'll have to be more strict with you. I sentence you..."

Suddenly, she rolled over, landing full length on top of him. "Sentence me to what?"

"Ahem. Young lady, what exactly do you think you're doing?" It was hell trying to maintain a properly judicious attitude with a naked nymph undulating against him.

"Throwing myself on your mercy?" She wriggled into a more intimate position.

"That's not my 'mercy' you're on."

"Oh. Well...it'll do, won't it?"

"Yes," he gasped as her squirming enticed his flagging body back into life. "It'll definitely *do*."

BUT THEY COULDN'T make love all the time. Eventually they decided to get out and enjoy their stay in Julian. After a hilarious shared shower and quickly made sandwiches eaten at the rickety table, they wandered outside. The day was perfect for mid-April. Bright blue skies domed over a forest rich with the scent of pine trees and resurgent spring growth. Delicate mountain wildflowers painted sheltered corners with purples and pinks and blues. And on nearly every sun-splashed bank, hordes of yellow daffodils proudly waved in the breeze from bulbs originally planted but now allowed to spread in wild profusion.

"It reminds me of my grandmother's home," Mallory commented as they walked contentedly into Julian's minuscule downtown area. "She lived up in the Sierras, and every spring her yard had tons of wildflowers blossoming everywhere."

Cliff looked at her curiously. "I had the impression that you were raised back east, not in the mountains of California."

She turned to stare into the antiques displayed in a store window. "Mostly I was in boarding schools. My parents were always busy with their careers, so that was the easiest option."

He sensed something more behind her careful explanation. Delicately, he probed. "Easiest for whom? Them? Or you?"

She tossed her head, letting the blond strands he'd persuaded her to leave free fly across her face and conceal her eyes. "Oh, both, I think. My mother is an archaeologist and is forever off on digs in really remote places—especially in summer during school vacations. And my father is a concert pianist who spends most of his time on world tours."

Cliff chewed that over for a moment. "Sounds like they weren't home much," he finally said carefully.

"They weren't. But then, neither was I." She flicked back that strand of hair and met his gaze head-on.

"What about vacations? Did you ever travel with your parents then?" He guided her around a pair of tourists, stepping into the recessed doorway of another shop.

"Oh, no. What would a kid do in Eastern Europe? You can't just let a ten-year-old wander around unsupervised in a foreign city. And my mother's digs were generally in places you wouldn't want to take a child. No, I stayed home with my Gramma Lawrence."

He could think of a lot of things a child could learn and enjoy in Europe—or even in remote areas, on an archaeological dig. Funny. He'd always thought of his own childhood as deprived, but at least his mother, unsatisfactory as she'd been as a parent and family breadwinner, had cared enough to keep him with her. It couldn't have been easy for her to raise him by herself. While she wasn't the greatest mother in the world, at least somewhere inside he'd always known she wanted him. And that validated the feelings of loss he'd experienced at eighteen when she'd died, a broken and bitter woman who never had the chance to make it big.

It wasn't much consolation, but it was something.

"Want some pie?" He gestured at the etched-glass windows of Mom's, one of the several pie shops that, according to the Julian chamber of commerce, made the best apple pies anywhere. When she nodded, he opened the door and led her inside. It wasn't until he'd collected two orders of apple-cherry pie with coffee and seated her at a table that something clicked in his memory.

"Is that the same Gramma Lawrence you were talking about last Sunday in the car? The one who left you some kind of legacy?"

"Mmm-hmm." She took a bite of the pie. "This is really good." After swallowing, she added, "I inherited her house up in Sunfield. It's where I spent all my summers and school vacations until she died when I was twelve. It's beautiful up there. I had a great time with Gramma. I'll probably have to sell the house, though. If I get that network job, or any network job really, I'll be based in New York, not California."

Her casual statement was like a punch in his gut. *If she gets the network job, she'll be leaving for New York.* He knew that, of course. He'd always known she'd be leaving sooner or later. So why did that realization affect him so strongly now? She was too smart and too talented not to get what she wanted professionally.

He took a sip of coffee to moisten a mouth suddenly too dry. "Do you think you're likely to hear something soon? About the New York job, I mean."

She gave him an odd look he had no clue how to interpret. "Maybe," she said. "But we're having trouble scheduling a mutually convenient interview. It's possible they'll hire someone else without even talking to me."

She'll stay! He tried to disguise the bubble of elation that rose at the thought. "Oh. That's too bad."

She changed the subject. But while they wandered and shopped desultorily in Julian's tiny downtown area, Cliff felt as if he'd successfully dodged a bullet. Mallory was going to stay in town, at least for a while longer, and he could simply concentrate on enjoying their time together.

But he soon urged her to return to the cabin, where he made love to her all afternoon and into the evening.

CLIFF ENJOYED taking Mallory out to dinner on Sunday evening. They settled on a local restaurant and lingered over the meal, holding hands and staring into each other's eyes. It amused him to realize that anyone watching them would have taken them for a honeymoon couple. And that thought surprised him. He'd have expected to be embarrassed or irritated at such an assumption.

As dessert was served, he realized to his surprise that neither of them had shown the slightest inclination to discuss their jobs. In fact, the words *career* and *work* had been tacitly taboo for almost the entire weekend, as if both were trying to forget that such real-world issues existed.

It was the longest period in years that he hadn't even thought about his work.

But as Mallory dipped her spoon into her caramel flan, she asked, "I've been meaning to ask you how your meeting with your boss went last week. Did you clear up the problems that were bothering you?"

Cliff's gaze released hers and he shifted uncomfortably. "I guess. I understand better now why they're doing what they're doing." His answer was deliberately vague because he hadn't been able to tell Mallory anything specific about his problems—and especially not that they related to the infamous Bartlett murder case.

Actually the senior partner had been very sympathetic about Cliff's concerns, but had pointed out the hard facts. Client fees paid for the salaries and office expenses of the firm, and clients who were sent to jail often were irritated enough not to pay their bills. Not to mention that they often bad-mouthed their attorneys to everyone who would listen, which wasn't very good for business. Besides, it was in the honored tradition of American jurisprudence that every client—even one with tons of evidence against her—be provided with the best possible defense.

Cliff did understand. He always had. He wasn't one of those pie-in-the-sky dreamers who dashed around tilting at windmills and making everyone—especially themselves—miserable.

But this case still seemed different. The cop in question was a good cop, with an excellent record of more than twenty years of work. He had a wife and a couple of kids. No doubt the hatchet job Cliff's firm planned would hurt, maybe even destroy, the man's career. And his family.

"That didn't sound very certain," Mallory commented on his less-than-enthusiastic agreement.

"It wasn't. I still disagree with the tactics." No, he *hated* the tactics. And surprised himself once again for caring. "It's funny. All your life you work for something and then when you get it, it turns out to be very different from what you expect."

Her head tipped sideways, considering his words. "What do you mean?"

"Only that real life is different from what you see in movies or read in books." He gestured vaguely. "As a kid I saw all those rich, successful lawyers riding around in great cars and living in ritzy houses, and I thought, man, that's the place to be."

"And isn't it?" Her question was gently put, and her fingers closed around his.

"Not really." He gave a wry grin. "I never realized that if you're going to make money defending people from criminal charges, you end up spending a lot of your time hanging around with criminals."

"You mean your clients aren't all lily-white?" she teased.

"God, no. Some are merely rich enough to buy their way out of trouble."

He saw the question gathering in her eyes before she asked it. "Then how can you defend them if you know they're guilty?"

His lips twisted into a wry grin. "Because we're trained in law school that everyone—even the guilty—is entitled to a defense. Besides, I don't *know* they're guilty—we're also trained never to ask that question. Guilt or innocence is for the jury to decide."

She shook her head, but changed the subject. "Tomorrow's Monday. We have to go home then."

He nodded. "I know."

She shoved her dessert aside and stared at him through the golden candlelight. "I don't want to go back."

"Neither do I." It was true. Even the thought of facing the same problems again made his stomach clench.

Her wistful smile tugged at his heart. "I don't suppose you'd like to run away with me, would you? We'd never have to go back to the real world."

With all his heart he wanted to say yes. "Sorry. You'd miss out on your grand career plan. The network is waiting for you, you know. And I wouldn't make partner."

For a long heartbeat she stared at him. "And would that be so bad?"

"It's what you want, what you've always wanted. Isn't it?"

She studied his face for a moment without answering. Then she released his hand and pushed away from the table. "We'd better be going."

Her words were said with the finality of an epitaph. He knew she was right. It was time to leave this idyllic interlude and return to the things that really mattered. Their careers.

Their affair was well established now. They were comfortable with each other in bed and out. They had a genuine "relationship," a word which sent instinctive shivers up his bachelor spine but which also seemed right when it referred to him and Mallory.

Yes, this weekend had accomplished everything he'd wanted it to. So why was he so reluctant to put it behind him and return to what he truly loved?

9

LENNY'S VOICE abraded Mallory's ear. "They canceled, Mallory. They've found someone else."

It was three weeks since she'd returned from the trip into the mountains, and she'd kept the hope alive that her impulsiveness hadn't destroyed her chance to hit the big time. Obviously, those hopes were in vain.

She sank into her office chair and propped her forehead on one hand. "Are you sure? They didn't leave any possibility open that they'll change their minds again?"

"Not a chance. I won't repeat their exact words, but the general implication of their comments was 'unreliable.' You wouldn't do what they wanted and they were, uh, really irritated."

Absently, Mallory noticed that her hand was shaking. She stared at it as if it were an alien object. "That's that, I guess. Bye-bye golden network opportunity."

"Aw, kid, don't take it hard. Another chance'll

come up. Besides, I heard some rumors about this project I don't think you'd like.''

"Rumors?'' One of the many things she adored about her agent was his loyalty. "What are you talking about?''

Lenny dropped his voice to what he probably supposed was a whisper. It actually meant she could hold the receiver against her ear in comfort. "I heard this prime-time slot is for a real sleazoid tabloid show. Not in the news division at all—in the entertainment group. Don't know how well you'd have liked that.''

She really appreciated his attempts to cheer her up, so she went along with his story. "You're probably right, Lenny. I wouldn't have liked that much at all.''

"Don't worry. We'll find something better for you pretty soon now.''

Mallory said goodbye to her agent and hung up. It was just like Lenny to do his best for her, even when she'd been the one to let him down.

Doodling on a pad of paper, she contemplated her future. At the moment, it didn't look like much except a series of empty days and even emptier nights. Even her affair with Cliff had deteriorated since their return from Julian. He worked so much that they'd only managed to be together three times. And each time, he'd left her bed in the early morning before

she awakened, leaving her feeling lonelier than before.

Maybe she wasn't cut out for an affair.

Maybe she wasn't cut out for the "big time," either. Certainly those network guys seemed to think
that was the case.

She stared at her organizer where she'd penciled
in dinner with Cliff for that evening. The truth was,
she wasn't really depressed over losing out on the
network show. After three weeks of delays and stall-
ing tactics, she'd known in her heart that this time
she wouldn't get that job. She was a big girl now,
and she had to take the consequences of choosing a
weekend with Cliff over a last-minute interview with
the network.

While she regretted the lost professional opportunity, she spent far more time fretting over her relationship with Cliff. She wanted more than just an
occasional evening in bed together. He was a tender,
caring lover, to be sure, but when he disappeared
even before the sun rose, she ended up feeling
slightly used instead of satisfied.

The phone chirped, interrupting her disgruntled
ponderings. "Mallory Reissen."

"Hi. It's Cliff."

"I was just thinking about you," she said. Her
heart thumped heavily at the sound of his voice.
"I'm really glad you called."

"Good." Papers rustled in the background. "I wanted to talk to you about dinner."

Ignoring the warning frisson that shuddered down her spine, she said quickly, "Would you like to try that new Japanese place? Someone here at work said their sushi is outstanding."

"Mallory—"

Bowing to the inevitable, she let him interrupt her. A sinking feeling in her stomach prepared her for his words.

"I can't make dinner tonight. I've got to work."

Damn, damn, damn. It was the fifth time in two weeks he'd canceled a date with her. *But that's what you agreed to, dummy. You were going to be sympathetic and understanding when he has to work. Just as he's been when you had to cancel.*

True enough, but she'd only canceled once, when a huge fire raced through a downtown high-rise.

"Mallory? Are you there?"

"Yes." Her voice wasn't as controlled as she liked, so she cleared her throat. "I'm here."

"Look, honey, I'm really sorry. But I think this might be a major break for me. I have to get this work done tonight, but I'm hoping it'll get me noticed."

She cleared her throat again and blinked quickly. "That's—that's all right, Cliff. I understand. Would you like me to have something ready to heat up when you come in?'' One of their few evenings together had resulted from just such an offer. Cliff had arrived shortly before midnight, he'd gobbled down the re-heated meat loaf she'd saved, and they'd gone to bed. Of course, the next morning he was up and gone before six.

"No," he said, regret lacing his voice. "I'll probably be here into the wee smalls. I'll just send one of the clerks out for a sandwich or something."

"Oh."

"I'm really sorry about this. I know you were looking forward to dinner. I was, too."

Determinedly, she raised her chin. Sheer pride was keeping her going and strengthening her voice to a calm firmness. "Never mind. There'll be other evenings." *Wouldn't there?* "You get your work done and we'll see each other another time."

But after she'd ended the call she stared at the phone for long moments. The temptation to sweep it off the desk onto the floor was nearly irresistible—she had to curl her fingers until her nails stung her palms to prevent such a foolish action.

Her anger built into a flame that flickered higher. A quick rap at the door to her office sent her slewing around.

"Hey, Mallory, here's the latest from the boss on the sweeps results. We're doing really well so far. Up three points in the 24-to-35 age group." Janet

Powell, one of the station administrators, held out a memo to her. Janet and she occasionally shared a lunch at a local deli on slow news days. She was also the only person at the station who knew anything at all about Mallory's relationship with Cliff.

It took three deep breaths before Mallory could respond. "Good. That's good."

"Good? Girl, that's great. And most of the uptick seems to be a direct result of your series on traffic problems and population growth. People were really interested in what you presented."

"Terrific." A pounding headache was starting just behind her left eye.

Janet stared at her, then walked the rest of the way into the office and shut the door. "All right, what's wrong?"

She could have evaded the question. She even seriously considered lying. But at this moment, she needed to talk to someone. Janet was sympathetic. In her mid-forties, she'd also been around long enough to have useful advice.

"It's Cliff," Mallory confessed. "He just canceled another dinner date."

Drawing up the visitor's chair and planting her ample backside in it, Janet asked, "What is this? The third time, lately?"

"The fifth." Even saying the words made it sound worse.

"You think he's cheating on you?" That was Janet. Go straight to the heart of the matter.

"No. Except maybe with his work. He's just more devoted to it than to me."

"So he's got his work as a mistress, right?"

"No," Mallory said slowly. "*I'm* his mistress. His work is his wife."

"Honey, one thing I've learned is that the wife usually wins. Playing the other woman is like betting against the house. Sooner or later, it's going to clean you out."

"But I promised him I wouldn't come between him and his work. It was what we agreed to." Even Mallory could hear the wail in her voice.

"Why'd you agree to something silly like that?"

The question stopped her cold. Why *had* she agreed to it? Her reasons seemed remote and vague now, though she clearly remembered proposing the terms of their affair to Cliff herself. Why would she want a relationship in which she didn't even get to see her partner except occasionally? Why would she want a relationship just like her—

"Ohmigod."

"What is it?"

"I'm living my parents' life. They're really involved in their careers, barely are in the same city for more than a few weeks a year. Somehow, I've begun to model my life after theirs."

"Doesn't sound right to me." Janet thought about it. "Is that the life you really want for yourself? Waiting around for the man you love to toss you a crumb of his time?"

"Love? Who said anything about love?" Though she leaped to deny it, the heat of truth crept up her neck.

"Mallory, honey, I've known you for years. I've seen you date tons of guys—great guys. But I've never seen you so heated up over anyone. If this isn't love, I don't know what is."

"But—" Mallory shut up. Janet's unerring eye had revealed what she'd hidden from herself. She wasn't just resentful of Cliff's job. She wanted him to turn his attention to her because she wanted his love. She wanted him not to work so hard. She wanted him to eat more regularly, get more rest.

Be with her more.

She'd broken the biggest rule of all. She'd fallen head over heels for a man who didn't have time to love.

PETER ABRAMS, senior partner at Abrams, Dentwhistle, Farber, and Cox, patted Cliff on the shoulder. "Excellent work, Cliff. You've really done us proud."

Cliff tried to look appropriately humble. "I like to make a contribution to the firm."

"Well, we've all seen how hard you've worked on helping us prepare the Bartlett case. With the trial date now set for late June, it's time to fire up the defense team. My partners and I feel you'll be a great asset to us."

Cliff blinked. For all his misgivings about the defense strategy, this was still a major coup. A case like this would be a career-maker. Especially if they won. Still, he might have misunderstood. "You mean—"

"I mean that as of this afternoon you're officially part of the defense team for Fiona Bartlett." Abrams stuck out his hand. "Congratulations, Cliff."

Dazed, Cliff shook the older man's hand. Perhaps it was the combination of too little sleep and too much work. Or maybe it was simply the impact of being the only nonpartner included in the prestigious defense team. In either event, he walked back to his office in a daze, collecting congratulations as he went. He'd done it! He'd actually done it.

His first thought was to call Mallory. He'd felt bad about blowing off their dinner date yet again. These last few weeks he hadn't seen nearly as much of her as he'd have liked. Still, their time in the mountains had accomplished what he'd hoped, and he'd been able to attack his work with renewed vigor and enthusiasm ever since. Which had resulted, of course, in today's victory. In a way, he could credit Mallory for all this—and he couldn't think of a better way to celebrate than by taking her to bed.

"Mallory Reissen."

"Me again." The big sappy grin on his face wouldn't turn off. He twirled in his chair like a little kid.

"Cliff! I thought you were working late tonight."

"I was, but I decided to take the night off. I'm shoving all the paperwork into the circular file and shuffling out of here at a reasonable hour tonight."

A wary silence filled his ear. "What brought this on?"

"I'll tell you tonight. You can make it after all, can't you?"

"Well...to be honest, since you couldn't meet me for dinner I agreed to help out on a promo spot after the evening news. I won't be able to leave until at least eight or eight-thirty."

"That's okay," he said easily. "I have some stuff to do here before I can leave anyway. Why don't I meet you at the restaurant at nine? After we eat, we'll go home and get naked."

To his surprise, she didn't leap at the offer. Had he been mistaken when he thought she'd been disappointed at his earlier cancellation for tonight? "Cliff, maybe we should do this another night," she said at last. "I'm going to be pretty tired."

What was going on here? Didn't she want to be with him? "Mallory, is anything wrong?"

"No." Her voice sounded tired. Maybe she was merely feeling a little stressed. "All right," she capitulated. "But let's not go out. I'll stop by a take-out place and bring some food with me. I think we need some privacy, to talk."

"Great!" His mood restored, he sent her a smacking kiss over the phone line. "I'll see you around nine at my place. And, Mallory—prepare to celebrate, big-time. I've got some great news to share."

"I've got news, too," she said so quietly he barely noticed.

Idly, he wondered what her news was, then dismissed the question. He'd find out this evening. Meantime, he had six hours to finish up the paperwork cluttering his desk and get himself home. With renewed vigor, he pulled his legal pad toward him, flipped to a clean sheet, and started making notes.

MALLORY KNOCKED on Cliff's front door with her arms full of chicken lo mein and chopsticks. Nervously, she moistened her lips. This evening was going to be very difficult.

Ever since her revelation with Janet, she'd been trying to figure out what to do about Cliff. Did she want to continue a relationship that was inherently self-destructive for her? Could she bear to walk away from him?

Truthfully, she didn't know.

The door was flung open and Cliff pulled her inside, giving her a huge kiss and hug. "God, you look gorgeous!"

She handed him the bags of food and slipped out of the light jacket she wore against the early evening chill. "Sorry I'm so late. The promo spots took a little longer than I expected."

"Never mind. You're here now. I've got the table set and the wine's poured. Let's dish up the food and eat."

Silently she let him lead her to the dining area. Once they were served, she asked, "I gather something good happened at work this afternoon?" Maybe if she let him get his good news out first, he'd be in a mood to talk about their relationship.

He put down his chopsticks with a smile that threatened to split his face. "You might say that. As of today I am now officially a member of the Bartlett defense team. The one and only nonpartner so honored, I might add."

Oh, no. She knew what this meant. Instead of him being able to make more time to be together, the all-out effort for this trial would cut even further into his nearly nonexistent free time. Still, he was obviously looking for approval. "Cliff, that's wonderful.

I'm thrilled for you.'' Okay, so ''thrilled'' was an exaggeration. She genuinely was pleased he'd achieved what he'd worked so hard to get.

''This is going to be my ticket to the paneled offices, Mallory. They only wanted one junior member of the firm on the team—Fiona Bartlett always wants only the best of the best—and I'm the one they chose. I can hardly believe it.''

She leaned forward and took his hand. ''Cliff, there's not a doubt in my mind that you deserve this. You've been working so hard lately. They must have noticed your dedication.''

Smugly, he nodded, and regaled her with the details of how everyone in the office had reacted when the news was announced. Only when he was winding down did he appear to notice that she'd contributed little to the conversation.

''Mallory, didn't you say you have some news, too?''

She smiled weakly. ''It can't compare with yours, I'm afraid. It's just—the network isn't interested in me, after all.''

''What? I didn't even know you'd interviewed with them.'' Automatically, he shoved their plates aside so he could grasp her hand more tightly in his.

''I didn't. They wanted to talk to me the weekend we went up to Julian, but...well, I already had other plans. Since then, we've been getting the old run-around trying to schedule a meeting.'' She shrugged. "Lenny says they've now settled on someone else.''

"Why didn't you talk with them that weekend? I would have understood.''

She looked down at their clasped hands. "I decided I didn't want to cancel our weekend together. I thought it was important—you thought it was then, too.''

"Yes, but this was your chance at the networks. I would never have stood in your way for that!'' He looked profoundly shocked at the thought.

"I know that, Cliff. It was my decision, not yours.''

"I just don't understand. Why would you deliberately ruin your own chances like that?''

He'd moved the conversation to the one area she both needed to discuss and dreaded bringing up. She took a deep breath and came to a decision. "Before I answer that, will you tell me something?''

"Of course.''

"Will your new position on the defense team mean more work for you—or less?''

His surprise couldn't have been faked. "More, of course. As a member of the team, I'll have to double-check everything. I won't just be producing briefs, I'll be responsible for their accuracy and timeliness. I'll be working harder than ever.''

"That's what I thought.'' Her fingers clutched his

so tightly her knuckles ached. "Cliff, I want to end our relationship now, tonight."

"*What?*"

"Remember we said in the beginning that if I ever wanted out, all I had to do was tell you and that would be the end of it? Well, I'm telling you. I want out."

"But—Mallory—*why?* What's wrong? Whatever it is, let's talk about it. Surely we can fix it."

Her free hand came up to thread through his hair. "You said you'd never stand in the way of my career. You told me you'd support me in my decisions."

He paled. "Are you telling me you're going to New York after all? I thought you said the network job fell through."

She shook her head. "No. I'm saying I can't be so generous as that with you. I want nothing more than to tell you I don't want you taking on the Bartlett case. I don't want you working harder than you already are—in fact, I want you to ease up, work fewer hours." She took a breath that was more of a swallowed gulp. "I want you to have more time for me."

"I don't understand."

"Don't you see, Cliff? I'm as bad as Suzanne and all the other women you've known. I want more from you than an hour in bed when you can fit me in between your clients. If we don't break this off now, you'll grow to dislike me, just as you've disliked all those other women who were too demanding of your time and energy. And I can't stand the thought of that.''

"Mallory, I thought things were going well between us. Why can't we—''

His face dissolved in the mist of tears she refused to let fall. "Don't you get it, Cliff? I'm in love with you. I want all of you, not just the little pieces you're willing to share. I know I can't have that. It's not in you to love me. But at least I can leave before I make you hate me. That's why I have to go.''

Of course he argued. Cliff refused to believe that a compromise couldn't be worked out. But to his frustration, she stood firm against all his arguments. No, she wouldn't reconsider. No, she wouldn't change her mind.

No, she wouldn't stay.

In the end, he had to accept defeat. Not graciously. Not willingly. But he had to accept it nonetheless.

He won only one concession from her. She agreed to spend the night with him. He thought if he made love to her as tenderly and thoroughly as he knew how, she would understand how much she meant to him. And then her compassionate heart would realize how hurt he was that she wanted to leave him.

So they shared one last, loving farewell, a fitting

epitaph for an affair that had been nothing but inconvenient from the very first day.

And when he woke before dawn, she was already gone.

10

FOR THE TENTH time in the past week, Cliff picked up his office phone to call Mallory. His door was shut. His secretary had left two hours ago, at five-thirty. As far as he knew, only the janitors shared the office with him this Friday night. He was as safe from discovery as he could be.

This time, he actually punched in the numbers with fingers that trembled. Four soft rings later, he was almost certain he'd waited too late and she'd already left the station for the day.

"Mallory Reissen."

The sound of her voice, the first time he'd heard it in over a month, sucked the air from his lungs. He couldn't make a sound.

"Hello? Hello?"

She was about to hang up. "Don't hang up, Mallory. It's Cliff."

She was silent so long he wasn't sure she hadn't hung up anyway. "Hello, Cliff."

Now what? "I, uh, just wanted to know if you were all right. I've been thinking about you."

"I'm fine." While not impolite, the chill courtesy in her voice could have frozen a Popsicle.

"Oh. I'm fine, too."

"Good."

Had a more inane conversation ever taken place? He hadn't felt so inept since he was a thirteen-year-old requesting his first date. Which thought at least reminded him of his reason for calling.

"Mallory, I've been wondering. Would you like to go to dinner sometime soon? Maybe take in a movie?"

He measured her hesitation in heartbeats. Four long, thudding pumps later, she sighed. "Cliff, I don't think that's a very good idea."

"Please, Mallory. I'd like to see you."

"You see me all the time. I live right next door, remember?"

He ignored that. "Please."

Three. Four. This time it took five heartbeats for her to respond. "Are you still on the Bartlett defense team?"

"Yes, of course."

She sighed audibly. "Then I don't think it's a very good idea to start things up again between us, do you?"

"Dammit, Mallory, are you trying to punish me for being successful at what I do?"

"No, Cliff," she said gently. "I'm trying *not* to punish myself. That's all."

With a soft click, the phone went dead. Slowly, Cliff dropped the handset onto its cradle. With a groan that was torn painfully from his gut, he buried his head in his hands and stayed that way for a long, long time.

FIONA BARTLETT draped herself over the conference-room chair with the suppleness of a panther. She looked a lot like a panther, Cliff thought. All long, sleek lines and hungry eyes.

Unfortunately, the meal she hungered for seemed to be him.

"Cliff—you don't mind if I call you Cliff, do you?" Even her voice was a husky purr.

"Not at all, Ms. Bartlett. Cliff is fine."

"I was just wondering why I haven't had the opportunity to meet with you before now. The trial is about to start and I feel it's important that everyone on my team be on my side."

He rubbed his chin and wondered where the hell the paralegal was. He was sure he'd instructed her to be in the conference room at three o'clock on the dot. A quick glance at his watch confirmed it was now ten minutes after the hour.

Through some careful maneuvering and some plain, dumb luck, he'd managed to avoid being alone with the predatory Mrs. Bartlett until now. Apparently, his luck had run out. Along with that useless paralegal.

"We have met, of course," he said as smoothly as he could manage. *In large groups where I could be sure you were under control.* "And I'm only a very minor member of your team—more a support person than anything else. Hardly important enough to waste your time with."

She frowned and leaned sideways just enough to give him a glimpse of long, dark-stockinged leg stretched in voluptuous enticement. "But I thought you had something important to go over with me."

"I do," he assured her, ignoring her scarlet-painted pout. "But if you'll excuse me, I'll round up our paralegal. She has copies of the paperwork we need to go over."

"But—"

Before she could protest, Cliff slipped out the door. Hastily he stepped to a nearby secretary's station. "Where the hell is Lucy? She was supposed to be here—"

"Sorry, Mr. Young!" Lucy Davenwood dashed up, her arms full of papers and files. "Mrs. Bartlett told me on her way in that she needed at least a half hour in private consultation with you, so I thought I should—''

Of course. By this time Fiona Bartlett must know enough of the workings of her attorneys' office to know exactly how to sabotage his plans to avoid being alone with her.

Resigned, he just nodded. ''That's all right. You're here now.'' He took a stack of papers from her and guided her to the closed conference room door. ''But, Lucy, no matter what she says, you don't leave this room unless I tell you it's all right—understood?''

She nodded earnestly.

Grim-faced, he stepped back inside the lioness's den to discuss the depositions he'd been assigned to review with her. Was this what he really wanted to do with his life? Play dodgem with predatory women and defend them in court from the consequences of their own actions?

In his own mind he'd long ago realized that Fiona Bartlett wasn't merely guilty—she was as guilty as sin. From his reading of the evidence, she hadn't found her husband in bed with another woman and shot the pair in a rage. No, all the evidence pointed to a very carefully planned setup of both her husband and his lover—a woman who had once been Fiona's best friend.

And he was bound by oath to help Fiona walk free.

His hand groped in his pocket for the antacids that

were once again a staple of his diet. How he longed for Mallory's presence to help him sort through his life! She had a deep-rooted rational approach to sticky problems that he needed desperately. Yet after that one futile phone call, she'd started screening her calls both at work and at home. And messages from C. Young went mysteriously unanswered.

He never saw her entering or leaving her condo, though he made a point of looking for her whenever he was home—which was seldom. And just lately he'd been reduced to taping her nightly newscasts on his VCR, then watching a whole week's worth on Sundays, the only day of the week he didn't spend slaving at his desk. Sometimes he'd watch the tape over and over again, trying to decipher what she was thinking as she capably explained the day's events.

He wondered how she was doing. He wondered if she'd gotten over the disappointment of losing that network slot. He wondered if she was lonely, too.

He wondered if she'd found someone else.

To be on the safe side, he shoved two more antacids into his mouth. It was going to be another long afternoon. He only wished he didn't anticipate a lifetime of equally long afternoons in front of him.

"YOU LOOK LIKE hell, buddy." Todd Sinewski's blunt assessment only confirmed Cliff's own impression.

He'd answered the pounding on his front door with wildly beating heart. Maybe Mallory had had second thoughts. Maybe she was sorry she'd deserted him. Maybe—maybe it's only Todd at the door.

Disappointed, he turned away, a movement that allowed Todd to push his way inside and close the door.

"What the hell's wrong with you, Cliff? You look worse than the bum I gave a dollar to yesterday in the Gaslamp Quarter."

He shrugged. "I quit my job."

"I heard." Todd settled down on the large leather sofa. "Do you want to tell me why?"

Cliff shrugged and reached for the remote. He'd just started playing this week's tape when Todd's pounding interrupted his obsessive viewing.

"You look like you haven't shaved in a week."

"I haven't. Or maybe longer. I don't remember."

"Your hair needs a trim."

"So?" He pressed the start button on the remote, then used fast forward to whiz past the various commercials.

"Your cutoffs have definitely seen better days and could use a wash." Todd gave an indelicate sniff. "And so could you, from the smell of it."

"Get to the point." Cliff was barely listening. His attention was focused on the cool blonde on the screen. She had her hair down. He'd always liked it down.

"Will you give me that!" Todd snatched the remote and turned the tape and television off.

"Hey!"

"I'm not letting you go back to your wallowing until you tell me what's going on. Why has the city's most ambitious overachiever turned into a couch potato?"

Cliff's eyes, red-rimmed and burning, met Todd's gaze. "God's truth, Todd, I have no idea. One day I was kicking along just fine, well on the way to a partnership. The next thing I know, I hate my job, and I'm obsessing over a woman who loves me but doesn't want me anywhere around her."

"Mallory Reissen?" Todd gestured to the screen.

"Uh-huh." Suddenly, the words poured out. Cliff explained the whole sorry mess—the affair that was supposed to solve all his problems and how it had only created one larger than anything he'd ever dealt with in his life.

Todd listened in silence. Finally, after Cliff ran out of words, he said, "You say she said she loves you. Yet she doesn't want you to work so hard?"

"That's about the size of it. I tell you, Todd, I've just about gone crazy over her. I don't know what I'm doing anymore."

"Well, quitting your job doesn't seem to be a real bright move."

Cliff shrugged. "I haven't really quit. Just taken a leave of absence."

"In the middle of the biggest trial to hit San Diego? When you're on the defense team? *Are you nuts?*"

Cliff met his gaze straight on. "Maybe. Probably." He took a deep breath. "But you know what? I really *hate* being a big-time defense attorney. The clients are so slimy. If you know what I mean."

"Yeah, I got it." Todd took a deep breath. "You know, I never thought I'd live to see this happen to you. But I think you *are* nuts—nuts about Mallory Reissen. Maybe you should think about doing something about it."

"You think I haven't tried? She won't take my calls. She's virtually disappeared from her condo—I haven't seen her go in or out of there in weeks. About the only thing left for me to try is to lay siege to her at work—and if she really has gotten over me, that would humiliate her and me."

"It's a problem all right," Todd admitted.

"I'm in love with her, you know. It took a long time for me to realize it—too long. Now I can't even get her to listen to me long enough to try to apologize."

"Is this how you've been spending your time? Watching tapes of her over and over?"

"Pretty much. Wanna help me watch?"

Taking Todd's silence as acceptance, Cliff picked up the remote and turned the television and VCR back on. Silently, they watched the week's newscasts together, with Cliff fast-forwarding past anything that didn't have Mallory on screen.

It didn't take long for them to get to Friday's broadcast. At the very end of the program, the camera focused in on Mallory. Cliff caught his breath. How could he have been so stupid as to let her go? More to the point, how could he get her back?

On the screen, Mallory was talking. "—and I'd like to take a moment in my final broadcast here in San Diego to thank all the wonderful people in the city and especially here at KSAN television. It'll be a wrench leaving you all, but I'd like to wish everyone here in San Diego a happy, healthy life. Thank you for all your support." A tear glimmered in her eyes. "Goodbye. This is Mallory Reissen, signing off."

Stunned, Cliff turned to Todd. "Did you hear what I did? Did she just say that she'd left the station?"

Todd nodded. "That's what it sounded like to me."

Cliff picked up the telephone and punched in the number he knew by heart. Her office number rang and rang, until a taped voice came on the line and said, "You have reached an extension that is not currently in use. Please redial, or press 0 to reach the operator."

The operator confirmed that Mallory Reissen no longer worked at KSAN television, but could not—or would not—say where she had gone.

His hands shaking, Cliff punched in her home phone number. This time the recorded voice came on after only two rings. "The number you have dialed has been disconnected."

Without bothering to explain to Todd, he dashed out the front door and to hers next door. For the first time he noticed a small, discreet For Sale sign posted in the niche by her door. And when he peered through the now-curtainless window, he saw that no furniture remained inside.

Sometime recently she'd moved out.

Todd found him there moments later, sitting on the front doorstep, bitter tears etching his cheeks. In despair he looked up. "I've lost her, Todd. She's gone."

MALLORY SMILED up at the warm Sierra sunshine, her arms full of groceries. She'd been in Sunfield for three weeks and still enjoyed every moment. The small town was just as she remembered it from her childhood, filled with gentle people and a charming, low-key life-style. She woke each morning in her grandmother's house, trying hard to think only of her contentment in her new life, trying hard to forget that she'd left her heart behind in San Diego.

Every so often she wondered how he was doing. He'd wrapped himself so firmly around her heart that she knew she'd never break free of him. Nor did she want to. She treasured every moment of their loving. If remembrances were all she could have of him, remembrances would be what she'd make do with.

The nights were lonely, of course, and sometimes she would see a dark-haired man from a distance and feel her heartbeat accelerate.

It had all seemed so clear to her. When she realized she had to give up her relationship with Cliff, she recognized at last that she'd spent twenty-eight years striving for a crumb of appreciation from parents who simply didn't care.

She didn't really want that New York job—or at least she could live without it. What she wanted was a meaningful life with neighbors and a job she really loved, not one she did merely to impress her parents. She wanted children, too—PTA meetings and school plays and Jimmy-pushed-me-Mom squabbles. Most of all, she wanted to find a man just like Cliff, but one who also was willing to give up the "good" life of ambition for the even better life of love and family.

In the depths of the night when tears and longing were her only companions, she knew it would take her a long time to get over losing Cliff, but she had to try. For her own happiness, she had to forget him.

She'd had no choice except to leave him. She refused to let herself become one more woman he wanted to forget. He knew she loved him—she was glad of that. But her heartache and longing for him was private, not to be cheapened by painful scenes.

And she loved her new life. When she'd looked for a way to escape, she'd remembered the small college in the slightly larger town next to Sunfield. The communications department had been thrilled with her proposal to teach radio and television technology to their students. She was already looking forward to the start of classes in the fall.

She took her time as she walked the quarter mile back to her grandmother's house—*her* house now. There was no hurry; none of her groceries would spoil. And the day was beautiful—warm sunshine with just enough breeze to remind her she was in the mountains. As usual, her eyes drank in the picturesque setting eagerly, lingering on a quarrelsome squirrel here, a sassy mountain bluebird there.

So she was almost on top of the gold-colored Lexus before she noticed it.

His car.

Her steps slowed to a halt beside the front fender as she looked toward the front porch of her house.

"Hello, Mallory."

Her arms loosened and would have dropped the groceries if he hadn't stepped down from the porch and collected the bags. He set them on the porch, then took her arm and guided her to the swing suspended from the porch ceiling.

"Are you all right?" he asked solicitously.

"Cliff?" To her dismay, every nerve in her body seemed to have migrated to her elbow, directly underneath his protective hand. "What are you doing here?"

He shrugged, but his intense gaze belied the gesture. "Looking for you."

"How did you find me?"

His irises gleamed an intense pewter, a sign of some deep feeling held in check. Sunlight glinted off his dark auburn hair, but she noticed one or two silvery strands. And the tiny lines at the corners of his eyes seemed deeper.

"It wasn't easy. All I could remember was that your grandmother's house was in Sun-something. Do you know how many small towns in the Sierras start with 'Sun'?"

She shook her head, noticing the faint crease between his brows.

"Well, there are a ton of them. I had to check out

every one individually. Naturally, Sunfield was almost at the bottom of my list.''

''You found me, though.'' She started to reach out to him, then checked the gesture.

''Yes,'' he said, and even she couldn't miss the satisfaction in that word. ''I found you.''

''You're...looking good.'' Actually, he looked fabulous, though very tired. With an effort, she kept her fingers from smoothing the lines of weariness from his brow. Even his suit and tieless shirt seemed somehow appropriate for him, although he was the first person she'd seen in a suit since she'd hit town.

''You too,'' he said. From the way his eyes inspected every inch of her sundress-clad body, bare legs, and sandaled feet, she knew it was no casual compliment.

She tore her gaze from him and focused on the huge pine across the street. ''Cliff, why are you here? Is the Bartlett trial over?'' He heart hammered in her chest with hopes that suddenly, desperately tried to fly free.

He shrugged again. ''I don't know. I quit my job.''

That drew her attention. ''What? *Why?*''

''Because I realized I hated my work.'' He paused. ''Mallory, this can't be a surprise to you. We talked about how different it was from what I expected when we were up in that cabin in Julian, remember?''

"But—to give up your ambitions—I can't believe it."

"Mallory, my ambitions were making me ill. You were right about that, too. My doctor told me I was well on the way to building a dandy ulcer. I realized after you left that I was still trying to impress a ten-year-old kid from the wrong side of the tracks. My career was more for the kid I used to be, not for the adult I am now."

"Like me trying to impress my parents, instead of doing what I really wanted," she murmured.

His eyes lasered into hers. "And what is it you really do want? I thought it was a network job in New York."

Mallory's breath caught. She should have known he'd ask. Carefully, she kept her eyes on his hands, not quite willing to meet his gaze. "I realized I want something different from my parents. They wanted to prove themselves to the whole world."

"And you don't?"

She smiled a little wistfully. "Not really. I'll be happy if I can prove myself to myself. And maybe..."

"Maybe?"

"Maybe to someone else, too. Cliff, why are you here?"

A knot of tension visibly eased in his shoulders. "Because you're here," he said gently. He took her hand and a fortifying breath. "I wanted to ask you a question."

"What question?" Those hopes were beginning to flutter into her throat. It was hard to force her words past them.

"How do you feel about unemployment?"

"What?" Of all the possible questions she'd breathlessly imagined he might ask, that wasn't one of them.

"Well, you see before you a guy with no job. I sold my condo—and at a cut-rate price, I might add, because someone else had recently put hers on the market, driving up the supply."

Her hand turned, weaving her fingers with his. The thudding of her heart almost drowned his soft words.

"Where was I? Oh, yes. No job. No home. I sold all my too-expensive furniture. Just a used car and some clothes to call my own."

"A used *Lexus,*" she pointed out helpfully.

"Yeah. You know how expensive those are to insure and maintain? Like I said, a used car." He took a deep breath and leaned his forehead against hers. "So what do you think? Do my reduced circumstances put me completely out of the running?"

Her free hand traced the creases of his cheek. Her heart was thudding so powerfully, she could barely squeeze out a reply. "Out of the running for what? I understand Sunfield needs a new dogcatcher."

He shook his head. "Nope. I'm allergic."

"Oh. Well, what did you have in mind?"

"Maybe a small practice here. I used to be a pretty good lawyer, you know. And a proposition, really. Sort of like the one you once made me."

She groaned. "Not another great-sex-and-no-commitments affair!"

"Not a chance. How about great-sex-and-lots-of-commitments? How about you marry me and put me out of my misery? And then we'll talk about our affairs."

His suggestion sent her temper soaring. "You will *not* have affairs while you're my husband! No way!"

"Sure I will—with you. I figure if an affair is what you want, an affair is what you'll get. But only if you marry me first."

"And what if I want more?"

He watched her warily. "What do you mean by more?"

She took a deep breath. "Children. A family. What if I want that, too?"

His head lifted from hers and the wariness was back in his eyes. "Children? Mallory...you're not..."

She shook her head. "No, I'm not pregnant. Not yet, anyway." Her eyes searched his. "But would it be so awful if I were?"

"Pregnant..." He tasted the word slowly and the

thoughtful gleam in his eye worried her. His hand slipped down her neck to settle on her stomach in a protective caress. "My baby growing inside you…no, 'awful' isn't exactly how I'd describe that."

"How—how would you describe it?" Her hopes had reached her mouth and eyes, curving her lips into a smile and bringing the sting of joyous tears to her eyes.

"Heaven on earth. Mallory, marry me. Have my babies. Make me complete."

The smile on her face must have outshone the sun because she saw its light reflected in his eyes. Deliberately, she tried to lighten her voice. "Sounds like an okay deal to me. But, Counselor, shouldn't we negotiate some more?"

"Negotiate what?"

"Well, you haven't told me you love me yet. Seems to me that's an essential part of the deal."

"Oh. Well, maybe you're right."

He slipped to his knees beside the swing and pulled a small box out of his pants pocket. "I love you, Mallory Reissen, more than I ever thought I could love someone else. Please marry me." He opened the box and offered her a simple solitaire diamond that was not ostentatiously large, but perfectly shaped for her hand.

Gracefully she let him slip it on her finger, then

she slipped to her knees facing him. "I love you too, Cliff. I told you so weeks ago and every day apart has only made that love deeper and more a part of me. I could live without you, I'm sure. But I can't be joyful without you. I can't have the love I need without you."

His arms slipped around her and hugged her tightly against him. "Ah, Mallory, Mallory. How much I love you!"

For long moments, they stayed there, luxuriating in the simple pleasure of holding each other in their arms. Finally, Cliff said, "Uh, Mallory?"

"What?" Her lips had already started to explore his cheek.

"Could we get up? My knees are killing me."

With a burble of laughter, she helped her complaining lover up.

"Do I take it that we're in agreement at last?" he asked as she guided him toward her front door and more private—and comfortable—surroundings.

"Maybe," she said, pretending to ponder. "We've certainly adjusted the terms of our affair to some that are more to my liking."

His arm curled around her, he headed up the stairs. "Yeah. As I recall, we originally wanted an affair with great sex and no commitments."

She pointed out the door to her bedroom. "And

now we've got a great-sex-and-profound-commitments affair.''

He turned her to face him and looked into her eyes with an intensity and sincerity she couldn't miss. ''No, Mallory. Now we've got a love that will last a lifetime. Now we've got a marriage. And we're going to have a marriage and a family. And that makes all the difference.''

Mallory could only agree happily with his assessment of their circumstances. Love did make the difference. And she intended to spend a lifetime showing him—and herself—just how much a difference it made.

Do the Harlequin Duets™ Dating Quiz!

1) My ideal date would be:

a) a candlelight dinner at the most exclusive restaurant in town
b) dinner made by him even if it is burnt macaroni and cheese
c) a dinner made lovingly by me—to which he brings his mother and two ex-wives

2) If a woman came on to my ideal man, he would:

a) flirt back a little, but make it clear he's already taken
b) tell her to go away
c) bail me out of jail

3) The ideal setting for the perfect date would be:

a) a luxurious ocean resort with white sand, palm trees, picture-perfect sunsets
b) a desert island with just him and a few million mosquitoes
c) a stateroom on the *Titanic*

4) In his free time, my ideal man would most often choose to:

a) Watch sports on TV
b) Watch sports on TV
c) Watch sports on TV *(let's not kid ourselves, even ideal men will be men!)*

If you chose A most often: You are wonderful, talented and sexy. A near goddess, in fact, who will make beautiful music with just about any man you want. The only thing that could make you more perfect is reading Harlequin Duets™.

If you chose B most often: Others are jealous of your charm, wit, intelligence, good fashion sense and ability to eat whatever you want without gaining a pound. The only workout you need is a good evening with Harlequin Duets™.

If you chose C most often: Don't worry. Harlequin Duets™ to the rescue!

Experience the lighter side of love with Harlequin Duets™!

HARLEQUIN®
Makes any time special.™

 **HARLEQUIN®**
Makes any time special ™

 WIN A DREAM

In celebration of Harlequin®'s golden anniversary

Enter to win a *dream!* You could win:

- A luxurious trip for two to *The Renaissance Cottonwoods Resort* in Scottsdale, Arizona, or
- A bouquet of flowers once a week for a year from **FTD**, or
- A $500 shopping spree, or
- A fabulous bath & body gift basket, including **K-tel**'s *Candlelight and Romance* 5-CD set.

Look for **WIN A DREAM** flash on specially marked Harlequin® titles by Penny Jordan, Dallas Schulze, Anne Stuart and Kristine Rolofson in October 1999*.

 FTD

RENAISSANCE. COTTONWOODS RESORT SCOTTSDALE, ARIZONA

 K·TEL

*No purchase necessary—for contest details send a self-addressed envelope to Harlequin Makes Any Time Special Contest, P.O. Box 9069, Buffalo, NY, 14269-9069 (include contest name on self-addressed envelope). Contest ends December 31, 1999. Open to U.S. and Canadian residents who are 18 or over. Void where prohibited.

PHMATS-GR

COMING NEXT MONTH

HARLEQUIN Duets™

#11

HOW SWEET IT IS by Kimberly Raye

Delilah James had everything—friends, family, a career.
Once she'd wanted Zach Tanner...before she found out he was
a reckless, macho, sexy-as-sin bad boy. Little did she guess that
Zach, owner of Wild Man's Ribs, wanted Delilah, too. Even more
than he wanted exclusive rights on her cheesecakes. So when he
discovered she needed a fake fiancé, he decided to demonstrate
just how sweet a joint venture could be....

SECOND-CHANCE GROOM by Eugenia Riley

Bride-to-be Cassie Brandon had a funny thing happen on the
way to the altar—she fell in love with the best man. And now
handsome Brian Drake must prove he's the *wrong man* for
her. But when his plan for making her fall out of love backfired,
footloose-and-fancy-free Brian must face his biggest challenge of
all—love!

#12

HEAD OVER HEELS by Sandra Paul

Nicholas Ware had come back to Cauldron to banish tempting
Prudence McClure from his system—not to become engaged to
her! But when Halloween's magic filled the air, Prudence's
tempting spell was nearly impossible to resist!

PUPPY LOVE by Cheryl Anne Porter

David Sullivan's life was going to the dogs. He was amazed to
learn about his inheritance—and appalled to discover it was a
mangy, *very pregnant* little mutt. Then he was almost arrested
for dognapping! Luckily, he managed to convince gorgeous
veterinarian Emily Wright of his innocence. Now all he had to
do was convince her that he's more cuddly than his dog....

HARLEQUIN WIN A NEW BEETLE® CONTEST
OFFICIAL RULES
NO PURCHASE NECESSARY TO ENTER

1. To enter, access the Harlequin romance web site (http://www.romance.net) and follow the on-screen instructions: Enter your name, address (including zip code), e-mail address (optional), and in 200 words or fewer your own original story concept—which has not won a previous prize/award nor has previously been reproduced/published—for a Harlequin Duets romantic comedy novel that features a Volkswagon® New Beetle®. OR hand-print or type the same requested information for on-line entry on an Official Entry Form or 8 1/2" x 11" plain piece of paper and mail it (limit: one entry per person per outer mailing envelope) via first-class mail to: Harlequin Win A New Beetle® Contest. In the U.S.: P.O. Box 9069, Buffalo, NY 14269-9069. In Canada: P.O. Box 637, Fort Erie, Ontario, Canada L2A 5X3.

   For eligibility, entries must be submitted through a completed Internet transmission—or if mailed, postmarked—no later than November 30, 1999. Mail-in entries must be received by December 7, 1999.

2. Story concepts will be judged by a panel of members of the Harlequin editorial and marketing staff based on the following criteria:
   - Originality and Creativity—40%
   - Appropriateness to Subject Matter—35%
   - Romantic Comedy/Humor—25%

   Decision of the judges is final.

3. All entries become the property of Torstar Corp., will not be returned, and may be published. No responsibility is assumed for incomplete, lost, late, damaged, illegible or misdirected e-mail, for technical, hardware or software failures of any kind, lost or unavailable network connections, or failed, incomplete, garbled or delayed computer transmission which may limit user's ability to participate in the contest, or for non- or illegibly postmarked, lost, late nondelivered or misdirected mail. Rules are subject to any requirements/limitations imposed by the FCC. Winners will be determined no later than January 31, 2000, and will be notified by mail. Winners will be required to sign and return an Affidavit of Eligibility, and a Release of Royalty/Ownership of submitted story concept within 15 days after receipt of same certifying his/her eligibility, that entry is his/her own original work, has not won a previous prize/award nor previously been reproduced/published. Noncompliance within that time period may result in disqualification and an alternate winner may be selected. All federal, state and local laws and regulations apply. Contest open only to residents of the U.S. and Canada who are 18 years of age or older, and is void wherever prohibited by law. Any litigation within the Province of Quebec respecting the conduct and awarding of a prize may be submitted to the Régie des alcools, des courses et des jeux. Employees of Torstar Corp., their affiliates, agents and members of their immediate families are not eligible. Taxes on prizes are the sole responsibility of winners. Entry and acceptance of any prize offered constitutes permission to use winner's name, photograph or other likeness for the purposes of advertising, trade and promotion on behalf of Torstar Corp. without further compensation to the winner, unless prohibited by law.

4. Prizes: Grand Prize—a brand-new Volkswagon yellow New Beetle® (approx. value: $17,000 U.S.) and a Harlequin Duets novel (approx. value: $6 U.S.). Taxes, licensing and registration fees are the sole responsibility of the winner; 2 Runner-Up Prizes—a Harlequin Duets novel (approx. value: $6 U.S. each).

5. For a list of winners (available after March 31, 2000), send a self-addressed, stamped envelope to Harlequin Win A Beetle® Contest 8219 Winners, P.O. Box 4200 Blair, NE 68009-4200.

Sweepstakes sponsored by Torstar Corp., P.O. Box 9042, Buffalo, NY 14269-9042

Volkswagon and New Beetle registered trademarks are used with permission of Volkswagon of America, Inc.

Duets™ *Win a New Beetle®Contest!*

Starting September 1999, Harlequin Duets is offering you the chance to drive away in a Volkswagen® New Beetle®!

In addition to our grand prize winner, two more lucky entrants will also have their winning stories published in Harlequin Duets™ series and on our web site!

To enter our "WIN A NEW BEETLE®" contest, fill out this entry form and in 200 words or less write a romantic comedy short story for Harlequin Duets that features a New Beetle®.

**See previous page for contest rules.
Contest ends November 30, 1999.**

Be witty, be romantic, have fun!

Name

Address

City   State/Province

Zip/Postal Code

Mail to Harlequin Books: In the U.S.: P.O. Box 9069, Buffalo, NY 14269-9069; **In Canada,** P.O. Box 637, Fort Erie, Ontario, L4A 5X3

* No purchase necessary. To receive official contest rules and entry form, send a self-addressed stamped envelope to "Harlequin Duets Win A New Beetle® Contest Rules." In the U.S.: P.O. Box 9069, Buffalo, NY 14269-9069 (residents of Washington or Vermont may omit return postage); In Canada: P.O. Box 637, Fort Erie, ON, L4A 5X3. Or visit our web site for official contest rules and entry forms at www.romance.net/beetle.html. Open to U.S. and Canadian residents who are 18 or over. Void where prohibited.

Volkswagen and New Beetle are registered trademarks and used with permission of Volkswagen of America, Inc.

HARLEQUIN®
Makes any time special ™

HDBUG-EF